RACHEL AND ALEKS

Best wishes
Sylvia Smoller

RACHEL AND ALEKS

A Historical Novel of Life, Love, and WWII

SYLVIA SMOLLER

iUniverse, Inc.
New York Lincoln Shanghai

Rachel and Aleks
A Historical Novel of Life, Love, and WWII

iUniverse books may be ordered through booksellers or by contacting:

iUniverse
2021 Pine Lake Road, Suite 100
Lincoln, NE 68512
www.iuniverse.com
1-800-Authors (1-800-288-4677)

Because of the dynamic nature of the Internet, any Web addresses or links contained in this book may have changed since publication and may no longer be valid.

Certain characters in this work are historical figures, and certain events portrayed did take place. However, this is a work of fiction. All of the other characters, names, and events as well as all places, incidents, organizations, and dialogue in this novel are either the products of the author's imagination or are used fictitiously.

ISBN: 978-0-595-41727-8

Printed in the United States of America

In memory of my parents
And their unconditional love

PROLOGUE

When the air-raid alarm went off on that gray September dawn of 1939, Rachel, like many others, believed it was just another drill. How could she imagine there was no turning back, not for her, not for the world?

She left eight days later at an hour's notice, with Aleks and Rilka, in a car Aleks managed to requisition from the chief of police. But Sofie, her younger sister, refused to leave Warsaw. As the chauffeur pulled the large black Mercedes around the corner, she had a last glimpse of Sofie, standing in the doorway of their building, waving, her print dress blown against her legs by a sudden breeze, waving, waving.

PART I

EUROPE

-1-

Zarki—1918

The woods that encircled Zarki were fragrant in the early springtime with the fresh scent of pine, though the ground was still wet from melted patches of snow. Rachel walked along the mossy paths on Saturday afternoon, on her way to meet Helena, the only person who understood her. She considered Helena her best friend, in spite of the twelve-year age difference between them.

They met on the edge of the forest halfway between Rachel's house and Helena's. They embraced, and Helena, taller than Rachel by a head, bent down to kiss Rachel's cheek. There was a faint odor about her of dental paraphernalia. Helena worked Saturday mornings, mostly for the Polish peasants from the surrounding countryside, who always seemed to get toothaches just before Sunday.

"Don't be too late tonight. We have a visitor." Helena spoke in her throaty voice.

"I'll come as soon as I can. I can't leave before Shabbos is over," Rachel said. "Who is your visitor?"

"An old friend of mine," Helena laughed, and a slow blush rose from her throat to her high cheekbones. "Jakob. From the other side of Czestochowa."

"Who is he?" Rachel asked.

She thought how amazing it was that when you grow to love someone, you stop seeing them as they really look. Rachel was in the habit of thinking Helena was fairly nice-looking. Only now, when her friend's features were transformed by a certain softness, did Rachel recognize that ordinarily, Helena was really very plain, with her angular face, her too-thin body.

"He's interesting. He's a Zionist. You'll see."

Helena entwined her arm with Rachel's and they walked along with bouncy steps on the springy carpet of pine needles. Rachel stopped, threw her head back, looked up at the sky showing patches of blue through the trees, stretched out her arms and took a deep breath. At seventeen she was exploding with silent restlessness. Mostly, she was melancholy and serious, but sometimes she experienced such flights of inner exuberance that she thought surely her spirit, separated from her earthbound body, was soaring high above the tall trees of this forest on the edge of Zarki.

They came to the end of the path and emerged on the dusty road leading back into town. Beyond the road the vast, open countryside stretched north all the way to Czestochowa, a Catholic city with its shrine high on the mountain top, and beyond that, Warsaw.

The afternoon sun was low in the sky. Rachel looked off into the distance across the road. A peasant woman was tilling the fields and the furrows of freshly-turned rich brown earth spread outward in an inverted fan. The woman, heavy and shapeless, dropped her hoe, lifted her skirts and half-squatted, a heavy stream of water coming out of her. Presently, she dropped her skirts and resumed hoeing, her back bent over the earth. Rachel sighed. She alternated between despair, at the thought that she would live, marry and die in Zarki, and a firm conviction that she would escape, with the certain knowledge that she was on the verge of something.

"I will see you tonight," Rachel said to Helena.

"Not too late. Remember."

The highlight of Rachel's week was the Saturday night salon Helena had established shortly after she settled in Zarki to open her dental practice, but it was always a source of argument at home. On the evening when Jakob was to come to Helena's salon, Rachel had her usual disagreement with Papa.

"Why do you have to go there all the time? You should be meeting men suitable for marriage. Helena only puts wild ideas in your head." Papa leaned forward in his chair at the head of the dining table. Absent-mindedly, he brushed little crumbs of cake from his luxuriant beard.

"What wild ideas?" Rachel retorted. "They talk about Aleks Mischler; *you* talk about Aleks Mischler. They talk about Zionism; *you* talk about Zionism."

"Be respectful! They don't observe anything—not even Shabbos. You will become like one of them." Papa slammed his hand on the table. The tea glasses shook.

Rachel changed her tone. Papa was, after all, strict, and he was capable of forbidding her to go. She would not have dared to disobey him.

"Papa, it's just a little fun. You let Sofie have all her friends over and they sing and play the piano. These are my friends and my way of having fun. But I won't be late. Let me borrow your fur hat ... please, Papa."

Sofie, her younger sister, said helpfully, "Rachel, you can have my wool hat."

"No, I want Papa's tall fur hat—I love it."

"Take it," Papa said, as usual unable to resist Rachel. Mama, poised to intercede, relaxed and began to clean up after the evening meal.

Rachel ran out of the house and took a deep breath of the late March air. It was an exceptionally clear night. The stars were just beginning to multiply as the bright moon lit the street Rachel followed across town to Helena's. She passed all the closed shops: the fruit and vegetable stalls, tightly shuttered now; the fish market; the kosher butcher. Toward the end of the main street there was a fork in the road, and Rachel took the left branch down an unpaved street with small houses on either side. The other, the right branch led to the edge of town, where her father's leather-curing factory stood. All four of her brothers worked there after school but she rarely set foot in the factory—the smells were so awful. She wondered how they could stand it. Not that they had any choice, of course. Papa demanded work from all of them, the most from the eldest. Still, she recognized it was a good business and made them the wealthiest family in Zarki.

She approached Helena's house with a little thrill. It was brightly lit and voices from inside were rising and falling on the silent night air. Rachel knocked on the door to announce her arrival, walked into the foyer and scraped the mud off her shoes on the straw mat outside the living room. As she stepped over the small threshold into the living room, a man she had not seen before was in mid-sentence.

"You are all too complacent," he was saying. He looked up at Rachel for a moment, then continued. "I used to be like that. Then I woke up."

Helena, reclining on a chaise at the far end of the room, held up her hand, "Stop, stop for a moment, Jakob. This is Rachel. Come, Rachel, sit here next to me."

Rachel crossed the room and took her seat on a large soft footstool near Helena. She regarded the four other people in the room. Lounging on a chair nearest the door was Vitek, his long legs stretched out in front of him, arms crossed in back of his head. His unruly dark hair and thick eyebrows arched above the piercing black eyes; his muscular arms and the whole insouciant tilt of his body emphasized his seductive appeal. Next to him was Marta, his new girlfriend, a slender blond whose quick and lively wit was a match for Vitek's usual sarcasm. Opposite Helena sat Stanislaw, a student in economics, several years older than Rachel and rather unapproachable, with his slight air of superiority. He was home from school in Warsaw to visit his family for the weekend. The other person was Motek, the town pharmacist, a man of unprepossessing looks who had been in love with Helena for many years, starting back in Warsaw where they had both been in school. He seemed always attentive, helping Helena to prepare the cookies and little pastries when company came, and to clean up afterwards. He was unfailingly kind to Rachel, and now he headed off Jakob before he started talking again.

"Rachel, we are happy you came tonight. Jakob is visiting Helena this week. He is trying to get us all to go to Palestine. I am afraid Helena might listen to him."

There was an undertone of sadness in Motek's voice, despite his attempt at lightheartedness. Rachel looked at Helena looking at Jakob from under lowered eyelids. She said nothing, but took her hat off, curled her legs under her skirt on the foot stool and sat quietly as the talking resumed.

Jakob paced around the room with a fierce energy. He was shorter than Helena but taller than Rachel, with a powerful build, and he scowled as he spoke.

"Jews from all over Europe are going to settle Palestine. It is going to be a remarkable land. And you just sit here and talk!"

"Jakob," Helena said. "We are Poles as well as Jews. With Paderewski there's some stability in the government. Pilsudski is on our side. There is an independent Poland now. We have to support it."

"Ah, yes," Stanislaw inhaled deeply on a black cigarette. "Poland has a soul. Where else would a pianist head a government?"

"Independent Poland!" Vitek said bitterly. "All it means for us is more pogroms. We fought for Poland in the Great War and now they boycott Jewish stores and cut off the beards of our old men."

"They don't boycott them here," Motek said. "I have more business from the Polish peasants than ever. They come in from the country—from halfway to Czestochowa—on market day every week and practically buy out the store! I'm doing very well."

"You are all so short-sighted it makes me sick! You can only see in front of your nose. Though I must admit, for some people, that is a long distance." Vitek laughed.

"What a wit you are," Marta taunted him. "I don't see you doing anything but complaining."

"Well, you see all this talk just points out how powerless you are here," Jakob said. "It only underscores what I've been trying to tell you—we must have our own homeland. What you call Polonization … it's really assimilation, and it won't help. They won't let you assimilate even if you wanted to. And why should you want to?"

"I am Polonized," Stanislaw spoke slowly, with a slight accent, which Rachel considered an affectation. "In Warsaw it's quite different. We all speak Polish. We are part of the Polish culture, but that is not assimilation. Yes, there is anti-Semitism at the university. The solution is to take part in the government, to work for change from within."

"Yes, that's what Mischler says," Vitek unexpectedly agreed. "We have to form a strong political action movement."

"Bankrupt idea!" Jakob said vehemently.

Somehow, the conversation always ended up with talk about Aleks Mischler. Rachel was getting a little bored; she amused herself by looking at Jakob's strong arms, the muscles bulging under his shirt.

"Enough," Vitek said. "Come, Helena, let us eat some of your good cake. You see, our little Rachel isn't concerned about such things. Well, you should be, Rachel, you should be."

Rachel had expressed no opinions. She was happy to be there, in the midst of such important talk, but she was too secure in her close family life on the one hand, too full of her dreams on the other, to take their fears and political passions seriously.

They all filed into the dining room and Helena poured tea from a shining silver samovar which she polished every Saturday. They had vanillie-kuchel, the crescent shaped pastries coated with powdered sugar, and small cake puffs filled with preserves and prune butter, while they talked about village gossip and laughed a great deal. It was at times like this that Rachel loved being in Zarki. Loved it, because she was included in this circle, and because it seemed to her this was a prelude to some great adventure. But wherever life took her, Zarki would always be there, a home base from which she could fly away and always return.

"My God, it's eleven o'clock already," Helena exclaimed. "Jakob, be nice—walk Rachel home."

The party was breaking up. Jakob helped Rachel on with her coat and they walked outside into the cool, starlit night air. Rachel stepped gingerly through the mud till they got onto the main street and Jakob held her by the elbow to steady her. She liked the feel of his strong grip. He seemed so much older than the local boys she knew—he seemed like a man. Neither of them said anything for a long time, Rachel because she didn't know what to say and Jakob because he was preoccupied. Finally, he spoke.

"Rachel, you are a beautiful girl. When you walked in with that fur hat, those smoldering eyes … I was captivated. Why were you so silent?"

"I like to listen," Rachel said. "And to learn." Was he flirting with her or laughing at her? In either case, it made her uncomfortable.

"Well, I am going to be here for two weeks. There is much I can teach you—about Palestine, I mean. I will be seeing you at Helena's."

They had reached her house. "Good night," Jakob said and walked away.

❧   ❧   ❧

In the weeks that followed, Rachel went to Helena's nearly every afternoon and sometimes after supper. Jakob was always there. One evening while she and Helena and Jakob sat around the dining room table, having tea and talking about Palestine, Rachel's brother David rushed in, breathless from running all the way.

"Papa wants you home, now. Now!" he said in Yiddish.

"Speak Polish," Rachel said with annoyance. "I'll come after I finish my tea. Go home." Rachel sighed after the door slammed behind David. "I suppose it is late. I'll see you tomorrow."

Jakob walked with her across town. Only an occasional street lamp and the lights in houses along the way lit their path. They passed a Polish house with a crucifix on the door, the limp body of Jesus perfectly sculpted, hanging sadly there. Rachel averted her eyes. In the yard a small flock of white geese herded together, silent and ghostly.

"How do you know so much about Palestine? You've never been there. You don't have family there," Rachel said. "What will you do there? Palestine is a half a world away!"

"I will start my own family," Jakob said. "I will help build that country. It is such a stark, powerful landscape. It is barren now but we will make it green. I feel strangled in Poland—between the anti-Semites on the one side and those narrow, pious Jews on the other … I want to breathe!"

How she envied his certainty, his focus on something larger than himself, on an idea, a goal in life! Rachel had no concrete goals; she was a jumble of feelings. She thought of the future in some vague way as being in a larger world, but she didn't know where she would go or what she would do or whom she would marry. Jakob knew exactly where he was going, and to Rachel it was an aphrodisiac. She knew he found her attractive and she responded with a subtle flirtatiousness.

"You should go to Palestine," Jakob said. "A strong, young girl like you. You would work in the fields, picking oranges in the sun. You would be tan and healthy and bear many children."

"I can just imagine what Papa would say," Rachel laughed. She put her arm through his and their bodies touched as they walked. Everything was hard about Jakob, his chest, his arms, his powerful legs.

"Jakob, I don't want to work on a farm. In an uncivilized country! I want to get out of this small town. I want to be in a big city and have interesting friends and beautiful dresses and parties for important people. I want to run a salon, like Hela, but not in Zarki." Then she lowered her voice and backtracked a bit, thinking she had offended him. "You do make it sound appealing," she said. "Write me when you get there and tell me how it really is." She pressed herself closer against his side.

"Rachel, you don't know what's important. Beautiful dresses and parties are not." He stopped walking, but he held her wrist and she turned to face him, and met his gaze. She thought he was going to kiss her and her breath quickened, and she waited. But he was looking into her with such intensity, she suddenly felt he was evaluating the very core of her being, judging her. Was she just a frivolous girl, was she capable of a hard life given over to a purpose? Was she worthy of his interest? What was his verdict? She couldn't be sure. She lowered her eyes.

Jakob spoke softly in the silent night. "I'll be leaving next week, you know. On Sunday. But I will write you."

Excited by Jakob's promise, Rachel confided to Helena she thought Jakob liked her.

"I can see that," Helena said wryly. "It's a game for you."

"It's not just a game," Rachel protested. "He's so intense. I make him feel a little lighter." She fell silent. She knew that he would leave and they would not see each other again. Why was she leading him on so deliberately? Being a pioneer was not part of her vision and Jakob was not the man of her dreams. Why then? Was it just an exercise in power? She vowed not to flirt with him anymore. When Jakob departed for Palestine the following Sunday, Rachel decided she would forget him.

But the first letter that came from Jakob caused Rachel to blush with excitement. She read it secretly in her room. Now that Jakob was gone, he seemed attractive to her again. The letters began to come regularly, filled with descriptions of the Arabs and the British, and the kibbutz on which Jakob lived.

In the beginning Rachel read the letters to Helena. She could not help herself, in spite of a dim awareness that this was wrong. Helena was the only one who could possibly understand how alive these letters made Rachel feel, how desirable, how filled with possibility. But with each letter the romantic phrases, at first tentative, became so intense, that at last she stopped reading them to Helena.

Rachel answered his letters late at night, when the house was silent. In each letter she put a little poem she had written. Jakob did not ridicule her naïveté nor laugh at her awkward gropings to express the longings of her soul, and thus encouraged, her poems became increasingly more romantic. She had no idea where this was leading and it didn't matter. It was the notion of romance that thrilled her, not the reality. The actual Jakob had almost faded from her mind. Only the Jakob of the letters was real.

❧   ❧   ❧

Rachel was to take her gymnasium examination the following year in Czestochowa. While the boys in her family, exempt from the Polish school, went to *cheder* to have a Jewish education, Rachel and Sofie had no such religious responsibilities. They could never be one of the ten Jewish souls required for a minyan before prayers could start; they could not read from the Torah in synagogue; they could harbor no hope of becoming Talmudic scholars. Rachel had completed the public school of Zarki and had read whatever books Helena lent her, but still she wanted more, more. Papa could see no point in it. Already he was preparing to find a proper husband for her. What would she do with more education?

Still, though Papa had refused to let Rachel study in Czestochowa, he had agreed, after her pleading and stormy tears, to let her prepare for the examination that would lead to a diploma. Rachel awoke every morning at five, and in the dark made her way to the writing table in the bedroom she shared with Sofie. There she worked under the light of the dimmed lamp, when all was still, sometimes writing to Jakob, more often studying for the gymnasium examination, until the early morning sounds of an awakening household and the dawning light would signal that it was time to rouse Sofie. She was filled with tenderness for Sofie, blond curls spread out on the pillow, in those moments before dawn—the tenderness that comes before parting, when the other person does not yet know of the possibility of any separation.

Oh yes, in spite of all her protests and small rebellions, Rachel knew Papa was right—the pull to Helena's salon was the inexorable beginning of a long journey away from her family, but a journey she was not ready to begin. Or had she begun it already? The gymnasium diploma was the exit visa. Rachel was not unaware of that. Oh, but she wanted it, she wanted it more than anything—to be like all those friends she admired: Helena, Vitek, Stanislaw, even Motek, to be educated, set apart from Sofie's crowd and the boys who had merely gone to cheder.

One day a different letter came from Jakob. Rachel took the unopened envelope up to her room, put a chair against the door to keep Sofie out and sat by her open window to read it.

"My dearest Ruchele …" She was suffused with warmth for him, reading this. Only Mama and Sofie used this affectionate diminutive name for her, and Papa in rare moments.

Jakob wrote of the orange crop, of the life of sharing everything—all the work, all the fun. All the planning for the future, all the building going on in the settlement, four new houses now and a main house for dining and meetings, a children's house. Jakob had hopes it would be filled in a few years. Rachel kept reading:

Come to me, Ruchele. I am longing for you. Come and we shall be married here under the stars. There is a rabbi who travels around to the settlements; he will marry us. I can hear you objecting—I will brush away all your doubts. "I am too young," you say, but everyone is young here. This is a country for the young. "I cannot leave my family," you protest, but it is the way of nature for the young to leave their nest—and you have always said you want to get out of Zarki someday. The day is now!

"I don't love you," you say. No, no—that is the only thing I cannot brush away, but I could not believe that, even if you said it, after all those letters you wrote. Write me immediately to say you will marry me and I will make all the arrangements. I know it will take a long time before you receive this and before I receive your response. I shall put it out of my mind until then or else I would not be able to do a day's work. But I cannot truly put it out of mind … I await your reply.

With love,

Jakob

"He actually wants to marry me," Rachel marveled. Marry. She just couldn't imagine that a man actually had proposed marriage to her, a real man, not one of those Jewish boys from nearby towns whom Papa considered for an arranged match. But how had it come to this? She had really been play-acting, but now Jakob was suggesting that she change her whole life.

❈   ❈   ❈

Rachel knew she could not go to Palestine. What did he really know of her if he could imagine that kind of life was for her? She had told him she dreamt of big cities, not farms. Oh, but she yearned for him! Yearned for dancing in the starlit night, while in the children's house, the children slept. Perhaps he did know her. Perhaps it could be. Perhaps anything could be! She wanted to get out of Zarki, so why not to Palestine? She rushed over to Hela's.

"Come with me to the forest. I must show you something." She dragged Helena out and they walked along the shaded paths. Even as she gave Helena the letter, she had misgivings. They stopped for a moment. A small wind had risen up and the tops of the trees bent and rustled above them. It was the end of August, the beginning of fall, but not yet, not yet, thought Rachel, poised on the edge of possibility. After a time Helena dropped her hand to her side, the letter clutched in her fingers, and they walked on.

"How quickly he fell in love with you! How fast! It was just since spring, early spring. He didn't even know you! How much did you see of him, really—a couple of weeks?—and then you wrote him letters." Helena shook her head. She looked down. "I have known him for years. I would go to Palestine tomorrow if Jakob asked me." Her voice was barely audible, so uncharacteristic for strong, determined Helena.

Rachel was overcome with regret. "Hela, Hela, my dear, dear friend, how I must have hurt you—reading all those letters to you. I should have known!"

"You could not have known," Helena said softly. "I never let you see that."

Rachel hated herself with a physical revulsion that rose like nausea. What a fraud I am, she thought, making so much of friendship. Friendship means being the other person, dwelling within her soul, feeling her feelings, making a sacrifice. What kind of sacrifice is it to renounce Jakob when I don't want him anyway?

They walked back to town in silence, Rachel full of remorse, remorse toward Helena whom she had caused such pain, toward Jakob whom she did not love. For a fleeting moment she had a glimpse into his heart and she felt his loneliness and his need of her. She loathed herself anew for leading him to believe she could fulfill that need. But almost simultaneously she saw that he was so determined to live the kind of life he had chosen, she was essentially peripheral to that central idea of his: Palestine. Just as she had needed someone with a destination to lead her into a different world, so perhaps he needed someone passionate but unformed like Rachel, at his side, to complete his dream. Had he invented his own Rachel to fit the image, just as she had imagined for some brief moments that he would rescue her from life in Zarki? Perhaps his impassioned letters to her were really as impersonal as her own.

Helena and Rachel embraced at the edge of the forest and went in their separate directions. Some small balance had shifted between them, Rachel on the brink of possibilities, Helena on the edge of defeat.

Rachel ran home and wrote Jakob a long letter, full of explanations, full of logic.

"Hela adores you," Rachel wrote. "She would be at your side forever. She is my dearest friend. Friendship is more than love."

A month passed, and Rachel received a letter from Jakob with only one sentence.

"You have deceived me."

-2-

She was biding her time. It was a lush spring in Zarki that year. The days were unusually warm and the nights cool when the young people gathered at dusk in the square across the street from Rachel's house. There was a water fountain at one end of the square and the women from the farmhouses came to fill their water cans. They hummed Polish songs under their breaths, while on the other side of the square the Jewish boys and girls flirted. Rachel watched from the living room window. Sofie was out there, in the midst of them, almost every evening.

Papa's leather-curing business prospered and he had an outlet in Czesto-chowa, with plans to expand to Warsaw one day. Meanwhile, Rachel got a new tutor to prepare her for the gymnasium examination.

"Rachel, you must get married," her mother told her. "What will become of you if you go on this way? You are eighteen and you have no prospects."

Rachel, helping Mama make beds late on a Saturday afternoon, hugged the pillow she was holding and looked out the window onto the little square, already strewn with autumn leaves. No prospects! Could that really be true? Her only prospect that of marrying someone like one of her brothers? Not even speaking Polish properly? No, oh no! Still, she remained silent.

Sounds of singing came from downstairs. Sofie's clear soprano rose above the voices of six or seven of her friends, gathered downstairs as they frequently were on Saturday afternoons when Papa was in the synagogue. Someone was playing the piano and struck a wrong note. There was laughter amidst the momentary vocal disorder, like a crystal pitcher breaking, the fragments scattering on the floor.

Sofie, blond and plump and pretty, always surrounded by a group of young people, was pleased with the many prospects she had. Rachel both envied her and thought herself superior. She stood on the stairs, not quite able to join in, but wanting to be there. Rachel was on the fringe of Sofie's crowd; they recognized that she was not quite a part of them, that she was destined for some other life, not so easily joked with. She herself was never completely at ease with them. They did not understand her, as Hela did. Yet often when she looked in on them, singing and laughing in the living room, she had a sense of nostalgia for something that was still in her present. She heard Sofie's soprano blending with the other voices through a filter of time and memory and she fixed the sight and sound of it forever. She missed her family while she was still in the midst of it.

As evening approached, Sofie suddenly said in alarm, "Papa will be home any minute."

One of the boys pulled back the curtains and looked out the window. "He's on the corner. Hurry!" he said. Quickly the piano player closed the piano cover and the boys put on their tallis and pretended to *doven* the *mincha*, the evening prayer, amid suppressed laughter. "No frivolity on the Shabbos," one of them said sternly in mocking imitation of Papa. Rachel watched as Papa walked in, gave them a cursory glance, and went past her upstairs.

The new tutor's name was Pavel, and of course Rachel fell in love with him. But he was a *goy*, so she had to keep her dreams to herself. Papa would have banished him immediately if he had any inkling that Rachel was interested in him. It seemed rather odd that he shouldn't have been wary, since Pavel was young and nice-looking, tall and thin. A lock of his straight blond hair fell over his eyes and he had a gesture of brushing it away that Rachel found endearing. But the idea of a Jewish girl in Zarki, the daughter of Mordecai Wolf Jonish, being entwined with a Catholic Pole was so far from imaginable that it didn't even surface in Papa's consciousness. Mama, however, could imagine it, and she kept a watchful eye on Rachel.

Pavel came from Radom, a nearby town. "So," Papa said when he interviewed him. "You are living with Father Kosciuk. That is on the other side of the Church. And you will have enough time to teach at the Polish school and tutor Rachel as well? I have to get my money's worth. Tell me the truth. Think carefully. I could have taken one of the other teachers at the school, but they said you were going to teach at gymnasium in Warsaw next year—maybe even you could teach at the university. Is that true?" Papa could speak Polish if he chose, though it was heavily accented.

"Yes sir." Pavel's voice was soft but firm and respectful. "I hope for a position in Warsaw for next September. In a gymnasium. I'm afraid I'm not ready for university yet. I will have to earn a doctorate." He smiled gently and looked at Rachel. Something dissolved in her heart. "I am at the school only in the mornings. I will tutor your daughter every afternoon from noon to five."

For the first few weeks Rachel and Pavel exchanged conversation solely concerning mathematics, history, literature. During their one-hour break Pavel went back to the parish house where he lived until, one brilliantly sunny October day, Rachel suggested they walk in the woods. Pavel readily agreed. Her favorite subject was poetry and as they walked, she recited out loud the poems of Mickiewicz and Shakespeare, which she had been required to memorize.

As the weeks went by, Sofie began to complain that Rachel never went out with her and her friends anymore. Helena also commented on Rachel's less frequent appearances at the Saturday salon.

"I'm studying," Rachel told them both. "I'm studying all the time. I must get that gymnasium diploma. I must! I want to live in Czestochowa next year. I'll be nineteen. Papa will have to agree," she confided.

In truth, she was becoming bored with Sofie's parties and Helena's soirées. She cared less about discussing Aleks Mischler's views on Jews and Poles, or talking endlessly about Zionism. If she told Pavel about these things, he would think she was too parochial, too Jewish.

She walked in the forest with him every day now, on their one-hour break that sometimes stretched on into the late afternoon. They tramped through the silent woods, while afternoon sunlight filtered down through the trees, throwing mottled shadows on the ground and Rachel's clear voice rang out with passion amid the fragrance of pine and wild flowers,

"Sweet pain of love, bind thou with fetters fleet
The heart that on the dew of hope must pine!"

They had both stopped walking. Pavel moved toward her, and held her against the trunk of a tall pine. He bent his head and kissed her. They pressed against each other briefly. Then they walked back to town in silence, Rachel's heart beating wildly, seeming to chant, "He's gentile, he's gentile."

When Pavel came to give his lesson the following day, he said nothing, but Rachel relived in her mind that kiss in the forest. She wanted him to touch her. She didn't know what to do, and she could not even tell Sofie about this. She had never let any man touch her below the waist, but now more than anything she wanted Pavel to do it. She had never really understood the joking allusions to an experience she couldn't imagine, but it had been an idea in her head and now it was a desire of her body, though what it was she desired, she didn't know. Only Pavel's touch on her skin, only Pavel's hand on her breast.

All week Rachel thought about nothing else. On Sunday she walked past the church on the edge of town hoping to catch a glimpse of him as he came out, but he was not among the crowd of men with gnarled hands and lined faces, the women in their flowered skirts, filing past the priest out onto the street. He must have gone to early Mass, she concluded, disappointed but also relieved not to have seen him. What would she say? Why was she there?

She continued to go to Hela's salon but she felt somewhat removed from the regular group there. Vitek noticed.

"Rachel, dear little one, you are growing up. Are you leaving us?"

"Of course not," she answered. "Where would I go?"

"I mean in spirit," Vitek said. She didn't respond. The talk turned, as it often did, to Aleks Mischler.

"Mischler thinks the Minorities Treaty is a good thing. It legitimizes the status of the Jews. It allows a Jewish identity, Jewish schools and institutions," Helena said. Her angular features, her dark hair tied in a bun, imparted a seriousness to her face that Rachel lacked. No wonder everyone listened to Helena's opinions.

"And the Ukrainians," Vitek reminded her. "The Ukrainians are a minority here too. And they don't exactly love the Jews. And the Belorussians, and the Lithuanians. Well, we are certainly happy the Versailles Treaty insisted on an independent Poland. One good outcome of the war for us. But the minority rights part of the treaty—it's a sham. There will always be anti-Semitism. We'll see which minorities get the rights."

"You make it sound so abstract," Helena responded. "It's a change in the laws, and it has to benefit everybody, especially the Jews. All the minorities can have their own schools now, their own languages, even public funds. Why be so cynical, Vitek? Believe that something good will come of this. This treaty even allows Jews to keep the Sabbath—no legal business, no civic obligations on Saturdays! It's really quite amazing this has come to pass at last."

"Mischler is in favor of Polonization," Motek said. "Why should he think the Minorities Treaty is so important?"

"But he is not an assimilationist! They're the ones who don't support the Treaty; they don't want Jews to be distinguished from Poles. Mischler is acculturated, but he is deeply opposed to assimilation, to denying your own cultural heritage. Don't you see the difference? Read his editorials. He embraces Polish culture, but he identifies himself as a Jew, and he's a champion of the Jewish cause. The Minorities Treaty is *exactly* what he is for!"

"It's really segregationist. It will divide the nationalities inside the country," Stanislaw said in his slightly bored way. "Each little national group will vie for more rights than some other group."

"It's true pluralism," Hela countered. "It's the only hope."

"Polonization is a good idea," Rachel said passionately. "After all, we are not that different from the Poles. It doesn't mean we can't be Jewish also. Like they are Catholic." She blushed suddenly at the forcefulness in her voice.

"Rachel," Vitek looked at her with interest. "We had no idea you had such strong opinions. What have you been up to?"

"I read too, you know. I have my own ideas. And it happens I know a few Poles. They are just like us."

"Not quite," Vitek said.

Rachel kept silent.

Rachel and Pavel walked in the forest every afternoon, staying longer and longer, but whenever their hands brushed by chance, they each drew away. Rachel imagined she was in a harness, pulled by Papa sitting in his heavy chair in the living room, pulling, pulling on Rachel as she strained invisibly to touch Pavel, till at last on a cloudy, chilly day, pine cones dropping around them, yellow leaves swirling in a sudden wind, their bodies touched, and she lunged forward in her imagination with a force that pulled the ropes out of Papa's hands.

She faced Pavel and embraced him with such resolution that, surprised, he began to kiss her all over, her mouth, her hair, her neck. His hands caressed her body, his long fingers gently outlined her breasts. It was that instant which was so exciting, the instant of yielding after monumental restraint. He stroked her thigh, slowly, gently, through her thick skirt, moving from the outside of her leg inward, all the while leaning over her, kissing her neck, her ear, her mouth, his blond hair falling onto her cheek, tickling gently, softly. She took his hand away from her leg and placed it on her waist and pulled away.

"Stop," she whispered. "Don't."

Why don't, she thought at the moment she said the word. Why not? She was supposed to be a modern person, free of these old-fashioned prohibitions of the village—after all, surely Vitek and Marta did it, surely Helena and Motek—but they were older. Maybe even Sofie had done it, on those picnics in the forest with her friends. And there was nothing wrong about it—Pavel loved her; he was whispering it in her ear this very moment. As she went back and forth in her mind, her excitement diminished and of course she knew she wouldn't do it. She wasn't Helena or Marta or even Sofie—if Sofie really did do it. She pushed his hands away and kissed him. She didn't want to hurt his feelings or embarrass him.

"I can't, Pavel, I can't," she whispered and straightened out her dress.

He stepped away slightly. He was flushed.

"I'm sorry," he said.

They walked deeper into the woods, not wanting to part.

"Come with me to church next Sunday," Pavel said after some time.

"You're not serious!" Rachel was amazed.

"Yes, why not?"

Rachel laughed uncomfortably. "I can just imagine all those people staring at me. I'm not exactly blond and blue-eyed. Besides, everyone knows me in Zarki. Papa would have a stroke!"

"Well, then we can go to the church in Radom. No one knows you there."

"But why, Pavel, what for?"

"You should know about me. Certainly you should know about the Church. It's part of your education."

"Will you come to the synagogue?" But she didn't want him to come to the synagogue. The picture of Pavel, tall, standing with his blond head above the heads of her brothers covered by their enormous prayer shawls, swaying back and forth and chanting unintelligibly in Hebrew, made her shudder. Would they even let him in, a goy? And if he came, they would stare at him uncomfortably and resume their prayers. No, she didn't want him there.

"I'll come with you," she said. "I'll tell Papa we're going on a picnic."

❦   ❦   ❦

They took a horse-drawn carriage early one Sunday morning to Radom, Rachel dressed in a black woven skirt, nearly down to her ankles, and a white, high-necked blouse with lace at the throat. Her dark hair shone and little wisps blew round her face as the wind rushed past when the horses picked up speed. She was feeling very gay and adventurous, but when they entered the church in Radom she held on to Pavel's arm nervously.

It was dark inside and she had to wait for her eyes to adjust after coming in from the bright sun. A smell of incense wafted through the air and the cold stones of the walls and pillars chilled her and she buttoned her jacket all the way. People looked at her as she passed the pews, but then seemed to ignore her. Everyone around her knew exactly what to do, when to kneel, when to sing, what was coming next, and she had no idea. She didn't want to kneel. It was forbidden to her. She certainly couldn't cross herself and wouldn't know how in any case. She felt so uncomfortable, and sinful. What a foolish idea to come here. How different from the synagogue, with its throng of men, separated from the women, each one praying at his own rate, in personal dialogue with God. But she knelt when Pavel knelt, realizing she would be too conspicuous if she remained standing, though she didn't cross herself. She looked up at one point, when everyone else's head was bowed, and saw a shaft of light streaming through the high, stained-glass window, onto the figure of Christ, high on the Cross behind the alter, Christ suffering. The choir sang with unbearable sadness of the "Lamb of God" and then, with mounting joy, of hope and resurrection, the clear notes soaring toward the light. She felt a sudden stab of understanding in her heart, an unexpected compassion for all the sorrow of life on earth and the comfort of hope. But then she saw around her the lined faces of the men, the flat features of the women, the young girls, like herself, dressed in their Sunday finery, all these gentiles who had nothing to do with her, had no part in her life, perhaps even hated her. This was not her world; she did not belong here, she did not *want* to belong here; she was betraying her family. She wanted to run out of there, run into the sunlight outside, run all the way back to Zarki. But she sat still, her hands folded in her lap. This is for my education, she reminded herself, and tried to enjoy the hymns and beautiful melodies, so decorous, so solemn.

On their way back, after a long silence, Pavel asked "Did you like that service?"

"Yes, it was beautiful," she said carefully. "Very different from the synagogue."

"When we go to Czestochowa for your examination I will take you to see Jasna Gora. The church in Czestochowa is the most beautiful in Poland."

"Pavel, what is the point of this?" she cried. "I'm Jewish. It's hopeless."

"But you could convert."

"I would never convert! *You* could convert!"

"Rachel, you don't know what you're saying. I'm going to teach at university one day. It's hard enough to get a post at the university." A small frown appeared between his wide-set eyes, a few lines running perpendicular to his eyebrows.

"And impossible with a Jewish wife!" Rachel said, her voice rising. "Well don't worry, I wouldn't do it anyway."

❈   ❈   ❈

"Ruchele, be careful with your heart," Mama said gently one afternoon when they were sitting alone together at the little round table in front of the living room window, with its crocheted tablecloth hanging to the floor. They sipped their afternoon tea from glasses in silver holders. Mama reached out across the table between them and stroked Rachel's hair.

"Pavel is not for you. But you know that. He will leave you soon."

Rachel looked at Mama in wonder. Her shoulders sagged with relief. At least she could talk to Mama.

"But he loves me, Mama."

"He is a goy. You are a Jewess. To him you are exotic, different. That is not the same as love. And for you too, to you, he is different. But what do you know of that world? You are not comfortable in it. And they would never accept you in it. This can come to nothing. Leave it alone, Ruchele."

"Why, Mama, why couldn't I go to Warsaw with him? There have been marriages between Poles and Jews. If he was Jewish, you would be happy. He is everything you would want for me: intelligent, a gentleman, with a future. Why, just because he's not Jewish?"

"Pfft, pfft, pfft," Mama made spitting noises to drive away the demons. "You must marry a Jewish boy. You know that. Papa would throw you out forever. He would sit shiva for you!"

"Shiva, as if I were dead!

"When I was your age I loved a goy also. I was beautiful and he courted me. But he was never serious, and it passed. It will pass for you too."

"Pavel is serious," Rachel said, but a little tentatively.

"Oh, Ruchele, Ruchele, don't you understand he is playing with you, like you played with Jakob?" Rachel blushed. How did Mama know everything? "Pavel has more important things than you on his mind. He has his career. I don't want to cause you pain, but it will be less pain if you have your eyes open."

In the middle of June, Rachel went to Czestochowa to take her gymnasium examination with Pavel, and Mama as chaperone. Late that afternoon, when she was done, Rachel met them in the Cafe Bristol. She was deliciously happy. She thought she had done well on the examination and she loved being in Czestochowa, so much larger than Zarki, so much livelier. The streets were full of people—Jews and non-Jews. This was where things were happening. After their tea and pastries, on the way back to the train station, they passed a photographer's studio.

"Let's take a picture," Rachel said and walked right into the shop. Mama and Pavel followed her in. The photographer posed her and Pavel against a black velvet backdrop but Mama inserted herself between them.

"Ah, yes," Pavel said, "the chaperone!" They all laughed, in such good humor, as if this were not the end of something. Then the photographer took a portrait of Rachel alone.

"This will be an unusual photograph," he told her. "I will send it out to you in two weeks."

"And I will give it to you, Pavel, so you will never forget me," Rachel said when Mama was out of hearing.

By the end of the summer, Pavel was gone. Without a romantic interest, Rachel was restless. Now that she had finished her studies, she found herself at loose ends. She helped Papa with the bookkeeping and learned his business, and began to press him to let her live in Czestochowa. At last Papa arranged for Rachel to rent a furnished room in the house of a friend of the rabbi's. She had passed her gymnasium examinations and when she became settled in Czestochowa, she enrolled in the Commercial School, made friends with Wanda, a fellow student from Krakow, with whom she often took dinner and did homework, and in the afternoons did the bookkeeping for her father's outlet. And every Friday afternoon she took the two-hour trip by train and then a horse-drawn carriage to Zarki for the Sabbath.

-3-

Czestochowa—1920

One crisp winter Sunday after dusk, Rachel tramped through the streets of Czestochowa to the Social Club to hear a lecture by Aleksander Mischler. The street lamps, placed at a considerable distance from each other, cast her from light into shadow as she walked along, humming to herself, her breath making soft clouds of air in front of her. She wore high boots, the tops hidden under her long, close-fitted coat, and her father's tall hat which had brought with her. She had to balance herself and make her way carefully from her boarding house in a side street to the more even main street. Here there were more lights, more people, more brightly lit windows. She stopped to look in at the mannequins displaying new dresses from Warsaw, new hats, new boots. Rachel loved clothes. She would carefully save small amounts from her food allowance to buy a silk slip. She dreamed of furs and lace. She had just enough money to last her till the beginning of next week and would not be able to buy anything till then. But she was not discontent; she planned her purchases carefully and always within her means. She smiled to herself, burrowed her hands deeper into the large fur muff she carried, and walked on.

She arrived a little late at the Social Club. The lecture had begun and the room was filled. People stood in the back and along the sides but she spied a single seat in the middle of the fourth row and made her way past the other people. It caused a stir and Aleks looked down at the interruption and halted in mid-sentence until she was seated. She looked up at him on the podium. He had a nice compact build and an air of authority. It was only later when she spoke with him at the tea and cake reception that she realized he was only slightly taller than she.

His talk was on the differences between Greek culture and Jewish culture. The emphasis of the Greeks was on the visual and of the Jews on the auditory;

hence, Greek architecture and Jewish Torah, Aleks claimed. The discussion period produced considerable disagreement, particularly from a very vocal young man who disputed this distinction by pointing out that Christianity flowered within Roman culture, which in turn followed the Greek, so one could say that Church music, all that glorious sound of Handel's *Messiah*, Verdi's *Requiem*, Bach Oratorios—all had their roots, though distant, in Greek culture.

"But in a broad sense," said Aleks, "the distinction remains. The Church built glorious Cathedrals and produced paintings. The Jews revered the Word and gave us the Talmud and laws to govern conduct between man and man."

Rachel listened only to the flow of words and missed the substance. In any case, she was determined to meet Aleks in person. Here was the man whose writings they had discussed so ardently at Hela's. Through the entire lecture she schemed how she would approach him and what she would say. Directly, she decided. She came up to him during the tea hour, while he was standing in the center of the room surrounded by a small crowd (mostly of young women), talking to the young man who had spoken from the audience. Though she was shy in Zarki at Helena's salon, she had gained a new confidence living on her own in Czestochowa. Her true nature was evolving: a lack of self-consciousness, mixed with an awareness of her physical charms and a firm belief that if you entertained the possibility of not succeeding, you would not succeed. Rachel never entertained that possibility. All this enabled her to plunge right in and take the initiative, and so she stood before him, holding out her hand and introducing herself as an admirer of his from Zarki.

In the instant between her impulsive outburst and his slightly amused reply, she looked at Aleksander Mischler and found him attractive, in his stylish suit, well-trimmed mustache, dark hair well combed: a man who clearly cared about his appearance, a dignified man, with an air of self-assurance—and perhaps some experience with women. In the surprised silence of the group, Aleks looked at her, and she was both pleased and embarrassed to see that he understood her intent and she knew she had caught his interest even before he spoke.

"How charming of you to say that, Madame. I would be delighted to explain my position to you at some time." He bowed slightly at the waist and returned to his conversation, while Rachel, flustered, retreated to a nearby table and poured herself some tea.

Throughout the rest of the evening she caught him looking at her surreptitiously, but he did not approach her, and she wondered what to do next. Before she could decide, he had left the hall. She became aware of his absence suddenly and was angry at herself for not making sure she would see him again, for the lost opportunity.

But the opportunity was not lost. The Jewish community in Czestochowa was not that large. The Social Club was the gathering place of the more secular of the Jewish youth, and the Cafe Bristol was everyone's favorite meeting place. It was only a matter of time before she would run into him again. In the meantime she began to read his political columns. He wrote in the eloquent, impassioned prose of that time:

> Poland is, for the Polish Jew, his Fatherland, for which he has given his blood from time immemorial and through all insurrections, against all forces attacking Poland. There has been no historic event in Polish history in which the Jew has not taken part wholeheartedly, defending his homeland where his forefathers have lived for over nine hundred years. There must be equal rights for Jews in Independent Poland!

Rachel was moved by the romantic visions of men—a vicarious pleasure, since she herself did not imagine she was capable of having a greater purpose in life. She thought of Aleks as a romantic because he had a vision of a better Poland, a hope that it could be achieved, and a willingness to work for it. Yes, hope and work, she knew, were the essential components that separated the romantic from the dreamer, the true idealist from an idle complainer. It was the first time she associated "romantic" with action. But first there must be a dream. Jakob's dream was of Palestine, Aleks' of Poland. Both were sustained by the motion towards the vision, at their most convincing when in the midst of the process of becoming.

She ran into him unexpectedly one night, at the Cafe Bristol where she was having dinner with her friend Wanda. At the end of their long, leisurely meal, when it was quite late already, Rachel sipped her tea, steaming in the glass set in a silver tea-glass holder. The silver handle was hot and she had to put it down every few seconds. During a lull in their conversation, the waiter came over with a silver tray holding two glasses of brandy.

"For you, from the gentleman at the table near the window."

Rachel looked up and saw Aleks sitting there with a much older man. He smiled and bowed his head in her direction. She smiled back and inclined her head very slightly. Then she turned and resumed talking to Wanda as if nothing had happened.

Rachel held the bowl of the brandy glass in her cupped hand, and took in the strong aroma with a deep breath. She forced herself to sit still, glancing in his direction every once in a while. He was deeply engaged in conversation, but he looked up now and then, and their eyes met. After some time, his companion left the restaurant and Aleks made his way past all the filled tables, greeting people as he went along, to stand beside Rachel and Wanda.

"You are the charming lady who attended my lecture. May I join you?"

Without waiting for an answer, he pulled over a chair from the next table, sat down and motioned to the waiter, "Remy Martin, please."

And so their long and stormy courtship began. Aleks agreed to give her English lessons. "I will come to your house next Wednesday," he had said when he walked her home from the Bristol, after they had taken Wanda to her boarding house.

"No," Rachel said. "My landlord doesn't allow gentlemen to visit."

"Well then, you can come to my house. Next Wednesday at 6. I am at 24 Kopernika Ulica. The entrance is on the side. I will await you eagerly," he said gallantly.

She arrived at the front door, rang the heavy bell and waited expectantly. After what seemed a long time to her, the door opened slightly and a young woman, blond, attractive and just a few years older than Rachel, faced her.

"Who do you want?" she asked without a trace of friendliness.

"I am Rachel Jonish. Mr. Mischler is expecting me."

"Aleks is not here." The door began to close.

"Just a minute!" Rachel stepped forward with her hand on the door, "Just a minute, I am supposed to have an English lesson from Aleks. He is waiting for me."

"I am his sister and I tell you he is not here and he did not say anything about this. Please call him at his office tomorrow." This time the door was closed firmly.

Rachel stood there, flushed, furious, humiliated, helpless.

"Oh," she said, "oh, how could he!" She stamped her foot. She ran all the way home. Determined not to call him, she resolved he would have to pursue her if he wanted her. She had enough men interested in her. Friday she went to Zarki for the weekend.

Home, she felt removed from everyone, as if she walked inside a bubble, and all the sounds that penetrated were muffled, barely reaching her consciousness. Somewhere, dimly, she registered Papa's concern about some new business problems; preoccupied with her own thoughts, she hardly paid attention.

On Monday night, she went to the Bristol. Aleks was sitting alone at a table situated near the brass balustrade marking the aisle that led to the back of the restaurant. Rachel, passing his table, did not look at him, though her heart beat wildly.

"Rachel," he grabbed her wrist. "Rachel, I am sorry about last week. Ella just didn't know, and I was late. I looked for you at the Bristol the next night."

"You should have told her! If I am coming to visit you, you should have prepared your whole family. I should have received a fine welcome!" She faced him furiously.

He raised an eyebrow, "Really? I had no idea I needed to prepare my family."

Rachel blushed. "No, of course not. I have presumed too much."

"Please, sit down," he was gently pulling her. "I really am terribly sorry. Let us start over again. Come on Wednesday night and you will have a royal welcome … in addition to the English lesson."

She came around the balustrade and took a seat opposite him.

"Well, I will try you out again. But I will not come to your house. I will tell my landlord he must allow you to come to me, or I will move out, if he doesn't agree."

Aleks came to her apartment regularly on Wednesday nights. After the English lessons he stayed on while she made tea and they talked more personally.

"It's French you should learn," Aleks told her. "French is the language of the educated. If you were to live in Warsaw you would need to know French."

"English first," Rachel laughed.

"You don't take yourself seriously enough. What will you do with your life? What will you do when you learn English?"

"What do you mean? I'm running my father's business. Perhaps I shall go to Warsaw. Someday I will go to England. I will travel. I will marry—only the right man, of course. I will entertain important people."

"To what purpose? What goal? You should think about that, Rachel. But first, become educated. English is not enough. I will make you a list of books you should read. If you are going to entertain important people, you must have something to talk to them about." He smiled.

Purpose, goal, Rachel thought: men's words. She never saw herself as a mover of the world. She would derive her power from being close to its source, her status from her position as wife of a powerful man.

-4-

The years went by quickly with no commitment from Aleks. They saw each other at his schedule, which was busy and erratic. She would go to the Bristol for late afternoon tea, hoping to run into him; often she did, and then he would always be gracious, always invite her to join him no matter who he was with. But she did not feel foremost in his life. And though it exasperated her, it also attracted her, that he was a man of the world, dealing with matters of consequence, and romance was only one part of his life. In spite of the temptations of Pavel, she was still a virgin. She knew she should be married by now, have children even. Girls were married off by their parents at sixteen, seventeen, and here she was at twenty, ignorant of the most important aspect of adult life. She hoped Aleks would seduce her: he was so much older, fifteen years older, clearly experienced, interested in women. But he was very careful with her, too careful, and all they had exchanged were kisses. It was always he who broke away, always he who restrained himself. One night, in early summer, he took her out to dinner and afterwards, at the doorstep of her house, he put his hand on her breast. She felt its warmth as he pressed his fingers to her breast, touched her through her silk shirt. Her nipple hardened, her groin ached. He kissed her neck, but he went no further and he left Rachel moist and agitated.

She had finished the Commercial School course and now managed her father's leather outlet. Papa came to Czestochowa one day, appearing unexpectedly at her apartment in his long black coat, his fedora hat covering his thick hair. He said he was losing money; the only way out was to expand, to buy new machinery, and for that he needed money.

"Oh, Papa, why do you have to borrow always? If you are losing money you shouldn't expand; you have to consolidate. Let's concentrate on Czestochowa. We can cut the overhead here, get rid of Tadeusz. I can run it myself. We'll get more salesmen on commission. I hate to borrow."

"What do you know about business!" he said angrily, tugging on his beard. "You are still a child. A girl! You should be married. I made a mistake letting you come here."

"I will try, Papa. I will try." Rachel was contrite. "I will borrow from the bank for you."

"Why would the bank lend to you and not to me? No, you have to ask your friends."

"Don't worry Papa, I will do it somehow."

She decided to approach Frederik Malinowski, though she hated to ask him. He had pursued her when he was her teacher in the Commercial School and she had not been kind to him. Now he was president of the Bank of Czestochowa, just as he had predicted he would be in the days she had scorned him.

"Rachel Jonish!" he exclaimed with genuine pleasure when she appeared at his office on Monday morning. He was married now, just a little paunchier than when he was her teacher, more self-satisfied, clearly more successful. He could afford to be generous of spirit with her. Rachel understood that meant he no longer cared, and she felt a small twinge of regret.

"Rachel, sit down, sit down." He came around the large polished desk and pulled out a chair for her. "How is life treating you? I hear you are busy with Aleks Mischler. You see, I do keep up with your affairs of the heart."

Rachel laughed. She felt warmed by his presence. Now that there was no sexual tension between them, he could be her friend, perhaps her protector even.

"And Aleks, are you serious about Aleks?" he persisted.

"I shall marry him."

"Rachel, you are a strong-willed woman but you are wasting your energy. He has the reputation of being a ladies' man. He won't marry. I would not like to see you suffer."

"We'll see," Rachel's eyes sparkled.

"Well, what can I do for you?"

"Frederik, I want to borrow money—that is, my father wants to borrow money—to buy new machinery for his leather curing business. You know we have an outlet here and we are doing well. But in these days if you don't go forward, you go backward. You taught me that too—you can't stand still. He has to modernize."

"With what collateral, Rachel?"

"My word," she said resolutely.

"Your word ... Rachel," he sighed, sitting back in his chair." My investors would laugh at me if I told them I lent the bank's money on the word of a young woman I was once in love with. You know that's impossible."

"Frederik, I swear to you, you will have the money back and with interest, in two years' time. I swear it. But my father will make his factory building in Zarki the collateral."

"Rachel, it is against my better judgment to mix business with my personal feelings about you. Still, the economy is booming. If it's a sound investment I would consider it—not just on the strength of your beautiful dark eyes. Well, tell your father to come see me on Friday, with all the figures, and we will see."

"Thank you, Frederik. You won't regret it. But not on Friday. He must be home in time for the Sabbath. On Thursday."

"You drive a hard bargain, Rachel," he laughed. "On Thursday, then. At noon."

Frederik's bank lent Papa most of the money he wanted and Rachel felt personally responsible for paying off this debt. Still, the money was not enough. She managed to get some more on the black market, though it was at fifteen percent, a dangerous rate.

"Imagine," she confided to Wanda, "during the day I am with those black marketeers borrowing money for father and in the evening I am with the biggest society of Czestochowa—not only Aleks. There is Marcusfeld, the engineer, Andre who's a concert pianist ... the biggest society of Czestochowa ..."

Aleks did not approve, but he was not a businessman and for the first time Rachel was torn between her deep respect for his intellect and a slight contempt for his lack of business acumen. Of course, this feeling arose at least partly from her resentment against Papa's demands on her and her resultant overcompensation by defending Papa and his ways to Aleks. Aleks, meanwhile, was embroiled in his own family problems. He had three sisters—stepsisters really. His mother had died when he was a small boy and his father had remarried and had three daughters with his second wife. These stepsisters were close to Aleks, who felt responsible for them, but they did not like Rachel, for they believed she was pulling him away from his own family. In particular, Ella, the eldest, who perceived a serious competition for Aleks' loyalty, was caustic and unfriendly to Rachel. Lena was a beautiful, blond young woman who did not have any meanness in her and also not much brainpower. Jadwiga already seemed destined to be an old maid, with her prissy ways and mousy demeanor, but was not a threat to Rachel. Only Ella was a potential problem. At first

Rachel tried to be friendly, but after she was rebuffed on several occasions, she became haughty in her manner to Ella, encouraging further hostility.

In the meantime, Aleks' father had a stroke and left his porcelain factory to be run by Aleks, who had little idea of how to run such a business. But his sisters depended on him and so he gave up his post at the newspaper and took over the porcelain factory, much to Rachel's chagrin. He still wrote occasional articles on political matters, which were eagerly awaited by his audience who would sit in the Cafe Bristol when the weekly edition of the paper came out and discuss his views. However, now that he was the sole support of his sisters, his relationship with Rachel was not progressing. She despaired, fearing that they would never marry. Another winter approached and Rachel seemed to be standing still.

It was after Christmas in Czestochowa, mid-January, but the decorations were still in the store windows. Old Christmas trees were discarded on the sidewalks while tinseled streamers still hung in windows of restaurants and wreaths of holly were displayed on the heavy carved wooden doors of small apartment houses in the residential section of town. Pictures of Our Lady of Czestochowa shone from people's windows. Known as the Black Madonna, her face was darkened by a fire that had almost consumed the painting of her, but had left it browned by smoke instead. Dressed in robes of orange and deep blue, adorned with jewels, she looked out upon the world serenely but with grief in her eyes, while the little Saint Casimir she held in her arms bestowed his blessings with raised hand. Around their golden crowns, small angels danced. But her lips seemed sensual to Rachel, Clara Bow lips, full and slightly pouting.

How strange this Christian world was, Rachel thought, how foreign and yet familiar to her. She lived in the midst of it, but she was not part of it. She remembered how one sunny day she had been walking in the woods outside of Zarki and, looking down, saw a stream of ants across her path. She had stopped to watch them as they scurried in almost a straight line, determined and purposeful, clearly intent on some momentously important task, caught up in their own universe and totally unaware of hers. And yet she could have destroyed their whole nation with one footstep. She had hopped over them, careful not to disturb a single one in its mission. She thought of those ants as she walked along the streets of Czestochowa, thought of all the many different universes, each inhabited by its own creatures with their own purposes and problems, oblivious to all the others, separate. Her own personal universe centered on Aleks. She wanted to possess him and he would not yield to her.

❧　　　　　❧　　　　　❧

One Tuesday afternoon, after a fight with Aleks about his desire for freedom and her desire for marriage, she took the train home to Zarki in defeat, arriving dusty and tired after the half-hour ride in the horse-drawn cart from the train station, and in a gloomy mood. Mama was shocked to see how thin she was, how drawn her face. Rachel was glad to be home; it was all so familiar to her, so safe, so far removed from her life in Czestochowa. She longed to be back here again, and at the same time she felt like a trespasser, foreign. This was not her world anymore. She felt cast out of the other one by Aleks' coolness, but not a part of this one, nowhere, displaced, floating. Where did she belong?

Her family greeted her happily, surprised to see her in the middle of the week, but she didn't want to talk. She had not brought them any gifts, as she always did when she came home. They knew something was wrong, and uncharacteristically, kindly, they left her alone. She went up to her room, the room she had shared with Sofie, and after a while Mama came in. Rachel told her everything, and in the telling, thought, how shrill I have become, how righteous—always complaining, wanting, demanding. What man would want me? Why can't I be nicer, softer?

Mama said, "What kind of a man is that? What does he want with you?"

Rachel slept till noon the next day and they let her sleep. At noon, two dozen yellow roses arrived. The card had only one word on it: "Aleks." Rachel did not respond. She was not playing games now; she was just weary of herself, of Aleks, of this constant seething. Ah, but the roses, the yellow roses …

On Thursday night, Aleks arrived, and Rachel's resolve and despair vanished. By midnight they were engaged.

All the children and the neighbors from the house next door were woken up. Moniek ran across town to get Helena. Mama produced platters of chopped liver, herrings and black bread, and of course, slivovitz and bottles of vodka. They sang and danced and got drunk and welcomed Aleks, who brought class and learning and honor into their family. Rachel, twenty-one years old, flushed and happy, stood poised on the brink of her future filled with prospects of realizing all her inchoate dreams as the wife of an important man, an intellectual. It was 1922. Everything was getting better.

-5-

"Post coitus animus tristus est," Aleks said softly, looking up at the ornate ceiling of the bedroom in the Hotel Europeiska, Rachel's head resting on his shoulder, her breast against his arm.

Engagement had brought new status to Rachel and though no date was set for the marriage, they now made love wherever they could, often registering in a Warsaw hotel as Mr. and Mrs. Mischler.

"Why?" Rachel asked. "Why sad?"

"Man and woman were one flesh. Then God split Eve from Adam's rib and ever since they have been trying to get back together again through intercourse."

"You are laughing at me."

"No," Aleks said. "I am not laughing. The soul is sad because it realizes the impossibility of achieving oneness. We are all separate."

"I don't feel that way," Rachel said passionately, almost angrily. "I feel close to you. We can be as one. I am with you. You pull away."

"Rachel, enjoy your illusions. It is so nonetheless. At the height of the climax, you are alone."

"But after the climax, I am more wholly a part of you."

He sighed and she trembled a little at the glimpse of this dark side of his nature that mixed despair with hope. She made love to him freely but she sensed in him a yearning unsatisfied by climax, unsatisfied by her.

Life had not changed very much for Rachel in that first year since their engagement. Though their relationship was easier and Rachel confided all her thoughts to him, there still seemed to be some secret part of him not wholly accessible to her. Ella was not happy with the entire situation, though Rachel dutifully went to see Aleks' sisters once a week.

"He cannot marry you now," Ella told Rachel. "He has three sisters and Father is dying. He never really recovered after his stroke last year. Aleks has to give up this idiocy of writing for that paper for practically nothing. Just wasting his time. We have a porcelain factory to run. Who does he think will run it? You should be a good influence on him; after all, if he does marry you, you will need money to live on also. He can't make a living with his ideas."

Rachel laughed and gave Ella a hug. She really tried to make his sisters like her, but with Ella it seemed hopeless. Lena and Jadwiga were friendlier.

"Aleks is rich," Rachel said. "He told Papa he is a very rich man—he has a personal library full of the best books!"

"You can't live on books! You have to have key money for an apartment. And you can't live with us!"

"A marriage is a partnership," Rachel said, shuddering inwardly at even the notion of living with them. "I am working too. Anyway, Aleks will be going to Warsaw soon. We plan to live in Warsaw."

"Hah!" Ella said. "You are a frivolous, impossible girl. He belongs with his family!"

❦   ❦   ❦

"I am selling the Czestochowa outlet," Papa told Rachel. "I have debts."

"Yes," Rachel sighed. "I knew it would come."

Papa's business was declining. Cured leather was beginning to come in from South America at far lower prices and his constant expansions resulted in heavy debts.

"But I will give you ten thousand zloty for your dowry."

"Oh, Papa you don't have to do that."

"He'll never marry you if I don't. He doesn't have a groszen. Where will you live?"

Aleks had moved to Warsaw, rewarded for his service in Pilsudski's Legion with a position in the government, but he had no key money for an apartment. There was no more reason for Rachel to stay in Czestochowa, so she moved back to Zarki to wait. She wrote to Aleks after her dowry was deposited in the bank: "I have money for an apartment. We can marry."

"Soon," he wrote back. "First I must find an apartment for us. It is very difficult. In a year. I am getting established."

One day blended into another and in some ways it seemed as if time stood still while Rachel waited in Zarki. In the beginning, being home again, she was happy because clearly this was such a temporary thing—just until her wedding, just a few months, a year perhaps. She helped Papa with the bookkeeping and watched while the expenses mounted and the income diminished.

"Papa," she said one day, "I can't pay the bill for the last shipment of leather you received. There is not enough money to cover the whole shipment. Don't order so much the next time. We have to pay this first."

"Just pay a third this month. Next month we will have more money coming in. Maybe Aleks can do something."

"Aleks is not in the leather business!" she said angrily. But she continued to juggle the bills, burdened, responsible, resentful. She had already borrowed a lot of money for him from Frederik. How was she going to pay it back when Papa couldn't keep up with his monthly bills? She hated his dependency on her, then felt guilty for her resentment and redoubled her efforts to please him to make up for it. But why, why did he have to draw her into his problems, into his life? She had her own life to look out for. How would she be able to get away again? Oh, how she hated business. Thank God Aleks was an intellectual. Her life would be different.

Now that she was home again, she spent more time with Mama and began to see her in a new light. Mama, whose outlines were always a little blurred, soft around the edges, compared to strong, demanding Papa; Mama, whose very existence was to cook, care, love, keep things in order—Mama had a secret life. There in her bedroom, Rachel found a closet full of exquisitely hand-sewn, fashionable, rich dresses. She had ordered fine materials from Warsaw, velvets, silks, brocades, and had them made up by a dressmaker in the next village. And there they were in her closet: a plum burgundy velvet dress with white ermine trim, a black silk and velvet with shiny sequins glittering in the dimly lit room, silk-flowered taffetas with ruffles. What kind of life were these dresses made for? Certainly not the one Mama led. But she wore them to the synagogue, on vacations in Carlsbad which she took sometimes with Papa, sometimes with the rabbi's wife when Papa couldn't get away. Mama had her own dreams, Rachel realized, unfulfilled perhaps, but kept alive by those beautiful dresses. How poignant, Rachel thought, that her mother, like Rachel herself, had these unspoken yearnings.

Rachel saw Helena too, most Saturday nights. Now when she went to those weekly salons, she was a participant. She had lived in Czestochowa, she was engaged to Aleksander Mischler, she had opinions worth listening to.

"How you have grown up," Helena said to her one day, as they were walking in the familiar, rustling woods outside of town. "You are no longer the little mouse in the corner—if you ever were. I think you were just pretending."

Rachel laughed. "With Aleks I'm still the little mouse."

"I don't believe that," said Helena. "I don't think you believe that either."

"Maybe not. But I can't quite get inside him. There is some way he keeps me away. Why shouldn't he tell me all his thoughts? I tell him. Well, it is true he has taught me a lot. Sometimes I feel it was Aleks who brought me up, not my parents. I didn't know anything about the world before I met him. He knows everything."

"You will go far, Rachel. I don't worry about you. But you will still have one foot in Zarki. I don't know if one can ever get away from here, no matter where one goes. But I have something to tell you. I am going far too. I am going to Palestine."

"To Palestine?" Rachel stopped walking. "Jakob? He has asked you to come?" A million thoughts of the life she had given up flashed through Rachel's mind.

"No," Helena said. "I am going because he is there, but he doesn't know I am coming. He does not write to me. I don't know what he is doing. He may be married. But I have to go and see. I cannot stand it here anymore. There is nothing for me here. I like the salons and the visitors; I like to be at the center of the life in this town. You know, everyone who passes through comes to see me—but that is just it; they pass through and I am left. No," she shook her head. "I have to go to Palestine … I will be useful there. I am sure they don't have enough dentists or doctors or engineers or people who have special skills. I can be part of a larger life than just talking here on Saturday nights. And maybe Jakob is free, and maybe he will need me."

My God, Rachel thought, poor Helena. Rachel was a little shocked, but what really surprised her was that Helena also had dreams, like her mother had her own dreams. Rachel was not the only one. It seemed so obvious to her now. Of course. Everyone wants something; what is so amazing is that the something is so different for each person on Earth. In that instant she had the experience of the discrete, separate nature of every living being and she suddenly understood what Aleks meant when he said, "We are all separate." She felt even stronger the renewed longing not to be separate, to merge, to engulf and be engulfed, all the while realizing there was nothing she could say to her friend. She thought, Jakob will not want her now—he didn't want her then, and these things don't change. How sad she doesn't know that. Rachel was overwhelmed with pain for her friend, for her mother, for her father, for all those who yearn in futility.

The two friends looked at each other, so much unspoken between them, and put their arms around each other. They wept softly, underneath the fir trees, knowing they were parting, perhaps forever.

-6-

Rachel came home from the leather factory one Friday afternoon. She was furious. Papa had ignored her warnings and ordered a whole new shipment.

"You told me you wouldn't order any more till you sold at least half of last year's stock," she shouted. "You know we haven't paid for the new machine yet. And I have to send 600 zloty to the bank for the loan payment." Papa did not answer. "Why did you do that without telling me?" Her voice had risen to a high pitch.

"I am getting ready for Shabbos. I will not talk about it now."

"Shabbos, Shabbos, what do I care about Shabbos! You will be ruined!"

They stood facing each other, he nearly a foot taller, his beard, luxurious, black but already flecked with gray, his breath faintly scented with tobacco, his body solid, powerful, legs spread apart, and she small, firm with every taut muscle in her arms, legs, and face, bespeaking determination. He slapped her with an open palm, the fingers leaving white marks on her cheek.

"Get dressed for Shabbos."

She stood motionless, her hand upon her cheek. In a blinding revelation she had a glimpse of his weakness. It was not out of strength he slapped her. She could never unknow that about him from now on—and at the same time she felt a deep pity that he had had to reveal that part of him to her, and that he now understood that she knew. With that slap, everything was altered between them. He turned away and went upstairs.

Mama rushed in to the living room from the dining room where she had been putting on the finishing touches to the Sabbath table.

"What happened? What happened? Ruchele, why did you make Papa angry? What did he do to you?" She stared at Rachel holding her hand to her cheek. "Always before dinner! Why must there be such a commotion before Shabbos? Come, get dressed, we will talk all about it tomorrow. Everything can be solved if we talk about it. Come, it will be time to light the candles in seven minutes. Hurry."

"Mama, I am not having dinner tonight," Rachel said quietly. She walked past the dining room toward the stairs, feeling as if she were looking in at someone else's home, someone else's life. The table was set with a white cloth and china ringed with blue. The silver gleamed, the wine glasses sparkled, and two tall candles in the special silver candleholders waited to be lit at Mama's end of the table. The warm smell of freshly baked challah permeated the air, and decanters of red wine at each end of the long table cast rich, burgundy shadows amidst the glow of white and silver and crystal. A place was set for the "Shabbos guest."

Mama came into Rachel's room, halfway through the meal, with a dinner plate laden with slices of beef brisket and potato pudding.

"Eat, Ruchele, eat. You need your strength. Papa is already sorry he got angry at you. But his life is difficult. You must understand that. When you are older you will understand."

"I am not hungry," Rachel said. "And your life? How difficult is your life? Does he ever think of that?"

"My life is not difficult," Mama said. "I have a kitchen maid and a cleaning maid. I have wonderful children. I go to Zakopany on vacation, and to Carlsbad. Papa is respected in town. What else can I want? Business is always risky—sometimes it's up, sometimes it's down—but we have done well. You have fine clothes, you have an education, and you always have enough money for your pleasures. And you even have a dowry." She smiled.

"I hate business," Rachel said. "Papa has grand dreams, but what does he back them up with? Air, dreams and air."

"Children don't know anything about their parents. One day you may understand him … when you have children of your own," Mama said gently and left the room to rejoin her family at the table for dessert.

Rachel and Papa did not exchange a word all during the Sabbath and not till after sundown on Saturday, after the evening meal, did Papa even look at her. Finally, he said, "I am going to declare bankruptcy."

"You can't do that, Papa. That means the bank will only get paid forty groszy on every zloty owed."

"Yes, and so will all the other creditors. Everyone will get something."

Rachel was in despair. "Papa, I gave Frederik my word that the bank would be paid back everything on the loan. I cannot go back on my word."

"You have to pay the bank," Mama said. "If you don't, you will never be able to start your business again. If you don't pay the bank, no one will give you credit."

"Papa, the leather wholesalers and the chemical plants will want you to be in business. They get large orders from you, so it is in their interest to see you don't fail. They will wait for their money. But the bank must be paid. Frederik trusted me."

"The bank has money," Papa said. "The creditors have to pay wages. They may end up going out of business too."

"We will pay the smaller ones first," Rachel said.

Finally, reluctantly, Papa agreed to pay the bank and Rachel made out the check for the full balance owed. The creditors had to be stalled. Papa decided he would build up slowly again. But now he came home each night with a weary sadness in his face, not hidden by the full beard, as most of his expressions were.

The Sabbath meals grew less lavish. Mama did not go to Carlsbad in the spring. Sofie did not get new clothes at Passover, as she always had, but she didn't complain. She was quieter these days, and had fewer gay outings with her friends. Rachel looked at her sadly one day when she was helping Mama in the kitchen (they had to let the cook go) and realized that Sofie's liveliest years were in a household that was suddenly impoverished, whereas her own had been in a household of abundance.

Rachel continued to juggle bills, but now the chemical suppliers would not ship the materials he needed for curing the large inventory of raw leather he intended to sell off in order to raise the money to start again. Meantime, good leather was coming in from Brazil, at lower prices, now that imports were growing. Inflation was increasing. The zloty was falling against the dollar. Papa's situation continued to get worse.

He came home early one afternoon and sat down at the dining room table and put his head down on his folded arms. He was perspiring profusely.

"What is it?" Mama asked.

"I have some pains in my stomach … and my arm, my left arm. I have to rest a little. I'll be all right."

His face was white above the beard, his shirt drenched in sweat. Rachel came in from the living room, frightened. He belched loudly.

"That feels better," he said. "I am better." But he looked worse.

Rachel ran out of the house down the street, to the main thoroughfare, to the doctor's house. She summoned him to follow her home immediately. Waddling after her, puffing as he ran, his heavy body rocked from side to side. He was an elderly man, barely trained, a Jewish country doctor mostly ministering to colds and bruises, and attending deathbeds, his watery eyes full of sympathy since that was mainly what he had to offer.

"A heart attack," he proclaimed as soon as he saw Papa's gray face. "Bed and complete rest. Too risky to move him to the hospital in Czestochowa." Moniek and David carried him upstairs and Rachel saw how suddenly frail he looked, sweating and groaning softly.

"It is in God's hands," the doctor said.

Rachel spent every morning at his bedside in the darkened room. Papa could not talk. He lay under the cover, his beard spread out on his chest, his face yellow and perspiring. She moistened his lips with lemon water. She sat at the side of his bed, silently stroking his hand, then rushed off to the factory when Mama came up to be there all afternoon till Rachel would return in early evening. The other children came and went throughout the day. Sofie was frightened.

"Will he die?" she asked Rachel, her eyes wide in her pale face.

"I don't know. I don't know," Rachel wearily replied.

One afternoon, when Mama came up to the sickroom, Rachel went down to the little park in front of the house and sat on a bench, amidst the blossoming lilac.

"He will die," she thought. "My fault, my fault. I hounded him. I killed him."

How could everything be so beautiful in this garden, this world, how could the sun shine so brightly, every budding leaf on the branch so crisply outlined against the blue sky, when inside was death?

She took a small notebook out of her purse and wrote a poem which she sent to Aleks.

> "W ogrodzie wsrod ruzy i kwiaty,
> siedzi dusha i mazy o szczescie minione ..."

In a garden among roses and grass, sits a soul and mourns the happiness passed.

Papa got better. Two weeks went by and the doctor thought he was out of danger. But he still he had to remain in bed another four weeks or so. The days became routine. Rachel resumed going to the factory, which Moniek was closing down. They planned to rent most of the building to some other business for the income, and slowly, slowly, try to pay off their debts. Maybe they would even have to sell the building—if they could even manage to find a buyer. Moniek had already closed the outlets in two other towns and cut the payroll entirely. Now only the family worked in the business. They decided to tell Papa what they were doing after he was well. He didn't ask and they didn't speak about it.

A letter came from Aleks. "Rachel, you have your dowry. Give it to your father. It will get him on his feet again."

Rachel was filled with anguish. Without a dowry how could they marry? How would they get an apartment? But immediately, her heart shifted. If my fiancé wants to give my father the money, what kind of daughter would I be if I didn't? How could I even be so selfish for a moment? Of course, of course I will give it to him! She was full of gratitude to Aleks. His generosity shamed her but filled her heart to overflowing with love for him. Now when they told Papa what they had done with the business, it wouldn't be so bad; he would have the ten thousand zloty to start again, he had not declared bankruptcy and he had paid off the bank. Her spirits lifted.

When she told Papa about the money, he nodded and closed his eyes, and turned his head toward the window.

❧   ❧   ❧

Rachel grew thinner and paler and sadder, waiting for a wedding that seemed increasingly remote. With the dowry gone and no key money for an apartment, Aleks, busy and rising, seemed content to just let time slip by.

One hot summer Tuesday morning Vitek and Marta appeared.

"Come for a walk, Rachel. Don't go to work today. We have something to tell you," Marta said.

Rachel went gladly. There was no more laughter or singing in her house. She was grateful to Vitek and Marta for reminding her of Hela, of the old times at the Saturday night salons, of the heated discussions, the camaraderie, the days of hope and promise.

They walked through the market square. The stalls were open and the peasant women, with brightly colored kerchiefs on their heads, faces browned by the sun, bits of straw from their wagons still clinging to their full skirts, bargained with housewives. Rachel stopped at a cart, filled with new red potatoes covered in clinging earth, ripe red tomatoes with green stems, great bunches of green onions, parsley and dill. Marta and Vitek waited while she purchased a bunch of dill for Mama's chicken soup. Into the dusty street circled by old buildings came the fragrance of the fields outside of town.

"We are getting married," Marta said when they moved on beyond the square. "We are going to Warsaw."

"Well, she finally convinced me," Vitek said. "But, really, I feel hope now. Pilsudski believes in socialism and in pluralism. He doesn't want to amalgamate everyone; he believes in the rights of national minorities and we are one of those groups. Your Aleks must be happy." He looked sideways at Rachel.

"Oh, Marta, I am so happy for you. That's wonderful. Vitek, I am so happy. I wish you everything good. It's so wonderful!" Rachel kissed Marta and hugged Vitek. She wished her voice sounded stronger, more exuberant, to match her words. Zarki without them. First Hela, then Marta and Vitek ... only Rachel would remain, lonelier than ever.

"Come with us to Czestochowa tomorrow. Just for the day. I am going to get material for a dress for the wedding. And you will be my maid of honor. You must get material too." Marta put her arms around Rachel's shoulders.

"Of course, I will come," Rachel said. "It will be a lovely outing."

They got to Czestochowa by noon and immediately went to the Cafe Bristol for lunch. She looked around, half-expecting to see Aleks at the table beside the balustrade. Everywhere she walked, she thought she saw him. Czestochowa, once so familiar and exciting to her, was a dead city, full of strangers, without Aleks in it. How could a city change so much? Just knowing Aleks was somewhere in that town, even when she didn't see him for a week, made it home to her, and now it was empty and alien. She shook herself out of this mood. It was not fair to Marta and Vitek. They walked through town and passed the photographer's shop. Vitek stopped in front of the window.

"It's you, Rachel. It's your picture! How beautiful you are!" he exclaimed, almost with surprise, as if he saw her in a new light, his familiar, everyday Rachel.

"It's the picture I had taken when I was here for my gymnasium examination with Pavel," Rachel said. The photographer was using it as a display of his work.

The portrait was enlarged and set in an ornate gilt frame, like a painting. The girl who looked out at them with smoldering eyes seemed to be mocking Rachel. There was a wild beauty about her, with wisps of hair blowing about the smooth contours of her face, high cheekbones, perfectly proportioned nose, slightly parted lips. Her long neck was accentuated by the high neckline of her dark dress, coming all the way up to her chin. There was a sensuousness and determination about her dark, intense eyes, the blown hair, the proud thrust of the chin. But more interesting than beauty, there shone an expectation of life, and an eagerness to grasp it. Rachel shivered slightly in the warm sun. Where was that girl in the portrait? It shook Rachel's spirit. She was not going to go around moping, feeling sorry for herself. Enough! She was fortunate that her father was getting well, Aleks loved her, she had a glistening future—everything was ahead of her. Everything depended on her attitude, and she had control of that.

"Let's go to the material shop, Marta. Vitek can do some errands of his own. I am going to buy material for my wedding dress too. Then I want to visit Aleks's family. We can meet back at the Bristol at six and still get back to Zarki before it's very late." She was suddenly gay and energetic, and they walked down the street, three abreast, with Rachel in the middle, her arms entwined in each of theirs.

They passed a newsstand and she saw the headlines: "Mischler Struck by Doroshka." Instantly she imagined the horses' hooves flying, kicking Aleks in the stomach, the head. She grabbed the paper and read on.

Aleksander Mischler, political writer and now an official in the Ministry of Interior, was struck down by the wheels of a doroshka while he was crossing Marshalkowska Ulica with Senator Friedeman, who was unhurt. Mr. Mischler was taken to Warsaw General Hospital where he is being treated for suspected internal injuries. His condition is good. Mr. Mischler was recently appointed by Marshal Pilsudski to ...

She felt a hole in the center of her being, her stomach like a vast, empty crater. How perilous life was, how fragile! She might have lost him. Her father might have died after his heart attack and though that was terrible to contemplate, it was in the natural order of things—parents get old—but that Aleks might die was unimaginable. She did imagine, though, and once imagined, it left forever a strain of underlying, pervasive anxiety that she would always henceforth try to obliterate by action.

She ran to Ella's house, Marta following, and instead of the usual cold reception, Ella, glancing down at the newspaper clutched in Rachel's hand, uncharacteristically threw her arms about Rachel.

"He's all right. He's all right," she said. "We had a telegram. Just this morning. I was going to have it delivered to you. Here." She held it out to Rachel.

"Ignore newspapers. Stop. I am fine. Stop. Tell Rachel. Stop. Love, Aleks."

"I am going to Warsaw," Rachel declared. "Tomorrow."

But when she returned to Zarki, Mama said, "Wait. He will come to you." And a few days later there was a letter.

"Dearest Rachel," Aleks wrote,

I am recovering. And now for the best news: Pilsudski has asked me to be Counselor to the Minorities Groups in the Ministry of Interior. This means Ukrainians, Jews, all groups. It is a big promotion, a wonderful development for a Jew to have such a post in the government! Independent Poland is taking shape in a government built upon justice and freedom for all groups to develop their own identities, and I will have a role in that.

I know you too are anxious to start on a new life. Soon we will be married. My hand shakes as I write this. Married! But you are the only woman who has so captivated me that I want to share all my life with you. It will not be easy; a government official does not earn much. But I promise you will not be bored. You will not be just a housewife, quietly tending to her own private household. You will be among those who make things happen.

I want to look into your dark eyes and bring them to a deep smile. I love you and kiss you and hug you. Your devoted, Aleks.

"Soon," Mama said. "How soon is soon?"

"You have wasted your prospects," Papa said. "He won't marry you. You are too thin and you are getting old."

Rachel kept quiet. Papa was still convalescing but he was increasingly more difficult. Home all day, he mostly lay on the sofa in the living room, and Mama served him tea and little cakes and compote every hour. He would ask for milk with his tea after Mama had brought the whole tray and set it on the table in front of the sofa. Then he wanted honey and she had to run back to the kitchen. Then he wanted another section of the newspaper which he had discarded an hour before. By this time the tea was cold and Mama, uncomplainingly, would run into the kitchen to bring a fresh pot.

At last Aleks wrote, "I have an apartment on Hoza Ulica, near Marshalkowska. It belongs to the widow of a Senator and in February she is leaving to live in the country. No key money. It will be ours."

Rachel began to drink goat's milk and ate huge slices of cheese and bread spread with gobs of honey and her arms became round and firm again, her skin regained its rose tint under her natural olive tone, her eyes sparkled with anticipation and she returned to her old indomitable self.

-7-

Who was this man she was marrying? Rachel wondered the day before her wedding. Though she had wanted this more than anything in her life, at this moment she could not generate the appropriate feelings. She felt as though she were just another player in some drama external to her, having to go through the motions that defined her role. Who was Aleks? Did he know her? Did she know him? How was it that two such total strangers were about to commit their lives to each other?

That night there had been a dinner for the wedding party given by the rabbi's wife. Sofie bubbled with excitement.

"I'm going to wear your purple silk dress," she told Rachel.

"Don't be silly. It's much too tight for you, and besides it's too showy. Aleks has a Polish officer with him, Major Wojczek—you have to look proper."

"Proper? I never thought you'd say that. Are you worried about Ella? She'll be your sister-in-law tomorrow. She's practically part of the family."

"Ella?" Rachel said sharply. "Of course not. She's such a snob—she thinks just because she comes from Czestochowa she's special. And that simpering Jadwiga, well, she doesn't have an opinion of her own. Impossible to believe she is Ella's sister. Lena at least is beautiful. Dumb, but beautiful. And she keeps her mouth shut. They think they're so important. Well, I'm the one who's marrying Aleks."

Rachel was sitting in front of the mirrored vanity table, carefully applying black kohl to outline her eyes.

"I wonder if the Major is handsome." Sofie slipped on a dress of her own, in pale blue, with a high lace neckline. "He'll be in uniform. I love to look at the officers."

"He's a gentile, and he's not interested in you." Rachel turned from the mirror and looked at her sister, "Sofie, I'm going to be Aleks's wife! Wife, wife, wife. I can't believe it!"

"Oh, Rachel, you'll leave us. What will I do without you? I'll never see you." Sofie sat down on the edge of the bed, looking so forlorn that Rachel came over and hugged her.

"Of course you will. You'll come to Warsaw and stay with us. It's not so far."

"It's further than Czestochowa," Sofie said mournfully. "And Aleks won't want me around."

"You know, people are a little intimidated by Aleks. He's really soft inside. He struggles so." Rachel returned to her vanity table, but sat facing Sofie. There were sounds of people moving between rooms, water running in the bathroom, her brothers calling to each other about something, everyone preparing for the evening. She was glad to have this moment alone with Sofie.

"That's what I love most about him," she continued, almost to herself. "He wants to do good. Oh, I don't mean just in the political sense. In his own personal world, too. Sometimes I see him as if his shoulders were weighed down with all his responsibilities. He wants to take care of Ella and the others—I may get irritated by it, but I love him for it. I just wish they appreciated it more. They're so demanding. And he's all alone. I have Mama and Papa and you and everyone! He has no mother, and his father, his father only cared about his sisters and now he's gone too and all the responsibility falls on Aleks. He feels it so heavily."

"What do you mean he's alone?" Sofie said. "He's famous and important. He has hundreds of friends. Many more than you."

"You don't understand at all, Sofie. I mean alone inside. Well, now he has me. He won't be alone. And I'll be nicer to Ella and Jadwiga." She turned back to the mirror, feeling virtuous.

"You resent them because you want to be the important one," Sofie said quietly to Rachel's back.

Rachel stopped mid-motion, the fluffy powder puff giving off specks of loose powder in a little cloud around her. She recognized immediately that Sofie touched a fundamental truth about her. But only part of the truth, thought Rachel; the other part was true also—the tenderness that overwhelmed her. It was the struggle that touched her. She too wanted to be good.

"It's late," Mama called. "Come girls, we have to be there before the other guests arrive."

Rachel quickly returned to complete her makeup application. She stood up and twirled around in her lilac chiffon dress, her arms raised in exuberance.

"You look beautiful," Sofie said admiringly, "and so innocent." Her eyes twinkled.

Rachel laughed and kissed her sister. Suddenly she turned serious. "I'll never let you go, Sofie. I'll never leave you."

"You will," Sofie said.

"But you'll come to live with us. That's my plan. You'll live in Warsaw too."

"No, I'll marry here," Sofie said quietly, her life laid out before her, as certain as the coming of the Shabbos.

Rachel took Sofie's hand in silence, and together they walked down into the living room where Mama and Papa stood waiting.

At dinner at the rabbi's house, Papa rose to make a toast.

"I want to welcome my son-in-law."

"Not yet, not yet. Tomorrow." Mama was superstitious about tempting fate.

"Tomorrow, then," Papa continued. "We are honored that you, a man of learning, join our family. It is the highest good. Above money. But a little money won't hurt. I know you will have a brilliant career in the government. Business you can leave to us. And I know you have the highest principles, like Maimonides. I want to tell you all what a good man Aleks is. When I had business problems, Aleks insisted that Rachel give me back her dowry. How many sons-in-law would do that? I am happy to be here, to be alive, to give my Ruchele to you." Papa's voice faltered. There was silence around the table. He composed himself. He took a sip of wine. "But I wish that with all your learning you should still remember the Torah and keep a Jewish house."

Aleks cleared his throat and stood up, holding his glass of red wine before him. "The honor is mine. It is not easy to become a husband after so long being a bachelor, but I give up my freedom happily. I love Rachel and I shall do my utmost to make her happy. 'A good woman is more precious than rubies,'" he quoted. "As for a Jewish home … there are many ways of being Jewish, but the essence is the moral tradition. Rabbi Hillel, when asked to explain the whole of the Talmud while standing on one foot. said, 'Do unto others as you would have them do unto you—the rest is commentary.' That is what I strive for. In that sense, you may rest easy, for we shall keep a Jewish home."

"Yes," Papa interrupted, "but Hillel's full response is 'the rest is commentary. Now go and learn it.' He meant live by the Talmud."

"But now we are in such times that a greater task is demanded of us," Aleks continued. "We must work to make Poland a country dedicated to liberty, committed to giving each nationality within its borders the full freedom to keep its customs, its cultural heritage, without restrictions and without harassment. But we must work also to give all Jews who want it the opportunity to take a full part in Polish life, in government, in universities, in business. This is not assimilation, which some hold in contempt; it is Polonization. We are Jews and we are Poles. There must be no restrictions."

Rachel took his hand under the tablecloth. She squirmed at his didacticism.

"I toast my bride, her beauty and her spirit."

"He won't keep kosher," Papa mumbled under his breath, loud enough so Rachel heard.

❧   ❧   ❧

Two hours before the wedding the house was in turmoil.

"Oy," Mama cried, "We'll never be ready on time. Moniek, put those chairs out in the living room. Sofie, the flowers, the flowers. Get more vases. Run next door. Borrow some vases." She gave instructions like a field commander.

"Hush," she said at the top of her voice, "Papa is napping."

Rachel ran upstairs to soak in the bath. She let all the sounds and smells in the house envelop her. Every limb felt languorous and relaxed. Her hair fell in ringlets, damp from the steam, around her face. She was entirely happy.

Soon the house began to fill with guests. It seemed the whole town had come. Mama had been careful to make sure she offended no one and so left no one out.

Rachel sat in the parlor on the second floor in a large, high backed armchair, with gold gilded arms and gold claw feet, on a platform constructed by her brothers, the chair in which her father reclined at Passover Seders. She sank into the green and burgundy silk cushions, her long white taffeta skirt rich with pink lace appliqués, spreading out on the platform around her. The women guests flowed in, wishing her luck, offering advice. Tonight Rachel loved them all. Downstairs in the front parlor room, Aleks sat with the men of the town, her brothers, and the Rabbi, chanting prayers; even his Polish officer friend was there.

Lena walked in to the room, gently made her way through the group of women surrounding Rachel, and took her hand.

"Rachel," she said shyly, "I am glad you will be my sister-in-law. I am happy for Aleks."

Rachel was touched. She squeezed Lena's hand, leaned over and kissed her on the cheek. "Thank you," she said gratefully. Lena, tall and blond and regal, was more Polish-looking than Jewish. She could be so imposing, Rachel thought, if only she weren't so simple. Jadwiga made a quick appearance.

"Good luck," she said in a perfunctory way.

Ella didn't enter the room at all. She remained downstairs with the other guests who had returned from their visit with either the bride or groom.

In a flurry of activity, of men singing and a fiddler playing, Aleks appeared in front of Rachel for the *bedecken*—to "inspect the bride," as custom says, and to veil her.

She wondered how many of these well-meaning women thought she was a virgin. She was sure Mama suspected she was not, but of course it was never discussed and she guessed most of the women would have been shocked. You're a hypocrite, she said to herself, a modern woman who wants an orthodox wedding, with all the ritual intact. Papa would have insisted on it anyway, but it suited her as well. And Aleks was happy to have it this way, but he didn't see it as hypocrisy.

"We are the link between the past and the future," he had said to Rachel. "A wedding is not a private affair. It is a public affair, a community affair. It is our obligation to acknowledge our heritage."

At last, everyone went down into the living room to take their seats or to stand at the sides, and Mama and Papa came upstairs to lead Rachel down to the parlor off the living room. It was March and too cold to have the ceremony outside under the stars. The rabbi was already standing under the huppah, with her four brothers each holding one of the four poles to which the richly-embroidered canopy of white satin and deep red velvet was attached. In front of the rabbi, on a small table covered with a fringed burgundy silk cloth, was a prayer book, a carafe of wine, a silver chalice, and a crystal wine glass.

Major Kazimierz Wojchek strode down the aisle which consisted of a white runner spread over the Persian carpet. He wore his full dress uniform with shiny black boots, his officer's hat casting a shadow over his forehead. His luxuriant black mustache accentuated the whiteness of his teeth as he smiled.

"A Polish officer for a best man!" Papa had bristled. "It's impossible. He must have a Jewish relative."

"Papa, Aleks has a right to pick his own best man. Kazimierz is his friend." Rachel had insisted, and so the wedding was a blend of the traditional and the secular—even the men and the women mixed freely.

Aleks's sisters walked down singly. First Ella, in her beige dress that blended with the color of her blond-brown hair, walking a little too fast, her face expressionless, then Jadwiga, with little steps, looking neither right nor left, then Lena, with measured steps, in pale green, her rich gold hair falling softly to her shoulders. They took their places, standing slightly to the left of the huppah. Then came Sofie, looking straight ahead and only once or twice stealing a glance at Kazimierz.

Aleks entered from the parlor to the right and began his walk to the huppah. Rachel, standing between her parents in the little room on the other side of the living room, looked at Aleks through her veil and her heart broke. He had no parents to lead him to the wedding canopy. Alone, she thought, he must walk to the huppah alone.

He walked slowly, with dignity, elegant in his dark suit and white shirt, looking taller than he really was. He took his place under the huppah in front of the little table, and turned to await Rachel, who stepped onto the white runner, with Mama holding her under one arm and Papa under the other.

"I am so happy," Mama had just whispered in Rachel's ear. "My eldest daughter, giving away my eldest daughter, the happiest moment, that I should live to do this, to bring my child to the huppah!"

Mama's cousins from Radomsk were called up singly to read the blessings. The rabbi held up the ketubah, ornately illustrated by the same scribe from Czestochowa who had prepared the wedding contract for her parents' marriage, and already signed by Aleks and his two witnesses. He read it out loud in Hebrew, and gave it to Rachel who gave it to Sofie to hold, the guarantee of her rights as a wife, including conjugal ones. Rachel, followed by Mama and Sofie, walked seven times around Aleks, to thwart away any malicious, envious demons. Aleks placed the ring on her finger and declared, first in Hebrew, then in Polish,

"Behold, thou art consecrated unto me according to the Law of Moses and of Israel." He had insisted on the Polish translation. And so they were officially wed with this simple declaration.

The rabbi raised the goblet of wine and pronounced the seventh of the seven blessings. "Blessed Art Thou O Lord our God, King of the Universe, who hast created joy and gladness, bridegroom and bride, mirth and exaltation, pleasure and delight, love, brotherhood, peace and fellowship. Blessed are you, O Lord, who maketh the groom to rejoice with the bride."

First Aleks, then Rachel sipped from the wine. The rabbi wrapped the crystal glass in a white cloth, put it under Aleks's foot, and firmly, lifting his foot high, Aleks stomped on the glass and broke it.

"Rejoice with trembling ..." say the Psalms. I will remember, thought Rachel in a shadow's flash, at the height of happiness, joy is ephemeral, fragile like the glass.

"Mazel tov, simmon tov," the guests sang at the breaking of the glass. Later, in the parlor, Rachel and Aleks received well-wishers, while the living room was being set up for the feast. The klezmerim played their lively dances, Moniek passed out glasses of whiskey and vodka, and a maid passed platters of food. A group of men surrounded Aleks in the open hallway and danced around him while in another corner, the women and young girls formed a circle around Rachel and swirled around while Rachel danced in the center with Sofie. Wilder and wilder the dance, till the dancers collapsed, breathless and laughing.

Ella was deep in conversation with Kazimierz, who was looking at Lena out of the corner of his eye.

"Do you find these customs quaint?" Ella said in her clipped Polish. "These people are so old-fashioned. We live quite differently in Czestochowa. You must come to visit us."

"Quaint? I wouldn't say that. Interesting, of course. But Aleks has told me much about what the wedding would be like before. I am delighted to be here. Yes, I would like to visit you," he glanced at Lena who blushed. "Next time Aleks goes home."

"Yes, do come," Lena said softly.

When the last guests left, Rachel and Aleks went to stay at the lodge on the outskirts of town where Aleks had arrived the day before. They made love in the four-poster bed, with a candle flickering on the fireplace mantel. They slept under a large down comforter, warm and safe, only half a mile from her parents' house. It was her last night in Zarki.

In Warsaw, settled in their new apartment, Rachel insisted that they go to the synagogue the following Saturday. They rode in a doroshka to the Great Synagogue, the horses clattering as they entered through the large iron gate onto the cobblestone courtyard. A compromise, riding to the Synagogue, thought Rachel, already abandoning the proscriptions of riding on the Sabbath, already abandoning her parents. But she wanted him to wear the silk prayer shawl she had given him as a wedding gift. She wanted to see him wrapped in the large tallit, as she saw her father each Saturday. He had the seat of honor, next to the Ark, as a newly married man, with the elders of the Synagogue around him. He stepped up to the platform and read from the Torah in a clear, unfaltering voice, his Hebrew precise, with no hint of Yiddish in it. Rachel followed the Polish translation as the congregation sang:

> Rejoice, O bridegroom, in the wife of your youth, your comrade,
>> Let your heart be merry now, and when you shall grow old,
>> Sons to your sons shall see you: your old age's crown;
> Sons who shall prosper and work in place of their pious sires,
>> Your days in good shall be spent, your years in pleasantness.
>> Floweth your peace as a stream, riseth your worth as its waves.

-8-

Warsaw—1925

It was the end of March. Rachel walked down Marshalkowska Ulica on a Saturday afternoon, her arms laden with flowers. On the main street of Warsaw the sidewalks were clear of snow, but from the roofs of the somber buildings, melting icicles dripped water. She stepped lightly around the puddles and breathed in the fragrance of the bouquets she carried, wild, exotic flowers, spring flowers, narcissus, and snapdragons and hyacinths. She had already had the florist send up long-stemmed gladioli and red and white carnations, but she wanted an excess of flowers for her first major dinner party, so she had walked twelve blocks to the most expensive flower shop and selected these herself. Offices and businesses closed at noon for the start of the weekend and the street was filled with people on their way home, walking with their heads down on this gray, damp day, while Rachel hummed to herself amidst the bunches of flowers.

She walked up the three flights to their apartment on Hoza Ulica and let herself in through the back door directly into the kitchen.

"Stefcia," she called out to the maid. "Please bring me four vases—the ones in the living room. And fill them with water. I want to arrange these myself." The cook was peeling onions and their sharp smell permeated the warm kitchen. Rachel, still in her coat, ran through the apartment to the other end where Aleks was writing in his study. He looked up from the papers on his large mahogany desk.

"Where have you been?" he asked.

"Oh, I still had a few things to buy for tonight. Aleks, I told the wine merchant you would pay him next week. I ran out of money. You only gave me thirty zlotys yesterday. I'm going to take a bath now. You should stop working and take a little nap before people come."

"Rachel, don't you think you spent a little too much on this party? These are friends of mine; you don't have to overdo everything. Everyone is going crazy in this house."

"I'm not overdoing! Just because they are friends of yours doesn't mean it's not important. Anyway, I don't know them all. I have to make a good impression."

"You're used to Papa giving you all the money you want," he sighed, "but we're on a government salary."

"But you make extra money from your writings. And you get money when you lecture. I don't understand why you don't give it all to me and I would manage it. A marriage is a partnership, but you give me an allowance, like a child. And Papa did not give me whatever I wanted. I gave *him* money! My dowry! Aleks, I hate to talk about money. I don't want to make life difficult for you. I could work. You have so many connections. Why don't you find me something? I love you."

She went around the desk and stood beside him and leaned down and kissed the top of his head, her arms holding his shoulders. He swiveled in his leather chair and embraced her around the waist.

She looked around her at the book-lined walls, the Persian carpet on the floor, the burgundy leather armchair with brass studs facing the desk, the dark wood paneling behind Aleks. This was his sanctuary, his escape, his world. Where was hers? In the Cafe Europeiska, amid the gossip and flirtations. She was trivial here. In Zarki at least she had been someone special. What nonsense! She was someone special here too: Aleks's wife.

She took a long, luxurious bath, in perfumed bubbles, only sporadically prickled by thoughts, quickly dismissed, of what she should be doing: inviting her parents to stay with them, making some sort of career for herself, doing more to enhance Aleks's position, not being demanding, being nicer to Ella. The thought of Ella brought a frown to her forehead. Ella was the one who was mean to her, with her pointed remarks about Aleks's obligations to his sisters and Rachel's selfishness which prevented him from fulfilling them. She recognized that Ella and Lena and Jadwiga all worked hard, and had no man to help them except Aleks, but they had such distorted perceptions about her. She could not think of any specific incident for which she could be faulted. She had done nothing wrong. On the contrary, she was always careful to be especially considerate, making numerous efforts, sending little presents. She always invited Ella to dinners; Ella invariably refused.

Rachel wanted Ella's approval, but she was coming to understand that the most profound hatreds are for the least logical reasons. And there was no way to deal with this irrationality. It was so intangible, nothing to grab hold of and fix. Still, she was the fortunate one while their lives were bitter, and even though it was through their own ill humor, Rachel resolved to be kinder to them. It occurred to her that her very kindness was resented, that perhaps they considered it patronizing, that they would like her better if they could be kind to her. Not Jadwiga or Lena, only Ella. Well, there was nothing she could do about that; she couldn't undo herself, erase herself, to please Ella.

A few hours later, she emerged in a black silk gown, long-leeved with pearl buttons all the way up to the elbow, her luminous skin showing in the deep décolletage of the dress, adorned by a small ruby and diamond pendant. She went into the living room for a final inspection. Vases of flowers were placed throughout, on the piano in the corner in front of the French doors which led to the balcony overlooking the courtyard, on the coffee table between the two facing couches, on the library table underneath the large mirror next to the door. The crystal chandelier sparkled, bathing the room in a warm light. Aleks walked in, fixing the bow tie on his tuxedo shirt, his jacket off, just as the bell rang.

"My God," Rachel said, "they're much too early."

"No—I think it's someone else."

Stefcia had opened the door and took an enormous box of flowers from the delivery boy. While Stefcia took the cover off to reveal eighteen long-stemmed yellow roses, droplets of water glistening on the petals, Rachel tore open the little card. "To my perfect love. Aleks"

"They're beautiful" she said, "I adore yellow roses."

He looked around the room, filled with overflowing vases. "Coals to Newcastle," he said quietly.

Aleks put on his jacket and began taking out bottles of vodka, slivovitz, and whiskey. The doorbell rang. There were voices in the little hallway off the living room, opposite the study, as Stefcia was taking coats and hats. The bell rang again and now the hallway was overflowing. Senator Friedeman walked into the living room, his belly leading the way, followed by his wife, a small dowdy woman with stringy hair.

"Aleks," he said as he reached out his big hand to shake Aleks's. He put his other arm around Aleks's shoulder." It's good to see you, and your lovely wife. Nice to be at a party instead of arguing with you at the club. Tonight, no talk of politics. Rachel, my dear, I don't think you've met my wife Henia, but you should know each other. She can tell you everything you need to know about where to go to get anything in Warsaw."

Henia shook Rachel's hand limply, but she said with warmth, "Of course, if there is anything I can help you with, I would be so happy. Aleks is very dear to us, and so you are too."

They were all exchanging greetings. Rachel was introduced to Rabbi Szteyn, who certainly didn't look like a rabbi. He wore full dress army uniform. He was tall, with black hair, bushy eyebrows and absolutely wicked, sparkling eyes. He bowed at the waist." Madame, a pleasure." He kissed her hand lightly.

"Leopold Szteyn," Aleks said to Rachel. "He will be the next Chief Rabbi of the Army. If he doesn't forget he's Jewish … Come, leave my wife alone and tell me what you are up to."

There were two other couples: Jerzy Witkowski, a journalist, and his wife Leila who owned a little boutique on Marshalkowska, and Nataniel and Wilma Zukowski, both lawyers. The last guest arrived after everyone was seated on the two couches, drinking vodka and eating little canapés of glistening black caviar topped with sour cream and bits of onion and hard-boiled egg.

"Karola," Aleks got up quickly and brought her into the circle. "I was worried you wouldn't come. Sit down, sit down. Let me get you a drink. This is Karola Rozman. You know the Friedemans. This is my wife Rachel." He went on with the introductions. Karola, who had given her coat to Stefcia in the hall, kept her hat on. It was a masculine style with a broad brim angled so that it hid the left side of her face while on the right side, her long blond hair fell to her shoulder and her sharp features were profiled against the black felt. She wore a long black skirt and a man-tailored striped jacket over a silk-satin white blouse. She immediately lit a cigarette in a long ivory cigarette holder that she kept between two ringed fingers with long red nails. She was not attractive but she was striking.

"Karola is writing a book on the Polish parliament," Aleks said, "Be careful what you say."

"It is you who should write the book." Karola looked at him. "A Jew in the Polish government has a special view of things."

"I will, I will, in good time. Right now I have other things I must tend to."

"Well, Aleks," the Senator boomed when they were seated at the dinner table, "I hear rumors that you will be promoted to Chief of the Minorities Section."

"It's premature to even talk about it," Aleks said, "I have competition."

Karola, on Aleks's right, touched his arm lightly. "You can't mean that idiot Janusz. He's Ukrainian. They need a Jew in this post."

"The Ukrainians are minorities too," Aleks said.

"Aleks, you have to see to your affairs more. You have to push yourself more; otherwise they will all step ahead of you. That's just fatherly advice." The Senator was expansive and on his third glass of wine.

"I thought you said no politics tonight. I want to make a toast." Aleks raised his glass."To my lovely wife, who makes this evening a special occasion, and for me every day with her is a special occasion. This is our anniversary."

There was clapping and everyone said, "Na zdrowie, na zdrowie." Rachel blushed as she removed Leopold's hand from her knee hidden by the long tablecloth, and raised her own glass.

They broke into song "Sto lat, sto lat, niech żyje, żyje nam," a hundred years, a hundred years, may they live a hundred years. The maid came around with the meat platter and the conversation broke up into private dialogues. Rachel saw Karola leaning toward Aleks at the other end of the table. They were deeply absorbed. He was frowning slightly and shaking his head. Rachel turned to Leopold, on her right, in retaliation. Rachel thought, I might as well be in Hela's salon in Zarki, sitting in the corner and listening. But she realized that was a ridiculous thought. She was mistress of this house and it was her dinner party, her salon. She was certainly getting enough attention. Henia Friedeman was kindly toward her, the Senator both paternal and gracious in his compliments, and Leopold flashed all kinds of unspoken invitations to her. But what was her life really? She had nothing her own, unique. When she was in Zarki she had dreamed of being close to power, in the midst of important people and important events. But now it wasn't enough. She had to have something of her own. She would have a baby. She would take a job. She would open up her own business. Even that little Leila had her own business. Why was she so restless?

The long, gray winters were broken by vacations in Zakopany where Rachel and Aleks spent days walking in the crisp snow in the village streets, passing rosy-cheeked skiers in their sporting clothes. They sipped hot chocolate piled with clouds of whipped cream and ate sacher torte and apple pastries in one or another of the many boisterous cafes where all the winter guests gathered.

At night they skated on the pond just outside the main part of town. Small fires dotted the shore as people warmed their hands and feet. Viennese waltzes blared from the loudspeaker in the recreation lodge. Aleks was a good skater and Rachel floated along with him exuberantly, feeling graceful, as if she were flying above the earth. But after a week, he had to go back to Warsaw.

Rachel remained, alone but not lonely. Several of her friends were staying at the same hotel and each night she was invited to the table of one of them, and Mama had arrived after Aleks left. She had invited Papa also, but he declined; he was expanding his leather outlets again and couldn't spare the time. Rachel suspected that he would not feel comfortable in this hotel, mostly occupied by gentiles and Polonized Jews. Mama arrived with her velvet dresses and embroidered capes with fur collars, those dresses that had been waiting in Zarki for just such an occasion.

In the evening they came down the ornate, curved staircase into the richly carpeted lobby, swept into the large, elegant dining room and paused in the doorway. At once, a distinguished gentleman with graying hair rose from his chair, approached Rachel and took her arm.

"Rachel, come, you must join us tonight. If Aleks insists on leaving you, it is his loss. And of course, your mother ..."

"No, thank you," Rachel said. "Mama and I have much to talk about. We will dine alone tonight."

"You are having a fine time without Aleks, I see," Mama said when they were seated at a table for two.

"Why not? I would rather he were here. But he rushed off. Anyway, I think he likes it that I have a good time. He is always telling me to be independent. I wish he were a little jealous. I am jealous of him." Her stomach muscles tightened as she remembered coming upon Aleks and Karola in the Cafe Europeiska last month, their heads bent together. She had approached their table with her head high and her eyes on fire, but they appeared delighted to see her and Aleks quickly pulled out a chair for her and summoned the waiter, ordering cafe au lait and a pastry for her without even asking what she wanted. But they stopped whatever conversation they had been having, and she felt excluded.

"Rachel, for heaven's sake, don't be so childish," Aleks had told her when she confronted him that night. "Karola is writing her editorials and I want to have some say in it. It is very important. And I have told her about my book. She thinks I should have it published in Germany. That is where it will have the biggest impact. After all, it is meant to shake the immense complacency of the

German Jews. God, how can they be so blind to what is happening? Oh, don't worry. It would be under a pseudonym. I won't be in any danger. I am going to go to Germany and see if I can get Lessing to write a preface. And stop being so suspicious of Karola. She is an intelligent woman and I admire her." Rachel had felt foolish, but not entirely reassured.

"Ruchele," Mama lowered her voice and put her hand over Rachel's slim fingers resting on the table, "Have a baby. You are getting close to thirty. Aleks is over forty. How long can you wait? I have seven children; you have none. Life is not complete without children. Life is not all play."

"Mama, I am going to work. Aleks introduced me to Herr Werner. He's a publisher of an encyclopedia. In Germany. He wants to open up the Polish market."

"To work! Why? You are married. You live well. You should have children."

"I will be setting up libraries for wealthy people. I will sell the encyclopedias and suggest other books—Aleks will advise me—and I get a commission on each set of encyclopedias. It is very respectable, and I will meet important people. I have entrée because of Aleks's name. Mama," she said abruptly. "Let Sofie come to Warsaw. We have a big apartment. Aleks will get her a job."

"Sofie must get married," Mama said. "A job isn't what she needs. I don't understand it," Mama shook her head. "She always had a dozen boys around her. Then they all went off and married someone else. It's you. You gave her ideas that they weren't good enough for her."

"Well, they weren't!" Rachel said.

"No, Ruchele, maybe they weren't good enough for you. Sofie is not you. It's simpler for Sofie."

"You are wrong, Mama. I know Sofie. She needs Warsaw. Anyway," Rachel said defensively "I'm going to work. You know Aleks just gives me an allowance to run the house. It isn't enough. Besides, I want to do something on my own." But she was suddenly overcome with sadness, regret at what she didn't have: children, a husband who took care of her in a way the rich merchants took care of their wives.

"Don't worry, Mama," Rachel said softly. "I will have a child, soon … just not yet."

-9-

It was 1933. Aleks published his book, Rachel had a baby, and Hitler came to power.

The week after the Reichstag fire, Rachel was preparing yet another dinner reception, this time to celebrate the arrival of the book. Cartons of copies had arrived the week before and Aleks cleared off one shelf in his study to accommodate them, leaving the remainder in the boxes that he stashed on top of each other in the corner. Rachel protested. She liked the study to be neat and imposing with its masculine decor of wood and leather and oriental carpet.

"It's my study," Aleks told her firmly. "It's for work, not for show."

Papa had arrived the night before. He was in Warsaw to borrow money for expanding his leather business.

"You should be more careful, Papa," Rachel said to him. "It's going well now; why can't you just continue for a while? Don't borrow now. Wait until you build up some cash."

"Ruchele, what do you know about my business? You haven't asked anything about it for years—since you left Zarki. I know what I am doing. Whoever lends me money will make a big profit." Papa sat in Aleks's deep, soft chair, stroking his beard, a relaxed smile on his face.

"Rachel's right, Papa," Aleks said. "The economy is in trouble. Why don't you wait a few years before you expand?"

"Aleks," Papa gave a little laugh, "you know about the politics, about your books, about all those important things, but you don't know about business. In business, if you don't go forward, you go backward. You have to grow or you shrink. You can't stand still. You write, Aleks, you work with your important people, and I'll make money."

Rachel shook her head in silence. How was it she felt so responsible for his troubles? Or at least responsible for rescuing him from them, but not enough so, she told herself wryly, to do anything concrete for him. Well, what, after all, could she do? Whoever listened to anyone else? We all do what we must and only listen to others' advice when it conforms to our own predilections.

It was Saturday night. The offices had closed at noon and Aleks was dressing after his nap. Papa had spent the day in his room, praying by himself. The synagogue was too far away to walk to and he would not ride on the Sabbath. He had relaxed some of his orthodoxy and though he was strictly kosher at home, he consented to eat in his daughter's house, though she prepared special meat-less dishes for him.

The guests filed into the dining room, trying to find their place cards. Aleks's boss, Suchnitski, took his seat at Rachel's left. Majkowski, the chief attorney for Aleks's division, held out the chair for his own wife Elyssa, next to Suchnitski, and went around to the other side of the table to sit down next to Suchnitski's wife who was already placed on Aleks's right. They were chattering and laughing, all gentiles, except Leopold, suave and charming in dress uniform, pulling out Rachel's chair with a smile and a courtly bow. Papa, who barely spoke Polish, and then with a heavy Yiddish accent, looked as if he were lost. What they must think, Rachel mused, looking around at her guests. He's from a different world. They know nothing of it, except all that anti-Semitic propaganda. Well, he's my father! I'm not ashamed of him.

"Papa," she tugged at his sleeve, "here, next to me, this is where you sit, on my right." She turned to Suchnitski and added, smiling sweetly, "the place of honor, for my father."

He sat silent most of the evening, his long beard flecked with gray hiding all expression. In the old days she would have thought he was disapproving. Now she saw him as weaker, somewhat confused.

"Your book is timely, Aleks," Majkowski, the attorney, said. "That Reichstag fire is just another step to power for that hoodlum Hitler. I don't believe for a moment it was set by the Communists. A trumped-up story. A good excuse."

"Yes. A good excuse to give Hitler all the powers to arrest—and kill legally Well, tomorrow are the elections. We'll see if the Germans are taken in by the Nazis," Aleks said. "But my book is meant for the German Jews. They think they're safe. They think they have power. Some of the industrialists even support Hitler. It seems no one has read *Mein Kampf*."

"It's not just the Jews who have to worry."

"But the Jews first," Aleks said. "Always the Jews first. But complacency is a disease that afflicts the Germans too."

"Not complacency," Majkowski said. "Panic, fear, this mania that the Bolsheviks will take over. Hitler is a master at fanning that fire."

Stefcia passed around platters of roast veal and dishes of marinated cucumbers, with the sweet smell of dill. For Papa she brought in a plate of potatoes and carrots with prunes and a dish of mixed beans. He chewed on a piece of black bread, listening. A small strip of carrot was caught in his beard. Rachel gently brushed it away.

"My son is in Germany now learning new ways to cure the leather. He is at a chemical plant in Munich. The Jews are rich in Germany." Papa spoke up in his heavily accented Polish.

"Yes, that's what makes them so complacent," Aleks said.

"Well, Aleks, I'm afraid your book might fall on deaf ears in Germany," Suchnitski noted as he leaned back in his chair, looking well satisfied with the wine, the food, the talk. "In Poland the Jews are safe, with all the guarantees Pilsudski gives. And look at you—a Jew in such a high-ranking position in the Polish government! But you should be a little careful anyhow. You're too outspoken." He turned to Rachel. "Madame, you look particularly lovely tonight. I understand you are a big success—and not only at the Cafe Europeiska," he grinned broadly, "but also with your private library business."

Rachel hated him, his sneering, patronizing voice. She knew Aleks was dependent on him, so she smiled sweetly. He had tried to seduce her repeatedly, usually just being ambiguously suggestive. She didn't mistake the signals though, and she had to tread a delicate line, to keep him interested, to offer a possibility, a bare suggestion if only the timing were right, if only the opportunity presented itself. Surely Aleks couldn't mistake his advances, but what could he do? Sometimes it seemed to Rachel that Aleks rather liked it when other men showed an interest in her. She couldn't understand it. She herself had such a jealous nature; it drove her mad when she was suspicious of him. She suspected he and Karola were lovers, but she usually managed to put it out of her mind. But sometimes she thought about the imagined details of their imagined love affair. She too was tempted, mostly by Leopold, and after all if Aleks and Karola did it, then … Well, it hadn't happened so far, but flirtatiousness was permitted, expected even, and so, with great distaste because of her feelings about Suchnitski, she returned his attentions.

"Pan Suchnitski," she said, addressing him formally, "you are more of a flatterer each time I see you. I am doing modestly well arranging the libraries. And I have you to thank for some of my clients. I think maybe they are doing you a favor buying from me."

"No, you have the source for the German encyclopedias. Everyone wants them. It's snobbishness, if you ask me. Shows they're 'cultured'. I'm willing to wager your rich clients don't even open the books. It's the leather bindings they like—makes them look educated. Well, if Hitler gets going, I don't know if you'll be able to get all those books from Germany."

"Rachel doesn't need to worry," Aleks said, "she is going to have a baby."

"Aleks," Rachel cried, "how could you tell everyone like this? Mama doesn't even know! And Papa!"

Papa looked startled, but he quickly rose from his chair raised his wine glass and said, "L'chaim, l'chaim … a grandson! Mazel tov." He kissed Rachel on the cheek. She buried her head in his beard. She was unused to such a public display of affection from him. He had tears in his eyes. He sat down, murmuring, "L'chaim, L'chaim …" To life, to life.

"What better time to announce it?" Aleks asked. "I gave birth to my book as you will give birth to a child, and Papa is here to celebrate with us."

Everyone spoke at once. There were congratulations, good wishes, more wine. Stefcia came around with liqueurs on a silver tray.

Now that it was publicly announced, Rachel finally believed she was having a baby.

❦   ❦   ❦

Throughout her pregnancy, Rachel felt an unaccustomed calmness of spirit. She had no need to flirt, no drive to be the perfect hostess, no jealousy of Aleks. Her skin glowed, her hair shone, her breasts swelled. She had only a few days of morning sickness at the beginning and she didn't mind at all. She relished every sensation of her body, dwelling on minute changes. She was so thoroughly content, her tempestuous nature so tamed, that Aleks commented on it one day.

"So that is the secret! I'll have to keep you pregnant."

And she had deep sexual urges. She touched herself in the middle of the day. She initiated sex with Aleks. While he read at night before going to sleep, she climbed into his bed, put her head on his shoulder and touched him, gently at first, then more urgently, until he responded. But it was over for him too quickly for her, and she, perspiring and breathless, beside herself on the crest of her desire, had to guide his hand until she came to orgasm.

Rachel continued working even when her growing belly broadcast her status. Lena said to her gently one day,

"Rachel, Kazimierz thinks it is not so proper to be showing yourself like this everywhere. Perhaps you should stay home a bit more."

Now that Lena had married Kazimierz Wojcek, it was he whose opinions Lena held as absolute. Ella had been displaced, which made her only more bitter; she now made acerbic comments about Kazimierz too, although basically she approved of him highly—after all, he was a Polish officer. But in this Ella concurred.

"Rachel, stay home," she said. "Only the Hasidic wives display themselves when they're pregnant. Otherwise they'd have to be indoors all their lives, they have so many children. You're an embarrassment to Aleks, flaunting yourself like that."

Rachel felt kindly toward Ella. "Ella, what can be more wonderful than to give new life? Everyone should know it." Placing her hand over Ella's, she added, "I want you to be godmother to my baby."

"What, not Sofie?" Ella, taken by surprise, softened. "Well, of course, I want to. That is nice of you. I think Aleks will be pleased."

Rachel had fashionable maternity clothes made out of silks and soft wools by her dressmaker, and she looked stylish and radiantly beautiful. She gave in with equal abandon to modernity and to superstition. Once when they were strolling on Marshalkowska Ulica on a Sunday afternoon, Rachel suddenly stopped and stared at a young woman across the street. She pulled Aleks across to the other sidewalk and stared at the young woman.

"What on earth are you looking at?" he asked.

"Her eyebrows! Look at her eyebrows! They are so full. I want our baby to have such eyebrows. You know if I look at her, the baby will have such eyebrows." Rachel's own eyebrows were sparse and she had to fill them in with eyebrow pencil.

"Oh, Rachel, Rachel," Aleks laughed. "You will never get rid of the Zarki inside you."

Aleks seemed lighter during these days of Rachel's pregnancy, younger somehow. They had less money now, since she had stopped working and she needed more, for the baby nurse, for a layette, for furniture. Aleks wrote a few pieces for a magazine and accepted some speaking engagements in small towns not too distant from Warsaw, and so they managed. She began to feel they were a family and he was providing for her as a husband should.

"Aleks, if we have a boy, you have to arrange the bris. I want him circumcised by a doctor. A Jewish doctor of course, and the rabbi will be there, but I don't trust the mohel. Suppose he makes a mistake? We have to make a list of people to invite to the bris. Mama will be here a few weeks before I'm due. She'll help you."

"You're already planning a party! Don't worry. I'll take care of the bris. But it has to be a mohel. That's the primal ritual —the covenant with God. It has to be done strictly according to tradition. But I'll find a doctor who is also a mohel."

She looked at him. "You really are a funny mixture. You won't speak a word of Yiddish and yet you want the full ritual."

"You know the old story," he said. "Every Jew has his own version of the religion. And speaking Yiddish has nothing to do with it. Just an excuse for people who won't learn Polish properly. Besides, it may be a girl."

A boy would be his, she thought. "Sons to your sons shall see you: your old age's crown …" The words to the bridegroom's song resonated in her head. Would he live to see "sons to his sons"? He was forty-five, too stubborn and opinioned for a son. They would fight and struggle with each other, but still, they would be inextricably tied to each other. No, a daughter would be more right. She could see him with a daughter, fondly spoiling her, amused, indulgent, but a little distant. A daughter would be hers.

The labor was hard—hard and long. She lay on the bed in the labor room watching the hands of the large clock on the wall in front of her going past the hour mark nine times. She listened to the screams of a woman in the next room. "Hail Mary, Mother of God … Help me, help. Oh God I am dying …" She would not scream like that, like some cow; she would bear her pain in dignity.

The contractions grew closer together, more intense. She held her breath as she felt one coming on. It made the pain worse. She thought she could grit her teeth until it passed, but it was constant. It came in waves: one was over; the next one began. At first she had dozed in between, but now it was impossible. The sisters in their starched habits came by and wiped her brow with a damp cold cloth, looked under the sheets covering her legs, spoke softly to each other and to the doctor who came in every once in a while. She tossed her head from side to side and little soft moans escaped her. She was barely conscious, only aware of that clock, the hands moving round inexorably.

A young nun all in white, like an angel suspended in clouds, held her hand. "Don't cry, don't cry, it will be over soon."

Rachel returned from some other universe as the sister's words registered. She was not aware she was crying, but now she felt the wetness on her cheeks. She was touched by the nun's words. She cared, she felt pity and sorrow for Rachel. Rachel wished to thank the nun for her kindness, but she couldn't talk. She was no longer in this world; she floated away.

When Rachel woke, she was in her private room with Aleks holding her hand. He bent over to kiss her and she was aware of her breath stale from sleep.

"A girl," he said, "we have a girl."

Rachel said nothing. Tears were rolling down her cheeks. She struggled against waking up. Something must be wrong with the baby—such pain, such reluctance to enter into life.

"It's fine, everything is fine," Aleks said. Neither of them had seen the baby yet.

The nurse came and told Aleks he could go for lunch while she made Rachel presentable. It was noon. The baby had been born at 6 a.m. When Aleks returned two hours later, Rachel was propped up on her pillows, wearing a pale mauve satin bed jacket over her lace nightgown, her hair combed, her face powdered, a blush of pale rouge on her cheeks. The room was filled with bouquets of flowers, gladiolus, long-stemmed yellow roses, deep red carnations, baskets overflowing with fruit, gifts sent by his colleagues, by their friends.

The nurse brought the baby in, wrapped almost entirely in white blankets. Peering out was the head, covered with black hair, the face red, wrinkled, ugly—ugly, not at all like the beautiful pink babies in pictures. The nun handed the baby to Rachel. She gasped as she unwrapped the blanket a bit. The baby puckered its face, contorted into even more grotesque features, and cried loudly, harshly. Rachel clutched the bundle to her breast. "My baby, my baby," she crooned. "You are my wonderful baby. I love you. I love you." Aleks turned his head away. Years later, when Rachel understood that Aleks's love for Rilka was as fierce as her own, she remembered this moment when she had taken possession of their daughter.

-10-

Everyone in the household was gripped by sadness. Stefcia wept copiously, wringing her hands, crying, "Jesu, Jesu, we are alone now, our Father is gone." Aleks was glued to the radio. The same message was broadcast over and over: "Marshal Pilsudski is dead." Rachel sat in silence at the dining room table, her tea cold and untouched, the child on her lap trying to wriggle free. Alyna, the governess, came into the room and took the baby out of Rachel's arms.

"Shh," she said to the child. "Shh, this is not the time to play."

"The Sanacja is finished," Rachel said quietly. The Moral Regime of Pilsudski was over.

"Maybe he was no longer as democratic as he once was, but it was the best we had. He wasn't anti-Semitic. He appreciated the Polonized Jews, he knew what we did for Independent Poland. We shall never have a leader like him!" Aleks too had tears in his eyes.

"What will happen now?" Alyna asked, not expecting an answer.

Rachel felt plunged in uncertainty, just as life had begun to seem smooth and predictable, even a little boring. With the birth of the baby her restlessness had abated. She was settled into a comfortable routine and at peace with everyone, even Ella. They called the baby Marja, which became Marilka, and eventually everyone called her Rilka. At the naming ceremony they gave her a Jewish name, Sarah Malka, after her great-grandmother. During the ceremony Ella held the baby who had lost her hair by then and had become more attractive. Rachel was pampered by Mama and by Aleks; even Ella was helpful, coming over after work almost every day with cake or fruit or some toy for Rilka. Their talks became more intimate and Ella began to confide her complaints about Lena and her Polish husband. She rarely saw them now; they were so busy with his friends. And Jadwiga, who worked in Ella's office, was so meek she would never get a raise. Ella had to look out for all of them. Rachel found she liked Ella better now; at least Ella had a definitive personality, was someone you had to contend with, not just mush.

Rachel nursed the baby herself. She didn't want to use a peasant wet-nurse. She relished the warmth of the baby's head against her breast, the hungry eagerness with which Rilka grabbed the nipple, the gentle sucking until she fell asleep, sated, and loosened her hold, the rich, tingling sensations. Aleks generally came home for the midday meal, looked in on the baby and took his short afternoon nap before going back to the office. In the late afternoon Rachel went to the Cafe Europeiska for tea and pastries. Back home again, she waited for Ella, who sometimes stayed for a late supper.

At night she told Aleks of her day. She was always doing small favors for people. She convinced the building superintendent to give the cook's son a job. She arranged for a nurse for a friend's elderly mother. She used her influence to get a scholarship to a Polish school for the son of someone she knew from Czestochowa. People called to ask her things, and she never refused, but more often she took matters into her own hands before she was asked.

"Why do you always have to put your nose into everything?" Aleks asked her. "Maybe it's not appreciated. Maybe they see it as interference."

"Don't be silly. I am only trying to help. It's my obligation to do something for someone if I can."

Aleks's day was filled with matters of greater import, Rachel thought, and she found herself jealous. Once she overheard him on the telephone with his secretary. There was some laughter over a matter known only to the two of them. His words on the phone were half sentences, unfinished phrases clearly understood by the secretary, a total mystery to Rachel. In a moment of illumination she saw so clearly what separate lives they really led, so individual, so personal.

What do I know of his life, she thought, and what does he know of mine? I'm not there when he pays a compliment to his secretary. I don't understand the little inside jokes, the nuances of office gossip. I don't exist for any of the people in his world except as a wife. The same day is completely different for him and for me. We only intersect in short spaces of time. How can it be that two married people are so individual in the particulars of their daily lives?

Sofie had moved in a few weeks before Pilsudski died. Rachel had at last persuaded her, and Papa agreed. There was no future for her in Zarki; how would she ever meet a man good enough for her in that provincial little town? Rachel wanted Sofie to have opportunities. Aleks got her a job in a large import-export firm. Rachel's household was full. Alyna slept in Rilka's room and Sofie had the spare bedroom. They were not rich but they lived well. Life was orderly, the future held promise—and then Pilsudski died.

The day of the funeral was sunny and cool, a May morning. Aleks had already left to be with the government officials and Rachel was going to join him later. Alyna and Rilka and Sofie were going to watch the procession coming along Marshalkowska Ulica. They all went downstairs together and walked toward the main avenue. At the corner, Rachel prepared to go in one direction, they in the other.

"Go toward the square," Rachel said. "You will see better. Hold Rilka tightly—such crowds." Even the side streets were filled with people. It was hard to get through. Women in babushkas wept silently; men in homburgs, fashionably dressed ladies, everyone pressed against each other. All of Warsaw was out on the streets.

They stopped on the corner before parting. Rilka was wearing her winter coat still, a pink wool with big round buttons and a soft little brown fur collar. Two brown fur pompons attached to a hood hung down the front. Alyna bent down and opened the top two buttons on Rilka's coat. The child took a deep breath. Rachel at that instant felt herself in her child's body, felt with pleasure the soft wind, with its hint of warmth and spring, against the bare skin of her neck.

At Marshalkowska they went their opposite ways. Rachel looked back after them, but they were immediately swallowed up by the solid mass of people. She felt a momentary panic but was comforted by the thought of Sofie. They wouldn't be separated.

She stood with Aleks, surrounded by his colleagues, as the procession passed in front of them, first the officers, the army units, the generals, the white horses bearing cannon, then the draped coffin, borne by the honor guard. Sounds of muffled drums blended with sobbing, but it was all as if at a great distance. The predominant tone was silence, a profound, bottomless silence. The winter was over, a new winter was begun.

-11-

After Pilsudski died, the city was gray and spring was slow in coming. Aleks seemed quieter, but he worked harder, kept longer hours, imbued with a sense that he must keep his finger in the dike to stem the flow of anti-Semitism. Rachel stopped giving dinner parties.

Leopold rang up one afternoon, sounding unaccustomedly brusque. "Rachel, I must talk to Aleks."

"He just went back to the office, Leo. Call in the evening. He'll be home the usual time, around eight o'clock." She imagined he was treating her so coldly because, though she flirted and teased him, she had never seriously responded to his advances. Leopold visited them at least once a month, appearing increasingly handsome to Rachel, in his army uniform and his polished boots. Really what appealed to her was his growing seriousness about his role as Chief Rabbi of the Army.

"Rachel, it's important," Leopold said. "I want to see you too. You have to know what is going on."

She relented. "Well, come for supper, then. We just have a light meal. Come around eight thirty."

"No, I'll come after, at nine."

She and Aleks had talked about visiting Ella and Jadwiga that night, but it could wait. They had had their customary main meal at two in the afternoon and after a short nap, Aleks had returned to his office by four. When he came home in the evening Rachel told him Leopold was on his way. They ate quickly, alone. Sofie had gone out with a young man from her office. Rilka was asleep. "Leopold feels his responsibility strongly," Aleks had said to Rachel only recently. "He is in a delicate situation—an officer, a Polish patriot, a Jewish symbol. But fortunately he has a strong code of honor. He'll come through."

"Aleks, I must tell you something very serious," Leopold said almost as soon as he entered.

"A little cognac first," Aleks said, pouring some into the large brandy snifters Rachel had laid out on the coffee table.

"Yes, yes, but listen, I don't know what to say to you. Aleks, what are you doing?"

"What are you talking about?" Aleks faced Leopold, holding the two brandy glasses.

"Szell told me you are bribed by the Agudah." Leopold took one of the glasses and emptied it quickly.

"Are you crazy? What nonsense!"

"He told me in secret. Aleks, I have to warn you. I am your friend!"

"Szell—that opportunist! And he's the staff Director of Agudah! It's a disgrace. He should be grateful; instead he spreads this malicious gossip!"

"He didn't spread it. He told only me, in secret. But I don't understand why you are playing such close games with the Agudah. They are ultra-religious; they are not your kind," Leopold said with exasperation.

"But you're wrong, Leo," Aleks said. "They have always supported Pilsudski, and their deputies' strategy in the Senate is to cooperate with the government. But they want to protect Jewish interests."

"Leopold, you should have been outraged for Aleks. You should have told Szell never to speak such a thing again. You know Aleks would never take a bribe." Rachel, flushed and angry, got up and went to the French windows for a breath of air. "Why would he say such a thing?"

"He doesn't like you, Aleks," Leopold said." He thinks you're too Polonized, you like Zionism, you're not religious, I could go on and on, but mainly he just doesn't like you. So it isn't true?" he persisted.

"Leopold, you don't understand," Aleks said calmly. "Let me explain to you. This vicious woman Janina Pristor, this Senator, proposed the law against ritual slaughter. They are going to vote on it. Now that Pilsudski is dead, they think they can do anything. Her rationale is that it's cruel, inhumane, barbaric, but that's just an excuse. It's another nail in the coffin of the Jews. They need ritual slaughter to keep kosher. If there is no kosher meat, they will have to import from abroad. Most of the villagers can't afford such a thing; even the Jews in Warsaw can't afford it. When an Agudah representative came to see me on some routine matter, I told him this law was going to be proposed. I suggested they hire poor Jewish students to translate foreign documents showing ritual slaughter was humane. The board met, they agreed, and they asked me to arrange it. I don't know what that worm is talking about."

"But you took money from the Agudah! That's what he says." Leopold's voice rose in pitch. He wiped his forehead. He got up from the couch, walked over to the sideboard and poured himself another drink.

"Leo, it is not what you think at all. I cleared it with my chief. The Agudah gave me money to pay these students over several months. I have receipts from every one of them. The translated documents are in the hands of officials in the government and the Agudah is sending them to the legislators. Pristor is preparing her case for a vote, but we will be prepared and we will defeat it. I may not keep kosher, and perhaps I see it as nonsense, but I know what the implications are for the Jews if it's forbidden."

"There is nothing wrong in what Aleks did," Rachel said. She turned from the window and came back to sit down on the couch. "This whole thing is really just idiocy."

"Szell is a pompous ass, a sycophant, and I told him so." Aleks said with a little smile of satisfaction.

"Oh, Aleks," Rachel said. "That's your problem, always. Why did you have to tell him that?"

"Because it's the truth and he should know it."

Rachel turned to Leopold, "That's how Aleks makes enemies. I ran into Szell at the Europeiska one day and he said to me 'Madame, your husband makes a fetish of the truth. If I want to know the truth about myself I can look in the mirror. From him I want a little flattery.' Really, Aleks, you should be more careful with what you say."

"This is foolish," Aleks said, "Let's just forget it."

"Well, I'm relieved, now that you've explained the situation," Leopold said. "I'm leaving for the East tomorrow. I can go without worrying about you. It's getting late. I leave at 5:00 a.m. Rachel, you beautiful creature, my heart will ache till I see you again. What a lucky man you are, Aleks."

They laughed together. The flirtation was ritualized now and no parting was ever complete without some sign of it.

"Aleks, I'm nervous about this," Rachel said after Leopold left. "This kind of gossip can do you harm."

"Don't worry," Aleks said. "Nothing will come of it."

❦   ❦   ❦

Two months later, Aleks returned from his office less than an hour after he had left in the morning. Rachel was still in bed. She was propped up on pillows, her dark, rich hair tousled, her lace and satin pale mint gown revealing her full breasts. Her knees were drawn up and she was reading *Gone with the Wind*. The room was filled with the scent of roses. The bright sunlight softly filtered through the gauze curtains lightly billowing into the room with the gentle breeze. She looked up in surprise when Aleks entered the room and put her book down, guiltily.

"Dismissed," he said quietly, looking at her with wide-open eyes. "Suchnitski said to get a lawyer. I am accused of treason."

"What are you saying?" She didn't understand him. She had to return from Atlanta, back into this world.

"I found my office locked. Suchnitski said they packed my things yesterday. I am fired! Treason! It's impossible." He stooped as if struck by a blow from behind.

Rachel gasped. "The Agudah, the bribery charge. Leo warned us. But treason! I don't believe it. I am going to see Suchnitski."

He didn't stop her. She dressed quickly, but took the time to put on her makeup carefully. She left Aleks making phone calls in his study and rushed out.

"Why did you do this to my husband?" she faced Suchnitski angrily." Why, why, why?"

"You ask why? Why did they put my brother in Bereza-Kartusa? Who knows why? I was told by my chief that Aleks had to go." Bereza-Kartusa was a concentration camp for political prisoners, no trials, no warrants, an instrument to get rid of opposition. It had been established while Pilsudski was still alive, when he was turning more totalitarian, and now it was being used with a vengeance by his successors, the OZON party.

"You know he didn't take bribes. You know you approved the students. How can you do this? Don't you have any conscience? And anyway, what does that have to do with treason?"

"Aleks was an official of the government, not an elected member of a political party. He gave away privileged information to an outside agency. He tried to influence the government."

"Even as a private citizen he can be opposed to laws the government passes. That isn't treason."

"But he was not a private citizen. Rachel, this is a matter for lawyers. Stay out of this. Get yourself a good lawyer. A criminal lawyer."

"A criminal lawyer! My God!"

Rachel called everyone she knew. At first disbelieving, she quickly faced the situation and sought advice, information, support. She was despondent only briefly; mostly she was a tiger in action. Aleks said to her one day,

"Stop talking to everyone. Majkowski is an excellent lawyer, the best criminal lawyer." He shuddered at the words. "This case will drag on and on. Meantime, we are using up our savings." He was the despondent one. She noted the subtle shift in their positions, but she brushed it aside. In some ways, he was more hers now. Their days were more similar and their worlds merged.

"Friedeman says the Jewish organizations have jobs. There are all those refugees from Germany and Czechoslovakia to be resettled. Why don't you go see him?"

"I will, but here's what I want to talk to you about. Majkowski says we have to bring a countersuit, a civil suit for libel against Szell. If we win such a case, they would have to drop the treason charge. We have to prove I didn't take bribes and we have to prove Szell said I did."

"Yes, oh, that is brilliant, of course. But how? Leopold said Szell said it."

"Leopold would have to be the major witness. Will he do it?" Aleks was dubious.

"How could he not? He is our friend. Of course, he'll do it."

"He's a careerist. This is delicate—it might hurt him. I don't know. Well, we'll see how good a friend he is."

They plunged into activity. They obtained a top civil lawyer, Paulus Brenek. Aleks contacted each of the students he had paid. Some had returned to their native villages and he tracked them down and traveled to see them. He and Brenek lined up Agudah officials to testify. Rachel made notes of everything. Only Leopold's agreement to testify had to be obtained. He came to see them when he was on leave from his unit.

"The trial date is set. Two months from tomorrow. You will have to ask for leave," Aleks said.

"Milk, Leo?" Rachel poured tea from the silver teapot Stefcia had brought in. She placed two butter crescent cookies covered with powdered sugar on his plate.

"What? No, no milk. I'm being transferred. I'll be stationed just outside of Warsaw next month." Leopold was distracted. His usually handsome face was gray in tone. Frown lines made his eyes appear closer together. He got up from the couch and paced back and forth across the length of the living room.

"I don't know," he said. "What good will it do if I testify? Rozanski should testify." Rozanski was the mayor of Warsaw and Szell kept him abreast of what was happening in the Jewish community. It was Rozanski whom Szell told that Aleks was bribed; it was Rozanski, who was not a Jew and who wished to stay in good standing with the ruling party, who brought this information to the government, to Suchnitski's boss.

"Rozanski will be called. Rozanski, that bastard, didn't even investigate what Szell was saying—just took his word. On the strength of Szell's word I am ruined!" Aleks's voice rose. Rachel was glad to hear the anger in it, far better than the monotone he sometimes sank into when he was in a despairing mood.

"Szell curries favors; always he was sneaky. Those darting little eyes. And he pretends he's so pious," Rachel wascontinued, getting wound up. "But the point is you heard it from Szell and that constitutes gossip and it's false gossip, so it's libel. You must testify what Szell told you. You must, Leo. If we lose this case Aleks is finished. A criminal charge. My God, he could go to Bereza-Kartusa!" she cried. In that moment she experienced for the first time her own powerlessness against forces that could inflict torture, pain, hunger, cold, on Aleks, her Aleks, her own dear flesh that she knew so well. She saw in the flash of a fleeting image, that no amount of arguing, pleading, shouting at officials, trying with her own body to force her way into the prison gates, against guards—nothing would prevail against Bereza-Kartusa.

"You must, you must help, Leo, oh my God, Leo ..." She faced him with tears and anguish.

"Yes, yes I will testify," Leo said emotionally, "My officer's honor demands it. Justice must be done. How could I live with myself if I failed to stand up for the right thing? I would have to kill myself! I will testify!" He came over to Aleks and put his arms around him. "You are my friend and you were wronged. Of course I will testify!" He came over to Rachel and held her weeping face up to his own and hugged her. "I will, Rachel. It will be all right."

They laughed together in relief. Aleks poured brandy. They raised their glasses and clinked them.

"To friendship," Aleks said.

"To friendship," Leo replied.

"To friendship," Rachel declared.

"I have thought about this for so long," Leopold said, "thought what I should do. Now, it is as if a heavy stone is lifted from my heart."

❦   ❦   ❦

Leopold did not show up in court on the first day of the trial.

"He'll come, he'll be here in time," Rachel said to Brenek. The trial proceeded on the first point, the bribery charge. Student after student testified. Dr. Shipper, President of the Jewish Students Organization testified. Signed receipts were marked as Exhibit A. It was going well. The judge nodded approval.

"Have you other witnesses?" the judge asked.

"Your Honor," Brenek addressed the judge, "Our prime witness on the libel issue, Lieutenant Colonel Szteyn, is not in court."

"Case is postponed for two months. New trial date is April the twenty-third."

Once again they were in court. Aleks had called repeatedly but Leopold was never available. Rachel had written letters. There was no response.

"He will be here, I know he will come," Rachel said.

Leopold was not there. Another postponement was granted.

For the third time Leopold did not come.

"Your Honor," Aleks said to the judge," Szteyn is hiding himself illegally. We have not been able to reach him. He is our star witness."

"He will be subpoenaed," the judge ruled. "New date in eight days."

On the fourth trial date Leopold entered the courtroom. In full uniform, he came down the aisle to sit at the witness table across from Aleks, Brenek and Rachel. Szell sat at a table with his lawyer diagonally across. Leopold looked neither right nor left; he walked stiffly straight ahead, not meeting Rachel's eyes, not glancing at Aleks. He took his seat. The courtroom was full. Spectators stood in the back and along the sides. The press corps was seated in a special section. Leopold took the stand.

"What did Szell say to you?" the judge questioned him.

"I do not recall."

"You have no memory of what was said about Mischler?"

"I walked for several hours in the woods trying to remember what was said. So many things were said. It is hard to be exact."

"Colonel, we have postponed this trial three times to give you time to recall. Search your memory," the judge said caustically.

Leopold shifted his weight and turned so that his back was half turned away from the table where Aleks and Rachel sat.

"I remember Szell said Mischler got money from the Agudah." His voice was barely audible. The press strained to hear.

"For what did Szell say Mischler got the money, for work or for a bribe?"

"I do not remember," said Leopold.

Rachel gripped the table edge with hands. She felt faint.

Aleks stood up and asked the judge for permission to address Szteyn. The judge nodded agreement.

"Colonel," Aleks looked at him directly," do you remember saying, on the night you agreed to appear as a witness in this trial, that you were so happy you felt as if a stone had been lifted from your heart? Do you remember saying otherwise your conscience would be so burdened you would have to commit suicide?"

There was perfect silence in the courtroom, a long silence, a communal holding of the breath.

"Yes, I remember this," Leopold said at last, in a clear voice, looking straight ahead. "I remember Szell said Mischler took a bribe."

There was a communal release of breath, an audible sigh from the press section, a shuffling of chairs, nervous coughs, whispering.

The judge said to Leopold, "Thank you for testifying. You may leave the room now."

Leopold walked down the aisle to the door, his shoulders back, smiling, obviously relieved that in the last resort he had acted with honor. He smiled.

The judge addressed the courtroom. "Gossip is like an avalanche. It can ruin a person, as it did in this case. The witness has said that the gossip weighed so heavily on his heart that he would have to commit suicide if he did not bring this case to justice. Mr. Szell, take heed of what you have done. You are sentenced to one year in prison. Since this is a first offense the sentence is commuted to a fine of five hundred złotys. Case dismissed."

Rachel wept with relief. The government case for treason was still pending.

Months went by and nothing was happening. Aleks wrote some articles, gave some lectures; they were together much of the time. Rachel was careful not to appear too impatient with him, but she wanted him to do something, to act in some way that would get results, though she didn't know what he could do. Again she took matters into her own hands, and again he let her.

"I want you to see the Attorney General and get him to finish with this," she told Brenek and Majkowski, the two lawyers.

"I have nothing further to do with this case. We won the civil suit," said Brenek.

"Rachel, let me and Aleks handle this," Majkowski said." We can't push the Attorney General. You know how the political climate is. It's too dangerous. We don't want Aleks to end up in Bereza-Kartusa."

"Are you afraid for Aleks, or yourself? If you won't see the Attorney General, I will!" Rachel stormed.

"Aleks, control your wife," Majkowski said.

"She's right," Aleks said, "I can't go on this way." But they were all helpless, Rachel realized. To have no power, no say about what happens to you, to have some external force in full control of your life and to be afraid to protest even—how intolerable! She felt caught in a maze, walls all around her, and on the other side, over the wall, a black abyss of fear. She could stand it no longer. She went to see the Attorney General. She came to his office every day for ten days, refusing to be put off by the secretary who always said he was unavailable. Finally, she gained an appointment for the following day. Aleks agreed she should go. She told Brenek and Majkowski and they arranged to meet in the Cafe Europeiska after Rachel's appointment.

She wore a close-fitting black dress, calf-length, the skirt flaring at the bottom like a mermaid's tail. Her thin waist, rounded hips, and full bosom were all accentuated, but subtly, softened by the demure white lace collar at her neck. She wore a little hat with a half-veil, under which her face shone with the intensity of her mission. The black eyes, outlined in dark kohl pencil, the beauty mark on her cheek, carefully applied, the red lips and the two dots of rouge on her fine cheekbones gave her the look and power of a beautiful but determined woman.

She was ushered into the Attorney General's imposing office and approached him as he sat bent over some papers on his large, cluttered desk, the top of his almost-bald head shining in the light. He looked up and smiled and she perceived this as a friendly gesture.

"My husband is not guilty," she said with passion. "He has won the libel case against his accuser, but his name is not cleared. I have a daughter. My husband is unemployed. This cannot go on. Clear his name or arrest him. But for the sake of heaven, do not leave this matter pending!"

"Madame, I will review the case. He will be cleared or arrested, as you ask so rightly. You may return in one week. With your husband."

Rachel rushed over to the Cafe Europeiska. Brenek and Majkowski were seated at an outdoor table, talking intently to each other. Aleks was drinking coffee, silent, tapping the glass table with nervous fingers.

"Well," he said as she approached.

"He's reviewing the case," Rachel said. She was suddenly gay. "I did better than you two," she added as she turned to the lawyers, "but it was your job." She was filled with contempt at their quaking, servile positions.

"We don't know yet how it will turn out," Majkowski said. "You took a gamble. Don't count your chickens yet. You may need me still." They fell silent. There was a chill in the air. The sky was gray.

❦   ❦   ❦

She read it in the paper first, before any official word. "The case for treason against Aleksander Mischler was dismissed."

Aleks was in his study. She burst in and put the paper in front of him. He looked up at her wordlessly.

"Thank God," she said.

The following week a letter came from the Ministry. How ironic, Rachel thought: a letter of promotion for Aleks, and six months' severance pay, but no job. Aleks's post was eliminated entirely.

"Well," Rachel said. "At least there is some satisfaction." The personnel director who had had Aleks dismissed for bribery was himself dismissed, and Rozanski ended up in a small town. The law against ritual slaughter was not passed.

"Was it worth it?" Rachel asked.

"It was worth it," Aleks replied.

❦   ❦   ❦

Aleks became director of the organization dealing with refugees streaming in from Germany, displaced, humiliated, impoverished refugees.

"A come-down," Ella pronounced. "You are nothing but a social worker!"

"But I have always been a social … worker," Aleks said.

❈   ❈   ❈

He was busy, he was always busy with the refugees. "They have nothing," Aleks said. "They are desperate. They cannot find work; what can they do? We must help them." When he wasn't away in the border town where the refugees first came, he was raising funds for the General Aid Committee he had started. He came home late almost every night. The situation was getting worse each day—first the Anschluss, and Austria was gone, willingly, happily they embraced the Nazis with garlands and cheers as the German army marched in. Aleks had warned them in his little book when Hitler first came to power, but no one had listened and now the Germans occupied Sudetenland and Chamberlain sacrificed Czechoslovakia. No one wanted to go to war. Roosevelt had said quite clearly America would not fight in a European dispute over Czechoslovakia. But perhaps Chamberlain did avert war; perhaps diplomacy would succeed. Then later that year: Kristallnacht, with the Jews hiding in their houses while the brownshirts smashed the stores, the windows, the synagogues, and the building superintendents gave away the hiding places, and the hoodlums dragged out the Jews.

❈   ❈   ❈

Rachel felt superfluous. She was determined to resume her business of arranging private libraries. Even though books were not coming in from Germany anymore, she could get better ones from England. Aleks would provide her with contacts. She regretted that her English was so halting. She would take a course after the New Year.

She bought a huge Christmas tree and placed it in the corner of the living room beside the French doors. Alyna and Stefcia brought decorations each had from her family, wooden dolls of peasant women, the baby Jesus carved in a gaily painted cradle, snowflakes cut out of shiny paper. Rilka was delighted to help decorate, but Sofie was scandalized.

"A Christmas tree!" Sofie exclaimed when it was delivered. "You'd better not invite Papa here till after it's gone. He'll renounce you! And Aleks? He permits this? Oh, Rachel, you have been away from your family for too long. What are you doing? All your friends are goyim."

"This is for Alyna and Stefcia," Rachel said. "They have to have a Christmas. It's only a tree, for heaven's sake! It's a lovely custom. Besides, I'm not allowing any crosses for decorations. Sofie, Sofie … you must become a little more worldly. You're not in Zarki anymore. I want you to meet some important men. You're just standing still in that office job."

"I'm not standing still! I'm doing very well. I just got promoted. In fact I meant to talk to you. By next year I'll be office manager. Then I'll make enough to get my own place."

Rachel was always a little startled by evidence of Sofie's competence, her growing seriousness. How had she turned from that carefree, laughing girl in Zarki into an office manager?

"Your own place? Oh, Sofie, what would you do living alone? No, you must get married. I'm going to talk to Aleks. He should introduce you. This Ludwik you're seeing … I don't trust him entirely. I think he's playing with you."

"You sound just like Mama," Sofie said, and came over to Rachel and kissed her on the cheek. "Don't worry about me. Ludwik is a very fine man. Anyway, we just have a friendship. We leave the office at the same time, so we go out for tea together."

Rachel embraced Sofie and held her tightly for a moment. If only she could make Sofie's life all right! If only she could arrange things for her, arrange love, children, security. There was that element of sadness about Sofie lately, of dreams unfulfilled, of time vanishing and a loss of hope.

She took Rilka to the cinema one afternoon. The screen was filled with a little girl, dancing, tapping her feet to a fast rhythm, her blond curls shaking, her round face smiling, her short skirt twirling. Rilka fidgeted in the darkened movie theatre, not quite understanding what the movie was about, but Rachel watched Shirley Temple intently, tapping her own feet to the music and squeezing Rilka's hand, kissing her, putting her arm around her.

"Look, darling, look; it's America," Rachel whispered.

At night, dressed to go to a New Year's ball, she sat on the edge of Rilka's bed and re-told her favorite bedtime story.

"We will be on a big ship. And all around, as far as we can see, there will be the ocean. And you will be dressed in a little pink dress, like the one you wear to ballet school, with blue flowers at the hem."

"A new dress," Rilka said. "I would like a new dress."

"Yes, of course, you'll have a new dress. The Captain will ask us to sit at his table, just like he did when I went to Palestine with your father. It will be a big round table, with shining glasses and flowers and silver gleaming. 'Who is that little girl?' people will whisper when you walk in. 'Why, that's Rilka, the star—she is going to Hollywood with her mother.' And everyone will look at you and smile."

Rilka snuggled into her down comforter, smiling happily, drowsily. "Where will you be?" she asked dreamily.

"I'll be right next to you. The music will play and the Captain will ask me to dance with him, and we will twirl around on the dance floor to a waltz. La-ra-ra-ra-rum, ra-rum, ra-rum," Rachel hummed in three-quarter time.

"And everyone will watch us dance, the handsome Captain and your mother. And people will whisper to each other, 'Who is that lady?' And they will say, 'Why, that's Rilka's mother. You know, Rilka the star.' And we will sail for many days and nights and then we will reach America."

"And then? What happens next?" Rilka held on to Rachel's hand tightly.

"And then … well, you'll have to wait and see. Tomorrow night we'll land in America. Now I have to go. Daddy is waiting. It's Sylvester. You know what that is. It's the end of this year and the beginning of a new year. We are going to a big ball and Daddy and I will dance." She twirled around the room, her taffeta skirt shimmering and rustling as she moved.

"And then, then what?" Rilka pursued.

"And then on the stroke of midnight a thousand balloons will be cut loose and they will rise to the ceiling, all different colors, and the corks on the champagne bottles will go 'pop' all around, and everyone will sing 'sto lat, sto lat,' and the strings of confetti will be thrown all around, and everyone will kiss. And one day, you will go to such a ball, one day in America, when you are a film star. Good-night darling. I'll see you tomorrow."

"Don't go," Rilka clung to her. "Stay with me."

"I must go. Alyna is here. Tomorrow morning you can come in to my bed and I will tell you every single thing that happened. Now, I must go."

And she swept out of the room, leaving a scent of orchid fragrance behind her.

-12-

London—1939

But it was not to America that Rachel went. It was to England. A letter from her Aunt Klara arrived one day inviting them for a stay in her house in High-gate. Her mother's sister had left Poland when she was eighteen and married well.

"I can't go," Aleks said." The Committee needs me; it is getting more desper-ate every day. But you should go."

"Without you?"

"But we're not joined together like Siamese twins! Of course you should go. And not just for a visit. You want to do business with English books, then learn English better. Rachel, I'm never home anyway. Go, enroll in a school. I'll come over with Rilka in the summer."

How quickly the inconceivable becomes the possible, Rachel thought. Could she leave Rilka? She consulted Mama, fully expecting Mama would be appalled. But surprisingly, Mama wrote her, "Go, Ruchele, go. You are young; whatever you learn will stay with you always. You never know what life will bring. Go and be independent if you have to. You will be with my sister. You will get to know your cousins. Time goes so quickly. Before you know it you'll be back, but you'll be back with something, English, something you learned. Go, Ruchele. You have Sofie there to watch Rilka, and Alyna. Go, Ruchele. I wish I could go."

In small steps the idea became increasingly acceptable. First Rachel wrote to her aunt, saying Aleks couldn't come, but maybe she'd come by herself. She wasn't really serious about it, but Aunt Klara answered her letter by return mail, full of plans for getting tickets to Covent Gardens, to Albert Hall, for tak-ing a motor trip to the Cotswald, maybe even to Scotland. Rachel toyed with the idea of getting on a train, arriving in London, being met at Charing Cross.

She ran it around in her mind like a piece of hard candy she might suck on, exploring its taste with her tongue, its sweet-and-sour flavor. Like she had toyed with Jakob in her youth, with the prospect of going off to Palestine with him, escaping to a new kind of freedom. But she hadn't done it then and she didn't really see how she would go off to England now. Certainly not to be away for months. But maybe just for a short visit to her aunt ... "See the head of the United Appeal for Jews in London," Aleks told her. Tell them firsthand how much we need their support. We need money for feeding the refugees, for training them for new work, for housing. You can get to see all the important people. Use you charm."

"Rachel, I am going to give you names of people to see in the leather business," said Papa. "See if you can arrange some leather outlets for me. I want to export to England. It's a good market."

People were relying on her. She had to go.

"Ruchele, go to business school," Mama advised her. "The time will pass anyway, and when a year is over, you'll be one year older. Better to be one year older and have something to show for it then just to be one year older and in the same situation."

Rachel wrote to the Pittman School asking about their commercial course. She wrote just to see what was available, just for information. And when the information came, she wrote back that perhaps she would enroll in the spring. They should save a place for her. And somehow, soon it was taken for granted that she was going. And finally that idea was integrated into her life, a *fait accompli*. Aleks is so progressive, Rachel told all her friends. He wants me to be independent. She herself had mixed feelings about independence. But soon she was saying with pride, "I am going to the Pittman School," as if it were Oxford rather than a secretarial course.

"It's just a vacation," she told Rilka, "just like Mommy went to Switzerland. And Daddy will be here and Alyna and Sofie. And before you know it I'll be back."

But when she saw Rilka playing alone in her room, her heart pounded. She seemed so alone. But now the wheels had been set in motion, now she had ordered her wardrobe, Aleks was making the travel arrangements, everyone was carrying on as if she had already left, and she knew she would not back out. She escaped thinking about it by reading in every spare moment. She did not allow her mind to dwell on the trip for an instant, but she proceeded with all the plans as if it were fixed immutably that she must go.

"In a few months, in the summer, when you are through with your kinder-garten, Daddy will bring you to England," she told Rilka. "And you'll learn English too. Then when you go to America to be a star, you'll know how to speak English. And we'll have a wonderful summer in England."

Rilka was quiet. Then she said, "Will Alyna come too?" And Rachel knew it was all right.

-13-

Aunt Klara, tall, slightly plump, with streaks of gray in her dark hair worn in a loose bun, with little wisps escaping around her forehead, Aunt Klara wore flowered housedresses, emanated softness, English gardens, early morning mists. Rachel was always startled by her English accent. She expected the familiar Yiddish to be spoken, or at least a Yiddish accent, but Aunt Klara's English was pure. Her household was calm and well organized, and Uncle Jakob with his rounded belly, his booming voice, and his inevitable cigar, took her entirely for granted. It was all very comfortable for Rachel. Not like the household of her parents in her childhood, which was turbulent and a little chaotic with the seven children making their strident demands and Papa acting stern or shouting for a little peace, and Mama trying to hold things together. This was a peaceful, well run household, orderly, smooth, the way things ought to be. How can this be my mother's sister, Rachel wondered. How can they lead such different lives?

Rachel checked in to the Mayfair Hotel acutely aware of her shabby brown suitcase. She always took great care to dress well, but she paid little attention to accessories. She should have gotten new luggage for this trip, she thought with some annoyance at herself. Around her were people with Louis Vuitton trunks, the women wearing Chanel suits, the men in their perfectly-tailored trousers and perfectly-cut shirts, gleaming gold cuff links. But here and there she spotted a fat man with his shirt just slightly hanging out of ill-fitting trousers, a woman with too much make-up. It was a manufacturers' convention, and there were all sorts gathering here. Rachel was splurging, having decided to stay in town for the meetings instead of returning to Aunt Klara's house in the suburb just outside of London. Uncle Jakob, who was in the textile business, had gotten admittance for her. Rachel thought she would learn valuable things here, and also she had in mind to make contacts among the users of leather.

"Your room isn't quite ready yet, Madame," the desk clerk, wearing gray cutaways, told her in clipped tones.

"What do you mean, not ready? I am scheduled to go to a meeting in half an hour and I must change and unpack. I reserved this room last week!"

"Madame, most of the rooms have been reserved for months. We were fortunate we had a cancellation and could accommodate you at such short notice. The present occupant was late in checking out. We have to prepare the room." He was politely condescending. "Perhaps Madame would like tea and crumpets in the salon while you wait. With our compliments of course," he added. "We shall look after your bags." He looked down at the brown suitcase and cleared his throat.

Rachel felt like one of Aleks's refugees and it angered her. "I hardly have a choice," she said haughtily, but with her Polish accent. She raised her chin and walked off to the lobby cafe at the left, separated from the rest of the lobby by a balustrade. She took a seat at a small table and almost immediately a waiter brought tea in a silver pot and a waitress came around with little cakes and jams.

Perhaps he thinks I'm a Polish countess, Rachel imagined, and turned her back to the arrogant clerk. An impoverished countess, she smiled to herself as she thought of her brown suitcase. The tea warmed her and she was soon enjoying herself thoroughly. A piano player in the center of the cafe was playing a soft romantic tune. Conversations in many different languages buzzed around her. People from all over Europe were staying here. She tossed her mauve soft wool coat with the large fox collar over the back of the chaise, took out a black cigarette and carefully inserted it into her ivory cigarette holder. Immediately a waiter appeared to light it. A gentleman two tables away, looked at her and smiled. He had an unruly lock of hair over his forehead and was nice-looking in an irregular sort of way. His face was mostly angles, except for full lips. She smiled back and blew soft smoke from her cigarette. She thought he might send over a cognac to her table, like Aleks had done so many, many years ago in Czestochowa. But he did not. In fact he turned his gaze away and spoke to a man seated at a table right next to him. It seemed to Rachel that he had not been looking at her at all, but past her at someone else, and she felt foolish, but also relieved. By the time a clerk came over to tell her that her room was ready, she was so relaxed and content, and she hated to leave.

In the afternoon, at a meeting on financing strategies in the textile industry, she stepped out into the hallway during a tea break. People congregated in small groups, laughing, talking, everyone seeming to know everyone else. For a moment she felt isolated, not belonging. With determination, she went up to one young woman who was holding some notes and pamphlets and conversing animatedly with a man who seemed very young.

"I'm Rachel Mischler," she introduced herself. "My English is not so good, but I'm here to learn it better. Are you in the textile business?"

The young woman laughed. "My English is not so good also," she said in a strong French accent, "Oui, I am in the textile business. I am buyer for a small house in Paris, but I want to have my own business sometime. Je m'appelle Lanie. And this is Marcel," she turned to the young man and Rachel held out her hand.

"Enchanté," he said and kissed her hand. "And I am the president of the 'small house in Paris.'"

"No," said Rachel, "you can't be. You are too young!"

"And the president's father is the owner of the 'small house in Paris,'" Lanie laughed. "But you are Polish. We have some Polish friends here too." She pulled Rachel over to a group of three men, of varying ages, thirty, perhaps, or forty. "Michal is from Krakow," she said,"and Tomas also, and Peter here is our English guide."

Soon they were all talking easily with each other, and they met again at the tea break mid-lecture. Michal and Tomas wore wedding rings. Peter's fingers were bare.

Peter said, "Come with us for dinner tonight, if you are free. Later we're going dancing. We're going to meet up with some others. It'll be a big crowd. A bit of fun. Do come."

Rachel hesitated for a moment only. What harm could there be? At the dance hall they sat at a long table with other people she didn't know. A band was playing on a little platform at the head of the large dance floor. Rachel danced with abandon, the Charleston, the fox trot, stopping every once in a while to sit down and catch her breath. Michal, from Krakow, was especially good at the waltz. Peter kept cutting in. Marcel, the Frenchman, took turns dancing with Lanie, the only other woman in the party, and Rachel. In one evening she came to feel Lanie was a friend. She didn't remember having as carefree a time as this since Czestochowa.

She was sitting at the table, catching her breath, when a tall man walked over. She looked up in surprise to see the man who had seemed to smile at her in the cafe at the Hotel Mayfair. He didn't appear to recognize her. Perhaps he hadn't even seen her before.

"This is Roman. Roman is Peter's boss," Lanie introduced them. "Meet Rachel. Roman, Rachel. Rachel, Roman." She giggled at the alliteration and went twirling off with Peter. Michal came over and grabbed Rachel as a polka started. They spun and slid along the polished dance floor, Rachel's hair disheveled, damp from perspiration, her face flushed with wine and dance, her eyes smudged a bit from the melting kohl liner. Every once in a while, as she flew past, she caught Roman looking at her, holding her eyes. She collapsed at the table and passed up the next dance with Peter. Roman danced with Lanie. Rachel watched him. He moved with confidence, smoothly, gracefully. His jacket was off and she could almost feel the muscular arms under his shirtsleeves. He was not handsome, but his face was compelling, serious, unsmiling, the jaw a little prominent, the eyes unreadable under rather bushy eyebrows, the look softened by his full lips.

The band played a slow, sinuous song. Roman came over, took her hand and led her onto the dance floor. He hadn't asked her, and in some vague way this pleased her. He was taller than she so that the top of her head reached to just below his eyes. His right hand was firm around her waist and he guided her surely and expertly. She tried to follow his intricate steps, short steps forward, then long glides, then back for a few steps, then forward and to the side, in no discernible pattern. She stepped on his foot.

"Sorry," she murmured.

"Relax," he said quietly. She realized how tense her muscles were and she tried to go limp. Then she began to feel the rhythm of the music and she sank into it. She anticipated his movements and bent in consonance with the bending of his body. His steps and turns became more intricate, more subtle, now a few beats in place, now back and forth, now across the floor. She was ready for each nuance. They didn't speak at all. She felt the muscles in his thighs pressing against her body as he moved her forward. She felt the hollow of his back with her arm around him, his chest against hers, her cheek brushing his jaw, a little rough, a little sweaty. The notes of the saxophone hung in the air, sultry, like their movements. She became aware that people were watching them, and their dance became a public thing, outside of that private, enclosed fragment of world in which they had been for a brief while. The music stopped and he brought her back to the table, said "Thank you," and didn't dance with her again. Roman left alone a half hour or so later. The rest of the party walked back together to the hotel, said good-night in the lobby, and Rachel went up to her room.

She was in the bathroom, putting night cream on her face when there was a knock on the door.

"Who is it?" she asked, alarmed.

"It's me, Roman. I've been knocking for five minutes! Let me in."

"What are you doing here? What's the matter?" She spoke through the closed door.

"Let me in," he said.

"I'm undressed. I'm in bed. I can't let you in. It's two in the morning! What is the matter?"

"Nothing is the matter, and I can't talk to you standing out in the hall here in the middle of the night. We are making a lot of noise. Someone will come along and complain. Now let me in."

She opened the door slightly and he walked in, past her. They stood in the center of the room facing each other. Rachel didn't know what to say, it was all so awkward, she standing there in her nightgown only barely covered by the sheer peignoir she had quickly put on as she went to open the door for him. She had no make-up on and her face was shiny with cream, her hair disheveled, but he didn't seem to notice at all. He was dressed in the same clothes he wore earlier in the evening, but his shirt looked crumpled now, his tie loose at the throat. They stood silent for a moment, then he said,

"I wanted to see you again. Alone. I liked dancing with you. I think you liked dancing with me." He smiled slightly.

"I liked dancing with you," she said slowly, looking directly into his eyes. They were hazel with flecks of green, a surprising color, changing back to brown as he turned in the low light of the room and put his arms around her. She stopped thinking. She banished the picture of Aleks that had come, unbidden, into her mind. Roman held her and she leaned her face on his chest. Her body felt soft and loose under her gown, and she liked the sensation of her almost nakedness against his clothed, hard body. His rough tweed jacket rubbed against her skin through the thin, sheer fabric of her nightgown. But she pushed Roman away and stood apart.

"I'm married," she said quietly.

"Yes, I'm sorry about that," he said, suddenly less brash, "I should have respected that. Pardon me for barging in like that. Let me stay a few minutes."

He walked over to the cabinet in the little sitting area of the room and took out a bottle of Napoleon brandy and two glasses.

"Well, we can talk for a while," she agreed. They sat down on the chaise next to each other and sipped the brandy. The room was bathed in a soft amber light from the two lamps on either side of the bed opposite the chaise. The heavy brocade drapes were drawn. They were alone, safe, apart from the rest of the world.

"Tell me about yourself," she said trying to sound gay but impersonal. "Lanie told me you are a very important man, very successful. Do you actually own the textile mill? My father owns a factory, leather, but he always has business troubles. I'm trying to help him here. But he was successful when I was growing up. He was very rich for our little town." She stopped. She thought herself ridiculous, prattling on like that. He hadn't said a word. She lowered her eyes. Her gaze fell on his lap and she looked up quickly as if caught at some forbidden thing. His lips were slightly parted and his eyes half shut. Her breasts swelled against the gauze of her gown as she shifted her position on the couch to face him. He put down his brandy glass, enveloped her in his arms and kissed her for a long time. She yielded, the upper part of her body pressed against him, her arm around his back, her lips trembling, her tongue searching his. His right hand slipped down her waist, caressed her thigh, her belly, through the gown. She was beside herself. She had to force herself not to grab his hand and guide it where she wanted it to stroke her. She strained against him, hoping he would find her.

He led her to the bed and as she lay on top of the silk quilt, waiting for him, mindless, he undressed quickly, dropping his clothes half on the bed, half on the floor, till he stood above her naked, his wide chest covered with curly ringlets of hair. She slipped the straps of her gown off her shoulders and slid it off from underneath her. He lay down next to her and softly touched her and she ran her hands over his body, through the hair on his chest, across his belly, looking so white, so exposed. She was moved by the vulnerability of his nakedness. But when he entered her, he was hard and sure. He filled her and she gasped with joy to feel all that power inside her. They made love for a long time and then lay together silently. Then she rolled over to the night table and took out a cigarette from the drawer.

"Don't smoke," he said, and she put it away.

He got under the quilt and tried to draw her to him.

"What are you doing?" she asked, sitting up.

"I'm going to sleep. It's four in the morning. We have to be up in two hours. Come, get some sleep."

"You have to go," she said in a panic. "You can't stay here. I can't have a man in my room!"

"Don't be foolish. I'm not going to leave in the middle of the night. I'm not staying in this hotel. Don't worry," he said more softly, "no one will see me leave in the morning. I won't compromise you." And he turned over.

"Roman, you can't stay here. You can't stay." But she knew she wouldn't budge him.

He fell asleep almost immediately while she lay awake, trying to move as far away from him on the bed as possible, trying not to touch him. She refused to let herself think about what happened. She just wanted to get through this night. She wanted it to be morning, day, normalcy. I'll think about it tomorrow, she said to herself. Like Scarlett O'Hara, she thought with a little irony. In the light of day, this will seem like it never happened.

❧   ❧   ❧

Uncle Jacob had purchased a table at the benefit ball in London for HIAS, the Hebrew Immigrant Aid Society, whose mission was to resettle immigrants. Rachel, dressed in her gown of black taffeta and tulle, a red velvet flower stuck in the décolletage of her dress, was happy to be going out. Nearly three months had passed since the night with Roman, which Rachel determinedly put out of her mind. She had enrolled in the Pitman School, threw herself into course-work, and wrote long letters to Aleks and short ones to Rilka. She was back on track.

The ballroom sparkled under large crystal chandeliers. Couples danced to an orchestra playing soft music.

"How beautiful," Rachel whispered to Aunt Klara. Then her face grew warm as she saw Roman quickly approaching them.

"Roman," Uncle Jacob boomed genially and put his arm around the man. "You're a heavy contributor too, eh? Of course you are. And you should be. We must all help these poor unfortunate souls, losing their homes, their status. Terrible, terrible. This is my niece, Rachel Mischler, from Poland. Oh, have you met already?" He looked surprised as Roman bowed slightly at the waist and kissed Rachel's fingertips.

"Madame Mischler," Roman's sea-blue eyes pierced her, "A pleasure to see you again."

"Yes, we met at that conference I went to in London, months ago," Rachel said quickly to Uncle Jacob.

"May I have this dance?" Roman asked.

"No, I'm sorry. We just came in. I'm not ready to dance." Rachel looked around her with a certain desperation, but of course she knew no one here. She could hardly hope to be rescued, except by her aunt perhaps.

"Go ahead, dear," Aunt Klara said, "have a bit of a good time. We'll meet you at our table later."

Roman led her out onto the polished dance floor and Rachel had to hold on to him at first to keep from slipping.

"Afraid to dance with me?" he smiled wickedly.

"No, I'm not afraid. I just don't want to see you. I am a married woman. What happened never happened. If you were a gentleman you would not have recognized me." She felt more comfortable being angry.

"I left you alone for months! What happened did happen. And besides, you're making too much of it. Come to my office Monday. Here is my card. I have someone for you to meet. He buys textiles from me and imports leather."

"I have school Monday."

"You'll learn more about business coming to my office." He pulled her closer and they danced in silence till the song ended. Then he took her back to the little group that had formed around her uncle and aunt.

"Thank you," he said to her, then turned to her uncle. "I have to do a little politicking, Jacob. So many people here. Good night."

She didn't see him the rest of the evening but she was so agitated she couldn't enjoy herself. The pull was there, and she looked around, through all the people, hoping he would appear, hoping he wouldn't. She sat through the interminable after-dinner speeches creating scenarios where she visited his office Monday, or where she didn't but wrote him a letter, or where she ignored him altogether, or where she just returned to Warsaw next week. She was happy when the ball was over.

"Uncle Jacob," she said to him Sunday evening. "Roman invited me to his office tomorrow. He says there is someone he wants me to meet, about leather. Do you think I should go?"

Her uncle chuckled. "Yes, yes, go. Roman is a sly old fox. If he's doing business with someone in leather, he'll come out on the top of it. If he takes a liking to you, he can help you."

"How?"

"With connections, with securing loans, anything. But if you're on the wrong side of him, watch out. He makes you think you're winning, but he always comes out ahead. Not above being a little shady either, I suspect. An interesting fellow, not much education, but a lot of know-how. Just don't get in the position where you owe him something."

Forewarned, forearmed, thought Rachel, and she dressed in her best suit, tight-fitting across the hips, a peplum jacket in a deep shade of green, a little hat with a half-veil across her eyes.

"Oh, you did come," Roman said. "Well, make yourself comfortable. I have business to do. You can stay here and listen. We'll have lunch later and I'll explain things to you."

They went to a pub around the corner for lunch and had cheese and bread and Pims.

"I want to meet that man in the leather business," Rachel said after the waiter vanished.

"Yes. He's coming next Monday. Be at my office by ten. This afternoon I am going to a bank meeting to secure a new loan. You can come and learn something. We'll have dinner at eight."

"I don't need to learn about loans," Rachel said. "And I have dinner at Highgate. But I will come next week. I must meet that leather man." She had more force in her voice than she intended. Roman looked at her with amusement. She blushed and summoned the waiter to distract him.

"No, no," Roman said. "In England, the gentleman calls for the waiter. Would you like more tea?"

"Oh," Rachel said. "You are so exasperating!"

She did meet the man in the leather business, and could hardly wait to write Papa that she had made a connection for him. Roman's friend agreed to consider her father's leather for import but would wait till he got samples. Rachel knew she was happier with this little accomplishment than reality warranted, happier because it justified her spending the day with Roman. She could make herself believe it was for Papa. But that little part of Rachel that always insisted on telling herself the truth inserted itself and she argued with it. Still, she said to herself, that is one reason I came to England, to help Papa—and this will help Papa, so it's not altogether untrue. What is altogether true? She could not, or would not, sort it out.

Rachel began going to Roman's office in the late afternoon, after her classes at the Pitman College were over, at first twice a week, on Tuesdays and Thursdays, then more often. Sometimes Roman would be away, seeing someone across town. Then Rachel talked to his secretary, Mabel, or to the salesmen who came in and out periodically, leaving reports for Roman or messages they asked Mabel to convey. Mabel seemed fond of Rachel and confided little details of her life. She was thirty-five, a round little person, with blond hair coiled in an upsweep, too much makeup, a little sloppy looking, her tight skirt pulling across her broad bottom. She lived with her pensioned mother, and wanted desperately to marry, but her boyfriend was a merchant seaman and was away for months at a time, so it seemed quite hopeless to Rachel. She imagined Mabel would go on living with her mother forever, always expecting her life to change, and never seeing that she was frozen in time like those youths gamboling about on Keats's Grecian Urn. This was her life: to live with her mother, to care for her mother when she got sick and old, to believe that her boyfriend would change all that. What was Rachel's own life? She didn't feel frozen in time. Quite the opposite, she felt fluid, formless, on the verge of possibilities. But how could she feel that? Her own life was in Warsaw, with Aleks and Rilka, giving parties, perhaps having a career and making some money, helping Papa, finding a husband for Sofie, going to the Cafe Europeiska—not here with Roman, adrift, as if she had no ties. Really, she must stop coming to his office. There was no point in it at all.

"At least on the days you come, I know he'll return to the office," Mabel said happily. "He's always traveling somewhere, always busy. He has no personal life, it's all this business. Well, I suppose if you're going to be rich, that's what you have to do," she said philosophically. Rachel was happy to hear Roman had no personal life.

"He's late—it's after five already. I can't stay tonight. Mum is having an old friend for dinner. Here, you give him these. Tell him I finished everything he wanted." Mabel handed a stack of papers to Rachel, powdered her nose, put on some lipstick, and bounced out the door. "Ta," she called over her shoulder. "See you next week."

When Roman returned he said, "Call your aunt and tell her you'll stay in town. I have tickets to the Haymarket. Noel Coward. You'll like it."

"Will I be able to catch the last train?"

"No, we'll have dinner after the show. You can stay in my flat. Oh, don't worry. I have two extra bedrooms and the housekeeper is there."

Why not, thought Rachel, why not? Roman took off his jacket and began going through the papers on his desk. "Here, read about the play." He handed her a folded newspaper.

"*Design for Living*," Rachel read, "with Diana Wynyard, Anton Wallbrook, Rex Harrison. A sophisticated comedy." Roman wasn't looking at her, nor she at him, but it seemed to her his eyes were burning into her. Without any specific gesture or sign, the air was charged.

Suddenly, he came around the desk, just as she stood up from the soft, large armchair in which she had been sitting. He kissed her, strongly, his mouth enveloping hers, his tongue deep within her. She held him tightly and pressed herself against him, aroused by his arousal. She, she alone, had that power to make him swell, to bring out that response, secret from the rest of the world, only for her. She felt warm and moist and pulsating. They were on the floor, on the soft carpet, Rachel still half dressed, her skirt bunched around her hips, her silk stockings held in place with the black garter belt, panties hastily thrown, a little pile of cream lace wrapped around the Queen Anne leg of his desk chair. He thrust into her with mounting intensity. In the last moments, before his final, shuddering gasp, she concentrated only on his rising excitement, his ultimate loss of control. It was that which most pleased her, the thought that this powerful, self-contained man, envied, hated, perhaps admired by some, but aloof from them all, private, inaccessible, this man was completely vulnerable to her. It was she who had made him grow hard, she who had the power to make him lose control. A controlled man, losing control. A powerful man, over whom she had power. In that moment he was fully hers.

He rolled off her, and put his lips on her breast, through the thin cloth of her blouse. She had not reached orgasm, but she pressed his fingers tightly to her, involuntarily moving against them, and in an instant felt the powerful contractions inside her, and the almost unbearable release. They lay on their backs on the floor, next to each other, breathing more slowly now. Already he was gone, already back to his public self, but still, they were enveloped in a secret intimacy that pleased her. She did not regret this.

Rachel came to Roman's office almost every day now. Sometimes they had a late supper and she caught the last train back to her aunt's. On those occasions she told her aunt she was having dinner with Lanie or with Tomas or with someone from school. But once in a while she said she was meeting with Roman. She wanted to be casual about it and not arouse suspicion by avoiding mentioning his name altogether.

"Is that rascal teaching you all his tricks?" Uncle Jacob asked. "He sells his goods to one wholesaler, tells him he's the exclusive customer, then undersells to the man's rival under another name. It will all backfire one day, but first he'll make a lot of millions. Well, some things you could learn from him. He doesn't expand unless he's sure of a market. He knows exactly what's going on in his industry everywhere. He doesn't dream, like your Papa. He's strictly a realist."

Rachel blushed, then said in what she hoped was an even, dispassionate tone, "Roman seems straightforward to me. I've heard him deal with people. He lays his cards on the table."

"Lays his cards on the table!" Uncle Jacob slapped his thigh and laughed. "Rachel, you are a naïve woman, but never mind; I like him anyway."

"Well, he has been very helpful to me. He introduced me to several important people." She thought she sounded defensive but she didn't know what posture to take. "I'm spending the weekend with Lanie. She has some friends with a cottage in the Cotswald."

Rachel had shut off her mind to thoughts of Aleks, of home. When she received letters from Aleks, she read them quickly, uneasily, wanting to be done with it. She had pulled down a screen that separated her mind in two unequal, non-overlapping parts, the larger part filled with Roman, the smaller ascending when the letters from home arrived. She was driven, compelled to see Roman, compelled to lie to her aunt and uncle. Though it seemed to her she had discovered passion, in some regard, she realized she was almost totally without feeling. She could not allow herself to feel, for what could she possibly feel? Love? Self-loathing? Guilt? She was like a lemming, blindly headed to the sea. In every spare moment she read, books, magazines, newspapers, billboards, anything so that she did not have one empty moment during which she could think. She just acted.

And yet, there were times with Roman, when she felt such completeness, such intimacy and fulfillment, that she could not imagine any other life. In the cottage he rented in the Cotswold they lay awake late into the night, talking. They walked along the cobbled streets, past lovely, flowering gardens, quaint houses, misty mornings, sunny afternoons. They had tea and scones in little tea shops. They made love before dinner. Back in London, she again felt the excitement of being in his office, watching him operate on such a large scale, taking her into his confidence, treating her like a partner, like a co-conspirator. In the Cotswold or in London, he focused on her. She was important to him. He gave his attention to her, even when he was in the midst of the most intricate business deals.

A letter came from Sofie. Rachel realized she had not had a letter from Aleks in over a week. Sofie wrote rarely. Perhaps something was wrong. She sat down weakly in the sunny breakfast room to read it.

Dearest Ruchele,

I miss you so. No one to really talk to. No one to laugh with, like we used to do at home. Remember when we would sit on your bed, and you told me you were in love with Pavel and I mustn't ever tell Papa? And I said you should go on our Sunday picnics to the woods and you would fall in love with one of our nice Jewish boys. How long ago that seems. Were we really girls? I am beginning to feel old—it's nothing but work and home. I am not seeing Ludwik anymore. He wants to go to America. He has an uncle in the haberdashery business there who wants him to come. Where does that leave me? I can't waste my time with someone who is just playing around and doesn't want to get married and is going to go to some place across the world.

Aleks comes home late every night. Oh, you don't have to worry about him; it is his work, not a woman. He has no time for anything else.

We had the Passover Seder last week and Aleks just didn't get there in time. You know I wanted to have it just like you would. Moniek was in Warsaw so he came. Of course I invited Aleks's sisters. Lena's husband is in training in the army camp. And your friend Wanda is in Warsaw with her husband. She came. And my Josef Tarsky and his wife, my boss. I took the day off from work and cooked all day with Stefcia. By eight o'clock Aleks hadn't arrived. He called to say he was arranging for his refugees to have some sort of Seder. He was placing them in homes and seeing that each one would have somewhere to go. There are so many of them and there is so much paperwork too.

We started the Seder with Moniek reading from the haggadah, and of course Rilka asked the four questions. But it was not the same without Aleks giving his welcoming speech to the guests and leading a discussion about the meaning of it all, and everyone grumbling a little for him to get through the talking and the reading so we could eat, and Aleks reprimanding the guests for not paying attention to the important things and you looking beautiful and telling everyone to be patient.

Oh, Rachel, I am getting so stupidly sentimental.-It's just that things seem to be falling apart. And it was better before, better in Zarki even. Maybe that was just because we were so young. We had so much hope for wonderful things to happen. We were just waiting. Oh, this is so stupid! I hate myself for writing you such gloomy thoughts.

Anyway, it was a nice Seder after all. Aleks came in just after we had finished the soup so he was able to conclude the Seder service. He looked so tired. He is obsessed with these refugees. It's all different when you are not here. But don't worry about us; really, everything is all right ... I guess I'm just disappointed because of Ludwik's going off to America. We love you.

Kisses, Sofie.

Rachel held the letter in her hand and stared out the window. A gentle April rain was falling on the budding forsythias outside the breakfast room. She felt dirty and sullied. How she longed to like herself again. With the now familiar stab of fear, she thought, there will be a war. I will be separated from them all. I'll never see them again. She was perspiring in the chilly room, filled with that empty sensation in her stomach, like a free fall. I will go back, I will go back, she thought. I will tell Roman today.

Roman cancelled their dinner date that evening.

"I have to go to Amsterdam for a few days. That bastard Winkler is reneging on his order—says he can get it cheaper. My mills are working on it already. I have a half a million pounds on the line! I'll fix him! I happen to know who he's dealing with ... I'm going to buy them out and he'll never get another shipment in his life. Well, I'm going to see him, maybe he'll see it the right way.

It will save us all a lot of trouble. Rachel, I'll be back Friday, we'll go to the house for the weekend." His voice softened, "I have something to discuss with you."

"Yes, I want to talk to you too."

There was a silence. "Hmm, well, till Friday then. Come to my office. We'll leave from there."

Rachel's stomach muscles were tense. Her jaw was tightly shut—it ached. Today she was completely determined to tell him she was leaving. She had rehearsed the scene in her mind. This was only Tuesday; how could she maintain the momentum of that resolve till Friday? But also, she was relieved not to have to face him just yet. Perhaps a few days distance would make it easier. She trained all her thoughts on Aleks. He was so above Roman in a moral sense, she thought. His concerns were the world, the human condition. But she pitied him, he did not know, he wanted her to be free, independent, whole without him, but had he thought where it might lead? She saw him as so alone, so at a disadvantage, being betrayed like that. Self-loathing flooded her. She visualized Sofie at the dinner table. She conjured up Rilka's image: Rilka playing on the swings at Łazienki Park, Rilka running, Rilka waking reluctantly to go to school. But the image had always a sad look; she could not frame a picture of Rilka laughing. She banished Roman's face, Roman's body, from her mind entirely.

Rachel slept so restlessly that night that the sheet covering her was all tangled at the foot of the bed. Half in, half out of sleep, she reached out to turn off the alarm clock and turned over onto her left side, away from the early morning light coming through the sheer curtains. Her heartbeat sounded like relentless footsteps, coming up some dim staircase, coming closer, pounding in her ear, ominous. She struggled to awaken, sank back into darkness, turned over again onto her other side and opened her eyes. She lay there for awhile, looking through the window at the lawn mottled with sunlight. How peaceful it was! Surely everything was alright.

She went downstairs to the breakfast room. Her aunt was measuring out tea into the warmed teapot. The scent of cinnamon toast wafted in the air, already heavy with spring blossoms.

Rachel sipped hot tea, looked out onto the garden, and read the Personals column on the front page of the London Times.

"Married couple, Jewish, still in Austria. Speak English. Must leave Vienna at end of month. Urgently seek position."

"Jewess, with eight-year-old boy, seeks any position in household. Well-educated, experienced music pedagogue, good cook. Must leave Austria immediately."

"I should go back home," Rachel sighed. "What if there is war?"

"It will be all right, dear," Aunt Klara poured more tea into Rachel's cup. "Everyone knows Britain backs Poland. Aleks will tell you if it is time to worry."

Rachel turned the pages of the paper, shivering in the cold March sunlight streaming through the windows. The real news was on the inside pages.

"First Court of the Season. The King and Queen held a Court at Buckingham Palace last evening." A full page devoted to the dress of the Royal Circle, the Diplomatic Corps, the Empire Representatives and the General Company.

"The Countess of Chesterfield wore an Edwardian gown of blue moiré, shot with a copper thread. A train of tulle bordered with moiré appliqué. A blue feathered fan." Rachel read out loud to her Aunt. "Lady Bowater: a gown of blue velvet embroidered with silver. A blue velvet train lined with silver. Jewels: diamond tiara and pearl necklace."

Does the Countess of Chesterfield perhaps need an educated Jewess fleeing from Austria? Rachel thought. Aloud she said, "Well, things can't be so bad if the King and Queen hold Court."

But the next morning at breakfast she announced, "Aunt Klara, I'm going back home."

Klara turned toward her. "But why, my dear? You haven't finished your courses yet. Aleks doesn't expect you back till December, you told me that yourself."

"Oh Auntie, I don't know. I am so uneasy. There's going to be war. The newspapers are filled with it. I just don't understand Aleks. He keeps writing me as if nothing unusual is going on."

"Well, my dear, we are concerned, of course, but after all Britain is pledged to guarantee Poland's independence. The Germans know that too. Aleks would know if there was real cause to worry. But why don't you send for Rilka? You could stay with us till things settle down. We have a big enough house. Aleks could join you then, if something happens."

How reasonable that sounded! But how impossible to think of Aleks and Roman in the same town! What had driven her to this? She longed to be back in Warsaw, back in her own life, her real life. She wrote Aleks that same morning, her pen sweeping across the linen stationery as if possessed, telling him she had to come back, now, right away, she couldn't bear to be apart any longer. She was frightened. There would be war. She sealed the letter, slipped on her coat and ran out to put it in the post box. She was relieved. There was no turning back.

On Friday, Rachel called Roman. "I can't go to the Cotswold. Someone is coming from Warsaw. A relative of Aleks's. Aunt Klara is having a dinner party Saturday. I'll meet you for dinner tonight."

"The Carleton at seven," he said very brusquely.

She thought she would weaken when she saw him. Her heart was beating against the wall of her chest when she entered the restaurant; the rush of blood in her ears muffled the other sounds around her. But when in fact, she did see him sitting at a table half-hidden in a red velvet alcove, she was calm. Her mind had already made that trans-continental transition and Roman did not have a place in that other place.

He pulled out the chair for her and she settled into the soft cushion, pulling off her gloves.

"Did you have a good trip?" she asked.

"Yes. We came to terms. Did you have a good week?" His eyes were opaque.

"I'm sorry about the weekend."

"Yes," he said. He turned to the waiter standing at the side of their table and ordered for her. "We'll each have Lillet and soda on the side. The lady will have asparagus and hollandaise, I'll have pate, then consommé, then rack of baby lamb for both of us. Chateau Margaux 1925 with the lamb."

"No, just a minute," she said to the waiter, "I'll have the beef roulade instead of the lamb please."

This evening was different from the one where he took her to dance without asking. If she acquiesced to the lamb, all would be lost.

They spoke of inconsequential matters.

"Aunt made creamed onions last night. My first time. Imagine! What a strange dish! Very English I suppose, like a ploughman's sandwich."

"Rachel, stop it! Stop it! No more creamed onions!" He held her wrist tightly and leaned across the table. "What is going on? Why are you so distant? I want to make love to you. What is the matter with you?"

"Roman, I am going home," she said, almost in a whisper.

They each let out a breath. They sat back in their chairs, staring at each other.

"Well," said Roman, "well, that is quite a decision. You were going to stay till December. What happened? Aleks suspects something? Tell him, then. It's time you told him."

"No, no, he doesn't know. I am worried about something happening. I have nightmares. I can't be away from home. And I hate myself." She looked down. "This is so wrong."

"Rachel, don't go back," he said more gently. "Of course you are worried. There will be a war. Maybe not this year, but it will come. You will be safer here. My cousin is coming from Warsaw next month. She can bring Rilka. I can arrange it all tomorrow if you agree. Rilka will have a good life here. She'll be educated in England ... it would be much better for her. You must know that."

"It's out of the question!" Rachel shuddered." Do you think I could just leave my whole family? For an affair? Because I want you, too? For me, just for me, not thinking of anyone else, just to satisfy myself? Of course I couldn't! And Aleks, how could I do such a thing to Aleks? If he ever found out ... Oh God, Aleks. He is my husband. I love him."

"Do you?"

"Yes," she said more calmly. "Yes. Oh, Roman, I love you too ... differently."

"Rachel, I thought you were a strong woman. One has to know what one wants in this world—and then take it, without all this wavering. What kind of a husband is this Aleks of yours, anyway? If you were my wife, I would certainly not let you go off to another country alone—and if I did, it would be for your safety. My wife would be the central part of my life. One woman ... I am a one-woman man."

"Roman, I couldn't leave Aleks. I don't want to leave Aleks," she said firmly.

"You want to leave me, then? You must leave one of us, Aleks or me. You are making a choice for the rest of your life!"

"It's not Aleks alone. Sofie—how could I leave Sofie? And my parents ... and my whole life ..." She fell silent.

He too was silent for a few moments. The waiter came over and poured more tea into their cups. He held a silver tray of chocolate mints. Rachel declined. A violin played *Oczy Czarnia, Oczy Krasnia*—Black Eyes, Beautiful Eyes. The notes hovered over the hum of a dozen private conversations in the large dining room.

"Oczy czarnia," Roman said softly, "Think it over, Rachel."

He rose and pulled her chair back. He helped her put the jade silk stole over her shoulders. She leaned her head down and brushed her cheek against his hand on her shoulder. How warm it was, how familiar.

He took her to her aunt's house, both of them silent in the back seat of the car. "We're here," the chauffeur announced. She stepped out of the car while he remained inside, hidden in the shadow. She leaned down inside the car toward him. Now she pitied him. She was leaving him, so now he too was alone. She kissed him, not full on the lips, but slightly off to the side. He pulled her gently towards him. She resisted, but not forcefully. His hand touched her breast and her nipple hardened in automatic response. She fought the impulse to get back in the car. She freed herself and ran up the steps of the building.

ᐁ

My dearest Rachel,

How foolish you are to write me with such panic in your tone. The situation is difficult here but negotiations are underway all the time and we have full hope that the matter will be resolved peacefully. In any case, we have England and France on our side. Even should talks break down, there will be plenty of warning and plenty of time. Then I will immediately send for you. But you need not worry yet.

I can understand your wanting to get home and that you miss Rilka and Sofie—and perhaps even your devoted and adoring husband. (I say this with a smile on my face, thinking how good it will be to hold you in my arms again). But, you set out to accomplish a goal, the goal of learning English so that you may be fluent in it, finishing your business course so that you can advance in your career, and being my goodwill ambassador to all who meet you. Everyone will laugh at you if you act like a little girl, frightened and homesick. To ease your mind, let me tell you how well Rilka is doing. Last week she won the prize in her school for her little ballet dance. I could not go of course, but Sofie took the afternoon off from work and went to see the performance. Sofie too is doing well. She is a little sad about Ludwik but she has met a fine young man who has taken her out to dinner several times. He is an assistant comptroller in her office and quite charming. Alyna is a good governess and takes care not only of Rilka but of me also. So there is nothing for you to be concerned about.

It is difficult to be apart, but love survives distance and grows stronger when the lovers are independent and come to each other of their own volition, rather than clinging to each other from weakness. You have your work to do and I have mine. But we are together in our hearts.

If you still want to come home, of course I won't prevent you. I send you my deep love and kiss you in a thousand places. Your loving husband, Aleks

Rachel wept silently in her room. The inside of her stomach trembled. How reasonable, how calm he was! How sure of her love! She couldn't bear it.

She dressed quickly and, without saying good-bye to anyone in the house, she slipped out the door, ran down the street to catch the double-decker bus to Marble Arch, rushed past the crowds of people on the street going to work, and began to feel some semblance of calm only when she reached the travel office and said to the clerk, "I would like to make arrangements to go to Warsaw, leaving immediately."

❦   ❦   ❦

Now as the train sped through the French countryside, taking Rachel home, home to Aleks, she determined to cut this part of her life out of memory. An affair was all it was, she convinced herself, just a culmination of the kind of de rigueur flirtations one had in Warsaw at the Cafe Europeiska, nothing more serious, not the grand passion of her life.

But what had really changed? Rachel wondered. One day Roman had seemed to her passionate, strong, decisive, and now, just a short time later, as she sat in her compartment looking out the window at the farmlands rolling by, he had turned into a crude, limited man, whose sources of sexual attraction, she realized, were money and power. And yet, Rachel thought, he loved her; she was important to him; in the midst of his pressing business he thought of her, he included her, he wanted her. But he was uneducated, even a little boorish, perhaps somewhat shady—at any rate, mysterious. How right she was to run away, how smart of her to be going home to Aleks: Aleks with his unquestionable integrity, his wisdom, his moral compass.

It seemed to Rachel that the smallest shifts in her heart could transform the very strengths which had drawn her to Roman into weaknesses from which she had to escape. Just a small turn of her mind transformed Aleks back into the man she had so ardently loved when she was young. What then was the reality?

The train she had boarded in Cherbourg was filled with Frenchmen and Swedes, with Poles returning home, with men who had missed the earlier mobilization hurrying back to Warsaw. A Polish journalist entered her compartment. "Przepraszam," he said when he jostled her trying to put his suitcase into the rack overhead, excuse me. He tipped his hat and replaced it on his head at a rakish angle. He offered her a little shot glass of vodka that he poured out of a silver flask. She smiled and accepted and the liquid warmed her. England receded.

A French family took the seats opposite Rachel's: a tall man wearing a plaid shirt unbuttoned at the neck, his attractive, tanned wife, and a girl about Rilka's age. They chattered easily, laughed, teased the little girl fondly. They pulled out a loaf of French bread and offered some cheese to Rachel. She declined, but she smiled in gratitude at their friendliness.

The train crossed the border into Germany and the atmosphere changed. The sky was gray and it was quiet now in the compartment. The French family had gotten off at the last stop. The Polish journalist went off to join his friends in another carriage. Rachel dozed fitfully. Fragments of dreams woke her in fits and starts. In her compartment, two men and a woman who had boarded the train in Berlin sat stolid and mute. Occasionally they spoke a few words in German to each other. They did not glance at Rachel. She began to feel uncomfortable and went into the dining car. It was filled. She waited in the lounge area for a table. It was eerily silent. The maitre d' seated a couple who had come in after Rachel. The woman was round and blond, her hair pulled into a knot in back. She wore a heather-green suit. The man with her was equally round, with a mustache, a bald spot on top of his head, and a self-satisfied air about him. He put a husbandly arm around her thick waist and propelled her in the wake of the waiter to their table. They so clearly belonged. Rachel sighed and went back to her own compartment. She was not hungry anyway.

She looked out the window and retreated into the protective shell of thoughts of home, home, Aleks and Rilka and Sofie. At last the train crossed the border into Poland. She felt safe.

-14-

Warsaw—1939

When she arrived in Warsaw, May lilacs were blooming alongside the walls of their apartment building on Hoza Ulica and the city was in a state of apparent calm. Rachel concluded her panic in London about the war was unwarranted. Even Aleks, faced daily with the refugees' stories of persecutions in Germany, believed war would be averted.

Rachel resumed her Polish life as though she had not been away. She took Rilka to a new Shirley Temple movie, trying to regain ground lost by her nearly six months' absence. She went for afternoon tea and pastries at the Cafe Europeiska. She hired a new helper for the cook and put her house in order. She cut Roman out of her mind and her heart.

Spring turned into summer and beneath the languor of the hot sunny days there was a new current of restlessness. The editorials in the Polish papers were full of brave, patriotic pronouncements that Poland would never capitulate to the demands of Hitler, proclaiming victory where there was no battle. The Polish Army Reservists had been called up.

"We have just seen a state fall because it relied on negotiations instead of on its own strength. Poles understand the tragic example of Czechoslovakia; therefore Poland is ready for war even against the strongest adversary," said the Polska Zbrojna.

Jan Kiepura, the world's most famous Polish opera singer, pledged 100,000 zlotys to the army, and also two large motor cars. He would give all his possessions for the defense of Poland if necessary, he stated publicly.

"Two motor cars!" Aleks laughed bitterly, convinced now of the real danger, as actually he had himself predicted in his book. "It's just posturing. They think Polish honor and Polish cavalry will defeat armed tanks! No, we must rely on Britain to stop Hitler."

Rachel felt herself moving as if through an underwater world. In spite of the shrill tone of the newspaper editorials, she heard only the muffled sounds. In spite of the heavy, silent sense of waiting, everything seemed to her so peaceful, so normal—well, almost normal. They had been issued gas masks. They had had a few air-raid drills. But it seemed to her like children's games, unreal and a lot of posturing. The Nazis and the Soviets signed the Non-Aggression Pact on August twenty-third and Britain and Poland signed a Mutual Assistance Treaty on August twenty-fifth. Just chess moves.

The days sped by like a silent film in fast motion. Rachel took Rilka and Alyna to Cziechochinek to bathe in the spa waters. Sofie joined her for the last week of August.

"You look so exhausted," Rachel had told her. "You must come, you can't work like that!" But they were both restless, overcome by the tension that engulfed Poland, that reached from Warsaw into this resort where fashionable women strolled in the gardens.

On a hot, sunless afternoon, Rachel, walking along the lakeshore road with Sofie, was suddenly tormented with a vision of Roman, bending over her, brushing her hair with his lips, so strong a vision, so real, that she could nearly touch him. She felt his warmth flood through her, but it was just the August heat, just a prelude to a summer storm. She let out an involuntary exclamation under her breath, a message to herself, an order. Stop, she said almost audibly, stop, enough. Sofie looked at her and slowed her pace. Rachel was already a few feet ahead, and she stood still, waiting for Sofie.

"You have been so distracted since you came home. As if you're somewhere else. What is the matter?" Sofie asked.

"I ... nothing, nothing."

"What happened to you in England?" Sofie persisted. "You're different. You used to laugh. You kept us all gay. Nothing got you down."

"It's just this awful tension about war. I wish it would come already if it has to!"

They walked on in silence, nodding occasionally to acquaintances passing by. How Rachel longed to tell Sofie about Roman! How awful to bear this secret alone. But as long as no one knew, it was as if it never happened. Why then could she not put Roman out of her mind?

"Rachel, there's a man. Is it Leopold? But when did you see him last? You've just come back. Tell me, Rachel."

Impulsively, Rachel grabbed Sofie's arm, and squeezed so hard, Sofie winced and shook herself free.

"In England. No, it's not Leopold. How could I do such a thing? Leo is Aleks's friend. Roman. his name is Roman."

"Tell me," Sofie said. And Rachel told her everything.

It was dusk by now and the strollers were returning to the hotel to dress for supper. Sofie had remained silent throughout, and Rachel, in the telling, was nearly oblivious of Sofie beside her. Now she reached out and took Sofie's arm. Sofie pulled away. Rachel looked at her, startled. Slowly, it began to dawn on her that Sofie was not just her sympathetic listener, her alter ego, the mirror of her soul. Sofie, her face dark and scowling, was looking at her unflinchingly.

"How could you?" she said at last. "How could you?"

Rachel recoiled. Immediately she went on the offensive; all her remorse, guilt, and regret vanished.

"You are a fine one to talk!" she said in anger. "You have no life of your own. You have not managed to be with any man! Just work, work, work. What do you know of love? How can you imagine what it is like to love two men—you can't love even one! Ludwik—that nonentity! That's not passion!"

"Passion! What you call passion is just sordid betrayal. Aleks deserves better than you." Sofie's voice was low and hard.

"You're in love with Aleks," Rachel said in amazement.

"No," Sofie said quietly, her cheeks reddening. "No. He is a decent man."

"Of course. I was gone for six months, and Aleks wasn't even anxious to have me come back. And you ... you wrote that stupid letter. It was just a cover, just a cover for your guilt."

"Rachel, you are saying wild things. It's not true. You are making excuses for yourself. Stop. What are you saying?" Sofie was trembling.

"Oh my God, what is happening? I thought I could tell you everything. My stupidity. We are all alone ... I am always alone." Rachel was crying, not quietly, not to herself, but in great sobs, loud whimpers, her body shaking. Sofie reached out and touched Rachel's arm, and led her to a bench a little further down the path. Rachel's crying subsided and they sat, silent now, looking across the still lake.

"Rachel ..." Sofie started.

"No, no, don't say anything." She put her arms around Sofie, who didn't resist, and she held her close.

"Oh, Sofie, Sofie, how could I say such things to you? You are right, of course you are right. I am so terrible. How I could I have? Sofie, I love youf ... forgive me."

"It's all right. It's all right," Sofie was murmuring. "I love you, Rachel. I am sorry. I should have tried to understand. You weren't yourself in London. You just did something you must forget about. It will be as if it never happened. Let us put this out of our minds forever. It's all right, Rachel."

Nothing will tear me apart from Sofie, Rachel thought. Nothing. But a gloom had settled upon them. When they joined the four other guests for supper at their table in the large spa dining room, they merely nodded hello and spoke little throughout the meal. After dinner, Rachel went to the library where Rilka, in Alyna's lap, was listening to the evening story hour. Rachel went in and kissed the top of her head, and silently walked out again. In the large lobby, she searched for Sofie, but she had gone to bed. Their little vacation suddenly seemed pointless. Rachel wondered what she was doing here. Really, she should be home. Perhaps she would resume setting up the private libraries, as she had done before England. Perhaps she would visit her parents in Zarki. Perhaps Aleks would go with her.

The next morning at breakfast Rachel said quietly, "We ought to be returning."

"Yes," Sofie agreed. "It's time to leave."

Though they were to have remained at the spa through the beginning of September, they made arrangements that day to shorten their stay, and on Sunday, they returned to Warsaw.

On Monday, August 28th, Papa arrived in Warsaw.

"There is going to be war, Ruchele," he said excitedly. "I am going to borrow money from any bank that will lend it. I will buy up all the leather in Poland. If there is a war, they will need leather. We will be rich. Give me all your money, Ruchele. I will make you rich! And Sofie too."

He rushed out on Tuesday morning, in his long black coat, his beard, all gray now, bobbing up and down. He was energized, hopeful. Rachel feared for his heart.

The banks were not lending money. If there was to be war, they would not lend money to Papa.

"Go home, Papa," Aleks said that evening. "Make preparations. This is not the time to expand. You should be home with Mama."

"So, my son-in-law is throwing me out of his house. This man you married, Ruchele? I will stay here as long as I need!" Papa stomped out of the room.

"Oh, Aleks," Rachel cried, torn between the two of them, like in the old days, "Of course he can stay as long as he wants."

"Yes, he can stay. Of course. But the war may start any moment. Then he won't be able to get home to Mama at all."

"But he won't leave till he gets the money."

"Rachel, don't you read the papers? You don't seem to understand how grave the situation is. There will be war! And he thinks he can make a profit on it! It's beyond understanding!" Aleks raised his voice in exasperation.

"Well, I am going to give him my money and Sofie will too."

Sofie had no such intention. When Rachel suggested it, Sofie was firm.

"He is dreaming again," she said. "He will just scatter it away. Rachel, I can't give him my savings. I've worked too hard and I need it too."

"But you don't need it now," Rachel pressed her.

"Maybe I'll go to America someday," Sofie said. "Who knows, Ludwik might still be single and in America it might be different with him. No," she said more vehemently. "No, there has to be a stop to it. Every time he wants something, you just run and do it. You don't even think."

"I do think. I think Papa says he needs money and I am going to give it to him!"

"What about Aleks, Rachel? He needs the money too. Since he got fired from the Ministry, it's not the same for him. You know this refugee business doesn't pay very much. You keep all your earnings instead of giving it to Aleks, and now you want to give it to Papa. Well, I won't do it!"

"Really, Sofie, you should hold your tongue! I don't keep all my earnings—I pay for my clothes, I pay for Alyna, I pay for …" She stopped herself. My God, she didn't want to quarrel with Sofie again!

"Do as you like," Rachel said quietly. "I am giving Papa my savings."

On Wednesday, August 30th, she went to her bank and withdrew her savings. After supper she gave the packet of money to Papa.

"You won't regret it," Papa said. She was to remember that in the dark years that followed. She never regretted it.

"Rachel," Aleks said to her in bed that evening. "You know I don't care if Papa stays with us for the weekend, or the month, or the year for that matter. But, if you want him to get home for Shabbos, if you want him to get home at all, tell him to leave now. The next day may be too late."

Early on Thursday morning, with an unreasoned urgency, she pleaded with Papa to go home to Zarki. It was August thirty-first.

"Don't leave Mama alone," she said.

"Well," Papa answered, "I will go this afternoon. I have seen all the bank officers I could. No one wants to talk to me even. I have done all I can. I was going to visit with you for the weekend, but I see things are a little tense here and Mama will be happy to have me home for Shabbos."

She saw him off on the train to Czestochowa. The platform was crowded with officers in full uniform, soldiers off on some assignment, kissing wives and babies, families with many suitcases, going … where?

"Do you have your ticket, Papa? Do you have your ticket?" Her eyes were wet.

"Yes. Ruchele, come to see us next weekend. Come spend Shabbos with us. Mama complains you never come home anymore."

"I will, Papa, I will. The weekend after next. I promise." The steam from the train rose up on the platform. She blinked through it. He boarded the train. It began to pull away while he was still standing in the doorway, waving to her, saying something. The noise drowned out his words.

"Goodbye, Papa, goodbye, goodbye. I love you Papa. I love you," she cried. She waited on the platform till the train was out of sight, the dim hum of the wheels the only evidence of its existence. Tears were streaming down her cheeks. The next morning, on September first, 1939, in the gray early dawn, the Germans invaded Poland.

PART II

IN TRANSIT

-15-

When the air-raid alarm went off, the household was deep in sleep. Rachel burst into Rilka's room and shook her awake while Alyna was already putting a sweater over her pajamas; she was being pushed and pulled like a rag doll, disoriented and only half-awake. In the hallway outside the bedroom door a stream of people ran through the apartment, coming in through the kitchen entrance, pushing past each other down the corridor, through the dining room, through the living room, out the front door. The maids and cooks and the neighbors from the floors above were using the flat as a passageway to the stairs leading into the courtyard, to take shelter on the ground floor under the massive arch of the building. Running, running, everyone was running. The large radio in the dining room blared out:

"The German Army has invaded Danzig. All citizens follow instructions. This is not a drill. This is not a drill."

Sofie, who was living with Rachel and Aleks in Warsaw at that time, appeared in the corridor outside Rilka's room, a sweater covering her bathrobe. She was shouting. "The gas masks, the gas masks!" Then Alyna and Rilka were running down the corridor, Sofie following, with Rachel and Aleks, behind them, holding the monstrous looking gas masks. They ran down the stairs and at last found themselves in the doorway that had been designated as the shelter for the building, together, amidst the throng of people. No one spoke. Only the drone of the planes broke the silence.

"Oh, my God," Rachel exclaimed. "Where is Rilka's gas mask? Alyna, I have yours. Where is hers?"

"I'll go up to get it," Alyna said.

"Stay here," Aleks said. "I'll get it."

"No," Rachel said. "If the building is hit we'll be separated. We'll all go"

A young woman, not from their building but taking shelter here, lightly touched Rachel on the arm and said quietly, "I'll get the child's mask. You mustn't be separated. Where is it?"

"Thank you, oh, thank you! How brave of you! How brave you are!"

She returned in a few moments and handed the small gas mask to Rachel. Overhead, the planes screeched as they dove down to drop their bombs upon the city. There was a rumbling as of thunder, off in the distance at the outer edges of the city. After a while the all-clear signal sounded and they moved silently out of the shelter, back up to the apartment. The radio still blared in the dining room. They huddled around the big mahogany box, neighbors and children from other apartments as well.

"German troops have invaded Poland. Stay calm. Follow instructions. When the alarm sounds, take your gas masks and proceed to shelter. If you are on the street when the alarm sounds, proceed to the nearest building. Stay in the doorway till the all-clear sounds. Do not panic. German bombers have hit Krakow, Radom, Czestochowa …"

All day, the news was interspersed with instructions, and with the Polish national anthem. "Jeszcze Polska nie zginewa …" Poland is not yet lost, while still we live.

The alarm sounded twice more that day. Each time they all ran down to the shelter, silently waiting, listening to the terrifying whistle of the falling bombs, the screech of diving planes. The incendiary bombs lit the sky and flashes of light burst in the distance. At night the city was completely dark. All the windows were covered with black paper, all the lights were out.

Two days later, Stefcia left tearfully to go to her family in the country. "How will you get there?" Rachel asked. "There is no gasoline. Are the trains running?"

"I'll walk," Stefcia said stolidly.

Alyna left too, but her family was just on the outskirts of town. She held Rilka and said, "I'll be back, I'll be home tonight. I just have to see if everyone is all right in my family. I'll be back, Madame, I promise. I won't leave you."

"German tanks are approaching Warsaw," the announcer intoned. The National Chorus sang, "Jeszcze Polska nie zginewa puki my zyjemy; marcz, marcz Dombroswski."

Aleks read the Polish Jewish paper *Nasz Przeglad*. "We are ready," the editorial proclaimed, "ready is our heroic army and ready is the civilian population … Nothing will weaken our will to victory." On the opposite page an advertisement announced the premiere of *The World is Beautiful*, starring Claudette

Colbert and James Stewart. On the radio, turned full volume, the National Anthem alternated with the defiance of Chopin's Polonaise in A Major.

On Monday, England declared war on Germany. The radio played God Save the King. The sirens sounded, the antiaircraft guns sputtered, the city was in smoke, but people rejoiced at the news. "It will soon be over now. The British will finish them off. Hitler is finished."

The editorial in *Nasz Przeglad* said "Polish Jews! At this moment in history it must be understood that we fight for a holy cause, for our fatherland, for honor, for our future, for freedom for all peoples and for the rebirth of humanity. Jews! Quietly and decisively, let us hurry to the ranks of the Polish Army and let us carry out, with courage and sacrifice, our soldierly duty."

Aleks, at age forty-nine, considered himself too old to heed the call, and believed the proud and highly anti-Semitic Polish Army would not welcome Jews his age, or any age, into its ranks. He had served in Pilsudski's Legions in the First World War, a post which eventually earned him a position in Pilsudski's Ministry of the Interior, and he knew the rigors of army life even in those golden days for Jews in Polish life under Pilsudski, who gave favored status to the Jewish minority. He decided to stay in Warsaw.

On Wednesday evening, a friend of his, a minor official in the current Polish government, came to the apartment, agitated, and urged him to leave immediately. The Germans were closing in. They would come for Aleks first thing. He was known to them as the author of the book *Der Antisemitismus in Der Deutsche Republic*, even though it had been published under a pseudonym in Germany, just after the Reishstag fire in 1933. The book warned German Jews not to be complacent about Hitler's rise to power. Aleks was an unknown, but the introduction, by the eminent Professor Lessing, gave the book credibility and some visibility. It was hardly a best-seller, and boxes of unsold copies were still stacked in the study. President Moscicki, the ministers, the whole government had fled to Nalechow, the summer resort near Lublin. It was clear the Germans would occupy Warsaw before the British finished them off, but of course everyone was sure women and children would be safe. After all, even in war, this was still civilized Europe. Aleks, however, must leave. The men would be shot or drafted into slave labor and Aleks in particular was in danger of arrest for his known anti-Nazi opinions. Aleks must leave immediately, the friend urged.

"Leave how?" Rachel asked. "There is no petrol, there are no cars."

There were no sirens the next morning, and in the early afternoon, Rachel went to the train station to see if Aleks could get a train out. On the streets families were walking with bundles of their possessions, some in carts, most on foot, towards the outskirts of town. At the railroad station the trains were packed. People pushed to get on as the train to Vilno pulled away. Buying a ticket was impossible. She turned back toward the center of town.

She was crossing Marshalkowska Ulica when the siren wailed. She ran into a doorway of the nearest building. "The shelter is in the basement," someone cried and pulled her along, down steps, inside a dark place. It was crowded, with a sweaty, pungent odor. The noise of the planes, the whine of the bombs, the brutal thunder as they hit, all seemed worse than in any previous raid. At last the all-clear sounded, but the drone of airplane motors still hung on the air when she emerged from the shelter.

Outside, fires were blazing against the twilight sky. She passed a huge crater in the earth, the building beside it a crumbled heap. "My husband is gone, gone …" a woman sat on the rubble holding her head in her hands, rocking back and forth. The streets were full of glass. It crunched under Rachel's feet as she ran, making her way around men and women and children running from the devastation. Fires flared in buildings and the smell of smoke was heavy in the air. A man sat on the sidewalk, weeping, stroking the head of his horse lying before him in the street, a large hole in the horse's neck bleeding. Stretcher-bearers and nurses carried the wounded to makeshift first-aid stations.

At last, she turned the corner of Hoza Ulica and saw the house was intact. She wept with relief.

A week later, Aleks, convinced now that the government had indeed fled the city, decided to leave Warsaw by whatever means possible. He walked into the police station across the street and demanded a car. The police chief, Ignac Wilgot, was someone he knew from his days in the Ministry.

In front of the police station, cars were lined up all the way down the street. Incongruously, some were being polished by uniformed chauffeurs. Outside Chief Wilgot's door, Rachel tucked her silk blouse into her black skirt, the satin sheen of the pale green fabric outlining her breasts. Quickly she applied fresh lipstick, and a spot of kohl to accent her beauty mark. It never hurt to look good.

As soon as they were ushered in to the Chief's office, Aleks said calmly and very firmly, "Ignac, I want a car and a chauffeur."

"You must be joking! Out of the question, Mischler! We have no extra cars. There is no petrol. Everyone wants to leave the city." Wilgot waved his hand toward the window, following Rachel's look. "Those cars were commandeered from private owners. They are at the disposal of the Army. Mischler, you've been a friend," he said more kindly. "But I can't do it. It's impossible!" He half-rose from behind his large worn desk to signal an end to this.

"You take it upon your own head to refuse me," Aleks said with a note of anger. "This is by order of the Minister of the Interior. The government is in exile. I am ordered to join them. Call him."

"You know perfectly well there are no communications lines open to Lublin." He looked at Aleks narrowly. "I'll call the mayor. He would know."

He picked up the phone. Aleks stood resolutely in front of the desk, his hand, hanging at his side, trembling slightly. Rachel, who used to claim with pride that she never perspired, felt wet under the armpits, the stain spreading on her silk blouse. A fly flew in through the open window, buzzed around the desk. There was the faint sound of the phone ringing on the other end. At last the Chief put the phone back on the hook and leaned forward.

"All right," he said. "No answer. I will take your word, bluff or not. Take any car down there. And pick your chauffeur. They're all waiting for assignments."

"Thank you," Aleks said and walked out of the office, his back straight, Rachel following closely behind him.

Six or seven chauffeurs were lounging in the hallway outside. "Pick a driver for me," Aleks said to Rachel.

Everything was going so fast. Rachel looked at the men. They straightened up as she and Aleks approached. One was short and looked surly. Another was fat with a beer belly and thin red veins on his nose, a drinker. They were peasants who had learned to drive. One was taller than the rest, broad-shouldered and trim, with unruly blond hair and serious blue eyes. His boots were highly polished, his uniform well pressed, his white gloves clean. He was the handsomest.

"This one," Rachel said to Aleks, and smiled at the man.

Rachel and Aleks came back from the stationhouse within an hour, and Aleks began to pack a small suitcase. He put one thousand zlotys in his wallet, half the money he had in the little safe in his closet, and gave the rest to Rachel.

"Take your fur coat," Rachel said handing him his long sealskin coat.

"Don't be silly," he said. "I'm going to the forest. What will I do with a fur coat? Besides, I'll be back before it gets really cold. Be good," he said to Rilka. "Listen to your mother. I'll be back soon." And then he was gone out the door,

Rachel running behind him, holding out a bag of sandwiches she had made, and Rilka following them both down the stairs for a final goodbye. Aleks kissed the top of Rilka's head and then kissed Rachel again as the chauffeur, Piotr, held the door of the large Mercedes open for him.

"Let's go," Aleks said.

"But your wife," the chauffer said.

"She's staying."

"You're running away and leaving your wife here?" he said incredulously. "The minute the bombings started I took my wife and children to her family in the country. I stayed here. Warsaw is getting the worst of the bombs."

Aleks stopped in mid-step, his foot on the running board of the car.

"Of course! Of course! Rachel, you must come with me. Quick! I must have been crazy to think of leaving you! He has more sense than both of us."

Within minutes Rachel filled a small bag with some clothes for her and for Rilka. She put a little drawstring purse around Rilka's neck, tucked into her shirt, with her name and age and address and a hundred-zloty bill, in case she got lost.

"Sofie?"Rachel turned to her sister.

"No, I'm not going. All the men are out of the office, digging trenches around the city. I have to run the office. I'll be all right here. Alyna will stay. We'll take care of the apartment."

Alyna knelt down to tie Rilka's shoe. She looked up and tearfully nodded in agreement. "I'll stay, Madame."

"You must come, Sofie," Rachel pleaded. "We must stay together."

"I am not going," Sofie said firmly.

Rachel hugged her and they clung to each other.

"Come," Aleks pulled at her arm.

And then they were inside the large black Mercedes, Aleks in front with the chauffeur, Rachel and Rilka in the soft cushions in the back. Rilka pressed her head against the window, crying, "Alyna, Alyna." The car pulled away. People walking in the street began to block the view of their building, but through the passersby, Rachel's last glimpse of Sofie was seared into her mind forever, Sofie standing in the doorway of the building, waving.

❦   ❦   ❦

They drove for several hours towards Brest-Litovsk, and by now it was dusk. They had come to a railroad track, stretching across the road, through the fields, vanishing over the horizon. A Messerschmidt appeared out of nowhere, flying low across the railroad tracks.

"Out, out! Get out of the car," shouted Piotr. "Lie flat, under the bushes!" He was already running towards a clump of mulberry bushes across the road. Aleks pulled Rachel and Rilka along towards another, larger bush, further away from the abandoned car on the road. They lay face down on the ground, Rachel's body covering her daughter's. The plane swooped down over the car, flew low over the mulberry bushes. They saw the black swastika on the underside of the wings. They saw the helmeted pilot as he banked and turned the plane.

"I don't want to die! I don't want to die!" Rilka cried out, and Rachel held her closer, saying "Shh, shh …" The plane flew over one last time, then rose slightly and flew off to the east, along the railroad tracks.

"All right. Back in the car," Piotr motioned to them, getting up from under his bush. "He's not interested in us. He's waiting for a train he can shoot up. But let's get out of here quickly!"

Several miles outside of Brest-Litovsk, Piotr announced he was going back to Warsaw.

"But you can't leave us here in the middle of nowhere," Rachel protested.

Aleks offered him five hundred zlotys.

"Not enough," said Piotr.

"A thousand," said Aleks.

"Not enough," said Piotr.

They settled on fifteen hundred zlotys and he agreed to take them into Brest-Litovsk. That left them with only five hundred zlotys for themselves.

In Brest-Litovsk they found lodging in a house where they became friendly with another refugee family, the Gordineks, similar in constellation, a mother, Ròzia, a father, Samson, and a daughter Lusia about a year older than Rilka. The first time Rilka saw Lusia, she was sitting near a window, facing a mirror, brushing her long blond hair. She seemed so beautiful. She didn't speak but continued to brush her hair in long, even strokes, until at last she turned and said "What is your name?" They became friends of a sort, though Lusia always seemed superior, more knowing; but they were the only two children among that particular group of refugees and they played together and shared secrets from their parents. It was not an unpleasant interlude. But Brest-Litovsk was only a stop on their way to Pinsk. They would wait out the war in Pinsk. Samson Gordinek managed to get a car large enough to accommodate the two families and they were driven to Pinsk in comfort, a happier trip for Rilka than the one out of Warsaw because she had a friend now.

Many refugees arrived in Pinsk as the weeks went by, and the Jewish organizations helped in settling them in various houses. After three months or so, they were told it was best for Jews to leave this town. The German army was advancing and there were already too many native Jews in Pinsk. It would be best if the new Jewish arrivals would leave. They must leave immediately, they were told, by a proclamation of the Mayor. After next week they would be sent back to Warsaw. But the Germans were in Warsaw. It was early winter already, bitter cold. They had no chauffeur now. How would they leave Pinsk? And where would they go? There was a freight train going through Stolin north to Vilno. There perhaps they would be safe, till Germany was defeated. But Stolin was in Russian territory and Russia had signed a non-aggression pact with Hitler just a month before, and the train went only once a week. Somehow, they were able to find a farmhouse on the edge of a small town on the other side of the border from Stolin. Rachel had no idea how that was arranged. Perhaps one of the Jewish organizations helping Jews to flee had a list of such safe houses. But Aleks was in full charge now. She was relieved he was making all the decisions. She loved him deeply; he was so strong and assured and tender. She did not question that they would be all right as long as they were together, the three of them, this small, tight little family in whose embrace she felt protected, as long as she could keep out of her mind what might have happened to Sofie and Papa and Mama.

One night at 2:00 a.m. Aleks wakened Rachel and Rilka. He had found two cart drivers. The women and children would go in one carriage and the men in the other.

"We're going to cross the Russian border. If they stop our carriage, yours will get through."

Rachel quickly wrapped Rilka, still half-asleep, in layers of clothes, and they stepped outside and walked in the dark to the gate opening up onto the road, where Ròzia and Lusia were already waiting. The men, Aleksand Samson and two others, stamped their feet to keep warm, waiting for the carriages to appear. In the dark, the snow was a bluish gray.

At last, the wagons silently came into sight. The women and children set off first, bundled up in blankets in the open carriage, drawn by two horses, their steamy breaths forming little clouds in the night. The men followed in the next carriage. Rilka began to whimper.

"It's an adventure," Rachel said. "Look how beautiful the horses are, tossing their heads."

They crossed the border to Stolin and the carriages stopped outside the station house. It was crowded with refugees from the surrounding areas who had made their way there somehow, all waiting for the train to Vilno. Inside the wooden station house people were lying on the floor, heads resting on makeshift pillows of their belongings, rolled up blankets, satchels. Rachel put her coat on a space she found on the huge pine table in the center of the room, to make a place for Rilka to sleep a little. A fire crackled in the wood-burning stove on one side of the room and provided some warmth.

Now the train clattered into the small station in Stolin and everyone was up, pushing, trying to get into the freight cars. In a few minutes it pulled out, with everyone on board, packed into the boxcars, headed toward Vilno. Now they would be safe. They would wait out the war in Vilno. Rachel would get word to Sofie somehow and they would decide if she would be safer in Warsaw or if she should try to join them in Vilno. She would get word to Papa and Mama and maybe even be able to send for them. But they couldn't endure a hazardous journey like this. No, they would be better off staying in Zarki—they were elderly and the Germans would leave them alone.

Sometimes it seemed to Rachel it was all chance: escaping, getting caught, life, death, everything hinging on some small, insignificant incident that leads to one path instead of another, each path equally likely, embarked on because of some random event, a word, a glance. At other times Rachel was convinced that she herself was indeed the instrument of fate. She, after all, had chosen that particular chauffeur. That chauffeur who had said to Aleks, "But your wife … You must take your wife."

-16-

Vilno—1939

In Vilno they were settled into a small apartment together with Ròzia and Samson and Lusia. Aleks, who once had been the dispenser of aid to Jewish refugees from Germany, now himself had to accept aid, from HIAS, the Hebrew Immigrant Aid Society, and from the Joint Distribution Committee. Refugees had flocked to Vilno as the last stop. Vilno changed hands so many times, it was hard to know when it was Polish and when it was Lithuanian or Russian. Within a few weeks of their arrival, Lusia and Rilka were sent to school and Rachel and Ròzia took turns walking them to the schoolhouse. The teacher was a young Lithuanian man, who was very kind and very patient. He was teaching them to read in Lithuanian.

Rachel began to sell off pieces of her jewelry, and eventually one or another buyer would ask if she had any more similar pieces and she said she would get some. She located someone who wanted to sell a bracelet or a ring and she found a customer for it. In all these transactions she made a commission and soon she had a thriving little business going, and they began to live a little better. But it was a dangerous business, because she might be paid in dollars, which were black market, and of course illegal.

"I'm in business," she exulted, her old verve back. She told the children stories at night when they were tucked in their cots in the living room. She found a dressmaker and had some clothes made. She sang in the mornings when it was her turn to make breakfast for everybody.

❧   ❧   ❧

Aleks looked at her intently one Saturday morning when they were alone in the apartment.

"You're amazing," he said. "You never complain."

"Why should I complain? Mama always told me to count my blessings. I am counting. We're healthy. We're together. We're alive."

"Still," Aleks said, "Ròzia is always whining that she doesn't have her maid, she has to wash dishes. Hannah is totally helpless; she won't go out to shop for food without her husband. They think they are still in Warsaw. But you, you go out and do business—and start to learn Lithuanian!"

"You've always underestimated me, Aleks. You thought of me as your lovely toy, a pet, a child, not to be taken too seriously. So now you're surprised I have a little strength."

"How can you say that? I've always wanted you to be independent. I sent you on all those trips abroad. I sent you to England! And I never complained about your little flirtations."

"I wish you had. I wanted you to be jealous … like I was jealous of Karola. You took her seriously. And besides," she continued, "you encouraged those little flirtations. It was a feather in your cap that men wanted me."

"No," Aleks said very softly, his eyes fixed on the bottom of his teacup. "No, I was afraid each time it would turn out to be something more."

Rachel was tormented by thoughts of Sofie. "How could I have left her?" she cried. "I took my own child, but I left my mother's child!" As soon as they had reached Vilno, she wrote Sofie, urging her to come, to find some way to get to them, but there was no response. After two weeks of fierce fighting, Warsaw, with little food or medicines or water, Warsaw, smoking and burning, had finally surrendered on September twenty-seventh. Still, Rachel was convinced that Sofie was alive and kept writing her letters, with little hope now that they would ever reach her. But in one of those letters Aleks sent an affidavit, claiming Sofie was his daughter from a previous marriage and requesting permission for her to join her family in Vilno. One day, miraculously, a letter came in Sofie's handwriting, uncensored. Perhaps the German efficiency was not yet in place.

I am all right. The building was not hit. There are no more bombings now. German officers have requisitioned our apartment. They came for Aleks. They confiscated all the copies of his book. The apartment is occupied by Polish women who service the Germans, but they are kind to me. I am allowed to stay in the maid's room and one night they protected me when some Germans were looking for Jews. They wouldn't let them in. They barricaded the door. I received your affidavit. I went to see Mama and Papa, to ask their advice. I gave money to the son of the Madam—he was driving a truck to Czestochowa and he let me hide in the back with the barrels of flour. I stayed a few hours and he brought me back. Mama wanted me to stay with them but I had to go back. They convinced me not to try to get to you—it is too dangerous. Everyday there are stories of people being shot when they try to leave. I am safer here. I cannot leave Warsaw. God knows where you are now or if this letter will ever get to you. I pray you are alive and will receive this.

❦   ❦   ❦

While Rachel ran her thriving little business of jewelry exchange in Vilno, Aleks traveled back and forth to Kovno, several times a week. There, in the capital of Lithuania, he was occasionally employed by officials who were issuing Polish passports to Jews who had arrived in the area with no papers, having escaped at a moment's notice and having brought nothing with them. These were stateless people. Many came into Lithuania, but they were not all from Poland. Aleks, as a former civil servant in the Polish government, was presumed to be able to tell who was Polish and who was not. If he vouchsafed that a person was Polish, a passport would be issued. As more and more such stateless people arrived, and as more desperate stories were told, he certified almost all who came as Polish. Then, as the Russians were approaching, and the flood of refugees kept growing, Aleks, together with a few others, began forging the Polish passports.

Early one Monday morning in the spring of 1940, two men in the uniform of the Lithuanian police knocked on the door. Rachel, still in her bathrobe, went to open it. Aleks was just getting ready to leave for Kovno.

"We must search this apartment," the taller of the two policemen said, half his body across the threshold. The shorter man was still behind him. "We have a warrant." Rachel stepped aside.

Aleks was accused of black marketeering, which although he vigorously denied it, was at least partially true. Rachel's business often resulted in black market exchanges of currency, and in fact some gold dollars were hidden at this very moment in a slit in the mattress.

"But that is a ridiculous accusation!" Aleks said. "I work in Kovno. I make Polish passports."

Rachel was horrified. What naïveté! Or was it stupidity, or honesty? Could he really think he was less guilty for forging passports than for trading in dollars? Why didn't he deny everything?

"You must come with us to the police station. The Chief of Police wants to question you." There was no further use protesting, but Rachel had visions of torture. And as soon as they left, with Aleks walking straight-backed between them, she ran into the hall and knocked on the doors of neighbors. Ròzia and Samson came in just then, followed by other friends of theirs. Being arrested by the Lithuanians was better than being arrested by the Russians, which would have meant Siberia at the very best, but still, everyone was worried. "We'll form a committee," Samson said, "and we'll get him out." Rachel, however, true to her nature, flew into action.

She appeared at the police station and demanded to see the Chief of Police. "Impossible," she was told. "He can't see you."

She went outside into the bright sunlight, and stood on the street next to the entrance, waiting for him to come out. She stayed till evening and when at last a man emerged whom she knew from photographs to be Chief Vicas, she approached him boldly.

"I am Mr. Mischler's wife. I plead with you to release him. He is innocent. You can't keep him in prison."

He looked at her carefully. She was flushed and her hair was disheveled and she was unafraid.

"Madame, if your husband is innocent, you have nothing to worry about."

"He is innocent." She pulled out an envelope from her purse. It contained a package of bills. "I hope this will enable you to speed up the process. So he can be released quickly."

He grabbed her wrist. His hold was strong. He was a man of her age, of medium height, with straight blond hair that fell over his forehead and piercing blue eyes. He had an open face, now clouded with anger. "Madame, you are trying to bribe me. I could arrest you for that! I repeat, Madame, if your husband is innocent, he will be released. Go home now."

"I am sorry," she said, "I am quite desperate."

His look softened. "Go home now," he said again and walked off quickly.

By that night, word had gotten around in the Jewish community that Mischler had been arrested. A committee was formed to help. They came to see her the next day. "We will protest," they said. "We will help."

"There is nothing you can do," she said. "I have it under control. I have seen the Chief of Police." They were always forming committees. She thought them useless.

On Tuesday evening she again waited outside the police station till Chief Vicas came out. He tipped his hat to her.

"What is happening? Are you going to release him?"

"We are investigating, Madame. Good evening."

On Wednesday night she was there again, but she stood across the street and she saw him pause and look around. She thought she saw a look of pleasure cross his face at seeing her. She went over to him. "Chief Vicas, it is three days already. My husband cannot be locked up like this."

"Be patient, Madame. It is getting chilly. You should wear a coat."

The "Mischler Committee" came over every day. They offered her money. Rachel said she didn't need it. The committee reported that several recipients of the passports had been interviewed and testified they were Polish and were issued the passports legitimately. The officials in Kovno testified they employed him and he was receiving a small salary. There was no word on the black market charges. She knew the investigation was proceeding.

On Thursday she was in her usual spot in front of the Police Station. Vicas greeted her warmly. "He is in more comfortable quarters. I had him transferred."

"But when will you release him?"

Vicas merely smiled. "Good evening, Madame." He bowed slightly.

On Friday afternoon, there was a knocking at the door. She opened it and Aleks stood in the doorway. Silently, they hugged each other. Another escape.

On Saturday afternoon, a message was delivered to Rachel. "My wife would like to meet you, Madame. She is impressed by your perseverance. Wilhelm Vicas."

Magda Vicas was a sparkling, warm woman, and Rachel quickly recognized her as a friend. They had a daughter Rilka's age, and the two families got in the habit of spending Sundays together. On one occasion, Vicas called to cancel their outing.

"I have a police mission. Magda isn't feeling well anyway."

"Oh," Rachel said, disappointed. "Well, why don't you come over for dinner tonight? I'll make something simple."

"No. I don't think Magda will be up to it. But you can come with me this afternoon. I'm going to make an arrest. You'll see what it's like. You can stay in the police car and observe."

She declined. She didn't want to leave Aleks and Rilka alone on a Sunday. She also felt a little uncomfortable at the prospect of spending an afternoon alone with him—although it wouldn't be alone, on a police raid, but what about afterward? She did not know if she could resist. Somehow, it had begun to seem inevitable to her that one day there would be no resistance on either of their parts. But how could she do that? She was a friend of his wife's. Aleks was very fond of him. How could she even think such thoughts?

On the radio that night the newscaster announced, "Police chief Vicas was killed this afternoon while making an arrest in a farmhouse outside of Vilno. Two officers accompanying him were severely wounded, as was the driver when multiple shots were fired into the automobile. The bandits were caught."

"Oh no, no, no!" Rachel cried. "Magda, oh poor Magda!" She gasped suddenly. "I might have been in that car! He asked me to go with him. My God …"

Aleks put his arms around her. "You were right to refuse him," he said softly. Rachel looked at Aleks.

"Not to go in his car, I meant," Aleks said in a steady voice.

"Yes," Rachel agreed.

"He was a good friend," Aleks said, "He was an honest man."

It was the summer of 1940; the Jews in Vilno were trapped. All of Western Europe was occupied; from the east, the Russians were advancing to annex those parts of Eastern Poland that Germany had agreed to give them in the Non-Aggression Pact. There was simply nowhere to go without a visa to another country. Rumors in Vilno spread with a rapidity unexplainable by any communications channels, and it was said that the Dutch consular official Zwartendijk was willing to put a stamp in the Polish passports of Jews: "No visa to Curaçao is required." It was a useless stamp, since no one could ever actually land in the Dutch colony across the world without a landing permit from its governor, and such a landing permit would never be issued. Everyone knew that, but no one wanted to go to Curaçao anyway and most had no idea even of where Curaçao was. To get out of Europe—that was the thing—just to get out of flaming Europe. Aleks managed to get his passport, which also included Rachel and Rilka, stamped for entry to Curaçao. But now what? Perhaps with that Dutch stamp in the passport there was a chance that some country would allow entry, in the knowledge that it would only be in transit to Curaçao. But no country wanted the Jews. And all the foreign consulates were closing, except the Japanese Consulate in Kovno. Perhaps the Japanese Consul Chiune Sugihara would issue a visa to Japan for transit en route to Curaçao.

And so Aleks stood in line outside the consulate along with hundreds of other Jews, day after day, waiting and hoping. On some days Rachel went with him to Kovno, leaving Rilka to stay with Lusia. Sometimes, all three of them went. It was a mixed bunch of people who gathered in front of the Consulate. There were well-dressed women, families of formerly well-to-do doctors and lawyers, the completely secular and the ultra-religious. An old man in a long frock coat, with a full beard, wearing a broad brimmed hat, reminded Rachel of Papa. Young men, pale, and speaking to each other in Yiddish, were familiar to her. A man such as that was offered her in marriage by the matchmaker in Zarki. It was what she had gotten away from; she had escaped such men who studied all day long and never did anything useful in her opinion, and expected God to take care of them—God or their wives. There was Warsaw and London and Aleks and Roman between Zarki and now, but here she was and it was all familiar to her and a part of her still. Zarki was still inside of her, just as Mama had said.

"You will never leave Zarki fully. It is in you always," Mama told her on one occasion when she was eighteen and stormily refused to meet any more of those young "scholars" who were potential husbands, and angrily shouted she was getting out, out, out of Zarki forever. "You belong to us," Mama had said.

And the enormity of her break with her past made her shiver in the August sun. She was hoping to go to Japan, a world away, a final escape from Zarki and from Papa and Mama. How could she do that? What kind of final betrayal was she about to perform? But to stay would be to die, and if she and Aleks and Rilka survived, she would somehow get Papa and Mama and Sofie out also and save them as well. It was her only comfort, even though in the depth of her soul she suspected it was a rationalization, as she stood with Aleks waiting for Sugihara to call them in to his office. She turned away from the young Jewish men with long beards and forelocks.

"They are from the Mir Yeshiva," Aleks told her, reading her mind. "They must be saved. Judaism rests on their scholarship. Their rabbis know that. They are not waiting for God; they are waiting for Sugihara."

❀   ❀   ❀

Rachel, standing in the long line, thought angrily of Sofie. Why, why hadn't Sofie come to Vilno? She could have left Warsaw with them. Rachel had begged her to come. Sofie was always stubborn, always doing exactly what she wanted to do, under the guise of being unassuming. Maybe she was really stronger than Rachel. After all, she had refused to give Papa her savings when he had come to Warsaw just before the war started. Rachel was the one who had rushed to the bank to give it all away. Well, Rachel didn't regret that; perhaps that money helped Mama and Papa survive. Oh, God, she thought in immediate remorse, perhaps Sofie's savings, those savings she kept, are helping her to survive. But then, after, why hadn't Sofie tried to get through the lines to Vilno? How could she think it was safer in Warsaw? Everybody here knew it wasn't safe anywhere in Europe; everyone was so desperate to get out. Sofie would be with her now, if only she hadn't been so stubborn, if only Rachel had been more forceful, more convinced, more convincing. What could have been in her heart that allowed her to just let go like that, to let Sofie stay behind?

The line in front of the consulate began to move. "He's issuing the visas!" The murmur swelled to a single sound of guarded hope as people began to come out of the consulate, passports in hand, showing the stamp of the red seal of Imperial Japan. The line surged forward, grew longer, stopped moving again, till it was dark and Sugihara's German secretary came out of the gate, and went up and down the line, saying over and over, "Closed, closed." Rachel and Aleks and Rilka went to spend the night at the apartment of one of Aleks' friends.

Next day, before the sun had fully risen, Rachel and Aleks took a sleepy, reluctant Rilka and went back to the Consul's house. The line moved more quickly this day, and in a few hours Rachel and Aleks were at the point where they had been the night before. Rilka was restless, but managed to find some other children on the line who weren't orthodox and who would play with her. The word flew down the line that Sugihara had stopped signing the visas. Japan ordered the consulate to be closed immediately. He was refused permission to issue visas.

This is the end, Rachel thought. We will not get out. She felt almost resigned. She would share Mama's and Papa's fate, and Sofie's.

But the line kept moving forward. People were going in. "He's signing, he's signing!" came the word down the line. "He's not listening to orders from

Japan!" And so they waited, and the line moved along more quickly all the time, until at last Rachel and Aleks and Rilka were standing inside the Consul's office.

Sugihara was a handsome man who looked like a diplomat, tall even when seated, fastidiously dressed, hair combed, posture straight. His expression was difficult to read; he might have seemed detached except for his eyes, brown and soft and kind. He looked weary and sad—like Aleks, Rachel thought, when he used to come home in Warsaw after a day of working at his refugee resettlement job. The Consul held out his hand for their passports. His small son stood next to him, peering over his shoulder, looking curiously at Rilka, and Sugihara put his arm around the boy's waist. A young Japanese woman entered the room, in Western dress, bearing a bamboo tray with a teapot and a cup without handles. She put it down on the side of his desk and said something in Japanese. Sugihara looked up at her. "Yukiko-san," he addressed her and she responded in Japanese. She took the boy by the hand and led him away, protesting. Chiune Sugihara smiled at Rilka.

"Where do you intend to go from Japan?" he asked Aleks in Polish.

"To Curaçao," Aleks said.

"Yes, of course," Sugihara said, stamped the passport before him with the official orange-red seal of Imperial Japan, and signed it. They had a visa, valid for a stay in Japan of twenty-one days while in transit to their country of destination! They knew Sugihara knew that they would extend the stay in Japan and that they didn't have a country of destination.

They rejoiced when they returned to Vilno late that afternoon and Rachel, who herself had no idea what Japan was like, began to describe a new adventure to Rilka. But Rilka was unconsoled at the prospect of leaving Lusia, since the Gordineks had not yet gotten a transit visa. Rachel assured her they were not leaving immediately; they needed to prepare and make arrangements and that would take quite a while. The tension in the refugee community was at a new height, especially among those who had no Japan transit visas. Rumor spread throughout the community with unbelievable rapidity that Sugihara was really closing the consulate and leaving Kovno. The Russians, in power now, had closed all the other consulates already. Then what would the Jews do?

Samson Gordinek traveled to Kovno and stayed there day after day. Sugihara was assigned to a post in Berlin, but he delayed his departure and moved to a hotel, where he continued, in spite of exhaustion unto illness, hands stiffened from the work, to stamp and sign the visas from dawn to midnight. And even as he and his family rode to the train station in the large limousine, and even as his train was slowly pulling out of the station, he kept stamping visas, held out to him by desperate people. He stamped two thousand visas, in passports valid for entire families. Gordinek at last received one of those visas.

One week after Sugihara left, the Russians annexed Lithuania and occupied Vilno. Rachel and Aleks were confronted with the next obstacle: how to get permission to leave Russia, for only through Russia could they get to Japan.

A letter had come through from Sofie, unsigned and somehow smuggled through the underground.

All Jews have been ordered to move to one section of the city, around Grzybowska Street. I have found a room here. We cannot leave the ghetto, except for the working squads. There is a guard at the gate. I have a working permit and am allowed out in the morning, to be back by evening. There is very little food and almost no coal. We fear for the winter. There are rumors they will seal off the ghetto. Then of course I won't be able to leave at all. The Germans ask for volunteers every once in a while for a labor force. Some people won't volunteer for anything because they heard terrible things happen to the volunteers, that they are killed. But others say they are sent to Germany to work in factories. So far I haven't volunteered. If things get worse, I will volunteer. What can I lose? Only my life. I received your packages before I had to move to the ghetto. They were a miracle. Now nothing gets through. When this nightmare is over, I will find you, my sister, my love, wherever in the world you are, I will find you.

The fall advanced; the days grew shorter, the air was colder. Rilka started school again, but now there was a Russian teacher instead of the kindly Lithuanian one and they began to learn Russian. The teacher was strict and they were somewhat frightened of him, but he gave praise lavishly when they showed some progress with the Russian alphabet.

They still had no word about their application for an exit permit. At last one morning a letter arrived, instructing them to come for an interview to the Narodny Komissariat Vnutrennih Del, the Soviet Commissariat for Internal Affairs. They sat silently in the small, crowded waiting room, till first Aleks, then Rachel, was called to come inside. Everything hinged on this interview. So many people were afraid even to apply, because once they declared an intent to leave, they were marked as enemies of the State, perhaps to be arrested, at any rate to be watched. Rachel had heard of the fate of the Jews of Lemberg: a small group had applied to leave eastern Poland early in the days after Stalin had taken over that part of the country. They were granted permission to move west and asked to board a train, which took them not westward, but eastward to Siberia and the labor camps.

Aleks needed to be inconspicuous to the Russian police. He had been connected with Pilsudski; he was known to be anti-communist, and so was at great risk of arrest. In fact it was most likely on that basis—of being an intellectual in known danger from both the Germans and the Russians—that he was one of the several hundred on the list of refugees recommended by the President's Advisory Committee to get an American visa. If they could get to Moscow, he would go to the American Embassy and try to get that special visa.

Aleks' interview with the NKVD was short. When he came out through the heavy oak door into the waiting room, his head bowed, his graying hair disheveled, he gave no sign of how it went. Rachel was called in next, and walked in holding Rilka's hand tightly in her own sweaty one.

The room they entered was sparsely furnished, with a large wooden table in front of two small windows covered with faded, dusty curtains and several tall backed wooden chairs occupied by young looking soldiers. Behind the table sat a man in his forties, looking as if he had been in his uniform for several days. His feet were stretched out under the table and Rachel could see the only threatening aspect of him, the way his pants were tucked into his well-polished leather boots. Otherwise he seemed quite benign and was smiling. Immediately, Rachel was on guard. She approached the table and stood silently, thinking how to start, when he said, in a mixture of Russian and Polish,

"So, tovarisch, you want to leave us. Why would you want to leave such a paradise? We bring you Utopia. You want to go to Curaçao? Come, come, tovarisch, what do you have against us?"

"No," Rachel said without flinching, "not to Curaçao. We want to go to America."

"Hmm. You have a transit visa to Japan en route to Curaçao. I do not see a destination visa for America in your passport."

"We have been told it is waiting for us at the American consulate in Moscow. It is not that we want to leave Russia, it is that we want to be united with my husband's family in America."

The soldiers spoke to each other in Russian. One of them laughed at something the chief official had said. The atmosphere appeared relaxed.

"Ah, tovarisch, such a beautiful woman! Your husband is old; you are young," he said, examining the passport. "Let your husband go to America. You stay with us."

"That wouldn't be right," Rachel said. "When I married him he was young and healthy. Now he is older and sicker; it wouldn't be right for me to leave him now. And I have a child. A child needs a mother and a father, and a family which we have in America." She emphasized the word "family."

"You are foolish," one of the younger men said. "You have a great future with us."

"We will consider your application," the chief said, in dismissal. "If it is approved your names will be on the posted lists outside."

It was well known that the Russians were trying to enlist many among the refugees who would potentially be agents for them in the Unites States. They solicited those who left family behind anywhere in the Russian-occupied territories as hostages. Aleks had not been approached, but perhaps that is what they wanted to do, perhaps that is why they had tried to persuade Rachel to stay. There was no hint whether Rachel alone, or all three of them, or none of them, would be on the exit lists.

At a party at the Polish Refugee Club for some friends whose names had been on the list and who were departing the following day, Rachel caught a glimpse in the dark mirrored wall of a small group of three people huddled close together, the man's arm around the woman's waist, the child between them. Startled, she realized it was herself and Aleks and Rilka. My little family, she thought, we are a family, a unit, not Aleks and I separately, but Aleks and I and Rilka, in this world together, a closed circle. She felt enfolded in that circle, what she had always wanted in those days of gaiety and independence in Warsaw, what had always eluded her. She had held Aleks responsible: he was not a family man, he never supported her, he belonged more to others than to her, he had a liaison with Karola who was more his equal than Rachel, he encouraged Rachel to live her own life. That is why she had those flirtations, that is why Roman … But now, observing the mirror images, she thought perhaps it could always have been thus, perhaps if she had accepted her life with Aleks as it was, if she had accepted him as he was, if she had understood him better. She had chafed under any restraints; she tossed her head in rebellion like a young horse. Even at this very instant she was rebelling against her own trend of thought—I would have had to obliterate my very self to be so totally submissive and I have a right to exist too, she reminded herself I have a right to want. But what she had wanted was in opposition to itself: to have her independence and freedom and at the same time to be taken care of. And perhaps she had had neither, her freedom curtailed by her guilt, her urge to passivity and submission never fulfillable because of that essential life force that drove her always to action.

But now, in the midst of their disrupted lives, she felt closer to Aleks than ever before. Their lives converged to their common good. Their love-making, infrequent and silent, in the crowded living arrangements, was infused with a passion and tenderness Rachel had not experienced before. There is only the present, Rachel thought the old familiar thought, finding it hard to imagine herself ever in London with Roman. She had fallen in love again … with her husband.

They had moved into a one-bedroom apartment in the Russian-occupied Vilno. The larger apartment they had shared with the Gordineks was requisitioned by the Russians. A Russian soldier, on his way westward, was billeted in with them, by order of the army. He moved in one day with his wife and two-year-old girl. They crowded in to the small bedroom, leaving the rest of the apartment to the three Russians. But they all used the kitchen and shared the bathroom.

"Piotr," the soldier said shyly, on the first day. "Marina, Olenka," he pointed.

"Aleksander, Rachela, Marilka," Aleks pointed to his family.

Everyone behaved with exaggerated politeness toward each other. No one wanted to offend; all were embarrassed by the enforced intimacy. Marina tried to keep the small apartment clean. Piotr tried to teach Rilka Russian. Rachel cooked them all chicken soup. "He's so young," Rachel said, "so tender with the children." She wept when they left, moving on toward the front, toward death.

"Sto lat, sto lat, niech żyje, żyje nam," they sang on Rachel's birthday at the lub. A hundred years, a hundred years, may she live a hundred years. It was December twenty-fifth and outside the bells rang, and the snow fell gently and crystals of ice formed on the windows of the club dining room. Rachel thought of the Black Madonna of Czestochowa, looking out onto a black world.

Rachel and Aleks lined up everyday in front of the NKVD office, taking turns in the cold, scanning the lists of exit permits. One day Rachel's name appeared but she did not see the names of Aleks or Rilka. It was nearly evening. Stunned, she couldn't talk about it and she went directly to bed. I'll think about it tomorrow, she told herself. The next days, on the new list, were the names of Aleks and Rilka. Aleks bought train tickets to Moscow.

-17-

Moscow—1941

Moscow in January was bitter, bitter cold. Rachel's breath condensed and froze around her lips as she walked in the crunching snow toward the American consulate to get the visas which they hoped were awaiting them. Rachel glanced at her reflection in the glass window of a shop and smiled with pleasure at the fur hat she was wearing. She had bargained, mostly through sign language, with its former owner, a man she had seen outside their hotel. Though the fur was worn and they had to conserve the little money they had, she simply had to have that hat.

"It's just like Papa's hat," she told Aleks. "I used to borrow it when I went to Helena's salon in Zarki. Jacob said I looked like a Russian princess in it. I loved that hat. It reminds me of Papa and Sofie. What dreams I had in that hat!" She fell silent suddenly.

At the American consulate, they were told the Ambassador wanted to see Aleks personally. They were ushered into his large office where he sat in a high-backed chair with gilt arms, his feet up on the fancy desk made of elaborately inlaid wood. He was a large man, with forthright face, blue eyes, and cropped graying hair that accentuated his rather prominent ears. He smiled expansively.

"Come in, come in." He motioned them to come closer. "Please sit down. Here. What a pleasure to meet you, Mr. Mischler. I like to meet you people who got this special visa from our President. And I read your book about the German Jews ... well, you certainly had foresight. You predicted this turn of events back in 1933. You have a fine daughter there." He handed Rilka a piece of candy. "She will grow up in a good country."

"We are very, very grateful to have this opportunity. You are saving our lives. Unfortunately there are so many others who don't have this visa, and others who have been promised the American visa but cannot get a permit to exit Russia. I fear they will be lost," Aleks said pointedly. "Everyone is terrified to ask for an exit visa and terrified not to ask for one—and be doomed to stay."

"I wish we could do more," the Consul said quietly then, more briskly, "Your train to Vladivostock leaves at the end of the week. I will be at the station to see you get on safely. You are not to acknowledge you recognize me. I will make no sign that we have met. We are all watched very closely here, and we don't know what is in the mind of the Russians. Be careful what you say in your room. The NKVD is everywhere. Goodbye and good luck to you. And by the way," he added, "when you go out, stop at the secretary's desk downstairs. She will give you three tickets to the Bolshoi for tonight. You might as well see something of the best of Russia."

"What a fine man," Rachel said when they were on the street. "But how strange that he had his legs up on the desk. I could see the soles of his shoes."

"To make us feel at ease," Aleks explained. "It's an American custom."

In the grand hotel, just on the verge of shabbiness but still reminiscent of Czarist luxury, they had a large room, with an oriental carpet, worn but in a rich red pattern, heavy brocade drapes, pulled back with a tassel, revealing floor-length windows looking out onto the city, with the Kremlin spires in the distance. On every floor a steward was always ready to pour tea from a large brass samovar standing on a small table with a white embroidered tablecloth. They spoke in low voices in their room, praising the Soviets, admiring the country, expressing delight with everything, all for the benefit of the hidden microphones, for Aleks was convinced the room was tapped.

In the late afternoon two days before they were to take the train from Moscow to Vladivostock, where they would board a ship for Japan, Rachel felt a discomfort, a growing pain in her abdomen. The three of them were in the tea-room in an alcove of the ornate lobby. The great chandelier in the center of the once opulent room sparkled, throwing light and shadow onto the plush, deep chairs and couches. Rachel loved sitting in this warm, sedate room, amidst the hushed voices of people conversing in different corners, while outside, through the long windows, she could see the snow swirling about on the street in the harsh blue light of an extremely cold day.

Then, as she was hit with a sudden pain, she cried out. "It's nothing," she said as the pain subsided. The pain began to mount and she said she was tired and would go up to the room. Aleks and Rilka went with her and she could barely stand while Aleks turned the key in the lock. She lay down on the bed, but a wave of nausea swept over her and she dragged herself to the bathroom. She grasped the sink with both hands, her knuckles turning white. She turned quickly to lean over the toilet bowl and retched and retched, without stop, trembling, shaking. She sank to the floor, damp with perspiration, while Rilka stood by frightened and helpless, and Aleks ran out to the floor lady to get a doctor. "I understand, I understand now," she said when she was lying in bed again a little more comfortable. "That is how it must be to die … you don't care … your body protects your mind … you just don't care."

A Russian doctor sent by the hotel was taking her pulse. Rachel was grateful to be in his hands, this friendly rotund man with a full bushy mustache who was poking around her stomach.

"Gallstones," he said in heavily accented Polish, "maybe the appendix, maybe woman trouble. You will stay in bed a week, two. We'll see. Maybe an operation. I am going to call someone else. We will have a consultation. Now try to sleep a little. I'll come back tomorrow, or sooner if you need me."

"No," Rachel said weakly, "we are leaving on Thursday."

He patted her hand. "No, no, you can't go anywhere. Sleep now. We'll see tomorrow."

She was in pain the next day, but not nauseous. She could bear the pain. "Aleks, I am one; we are three. If we stay, we will all be lost. If we go, at least you and Rilka will be safe. I am getting on that train, no matter what, even if you have to carry me!"

By the next morning the worst of the pains had waned. Aleks brought Maximillian, a doctor, a refugee friend of theirs from Warsaw.

"Eleven days on the Trans-Siberian railroad! Impossible," Maximillian said. "You have to wait until the attack subsides. Here at least there are hospitals." The Russian doctor came also, and brought another man.

"Too much risk. Your appendix could burst. Maybe poison gall bladder! No, No. You stay here."

"I am going," she said quietly and turned on her side. "I want to sleep now."

On the day of their departure, pale and queasy, frightened but determined, Rachel, leaning on Aleks and Maximillian, wrapped in sweaters and a warm coat, wearing her fur hat, boarded the train. On the platform, the American consul, standing near the steps of the second railroad car with two aides, as he had promised, silently observed their departure.

For ten nights and eleven days, Rachel mostly stayed in the sleeper compartment, drank weak tea and ate small portions of boiled chicken. Aleks spent the days talking to friends who were also on that train. Rilka found a playmate, but mostly she sat in the compartment with Rachel, coloring with crayons the hotel steward had given her, withdrawn into her own world. The train stopped at night in small stations along the way. The windows were frosted over and they could barely see out. Occasionally, the steam of the train swirling about on the station platform would part here and there in the black night, to make small groups of people visible in the eerie light cast by the train, and they would see peasant women, faces almost totally swathed in shawls, handing baskets of food to departing young men.

In the daylight they looked out at the Ural Mountains in the cold distance, and then at the boundless, frozen plains of Siberia. At Irkutsk, when the train stopped for a long period of time, Aleks became nervous that at any moment the police would burst in and arrest him. He sat quietly in the compartment, awaiting doom. They were so close, so close to escape, to life. But the train finally moved on, and Rachel and Aleks' apprehension eased and they looked in awe upon the grandeur of the scenery coming in and out of view through the frosted windows as the train wound its way along the rock ledge around Lake Baikal. At last, in pain, but triumphant, Rachel arrived in Vladivostock, leaning on Aleks, holding Rilka's hand, almost safe, almost, almost.

The journey from Vladivostock to Japan took two days. When they arrived in Tsuruga there was a cold wind and the air was damp and penetrating. Rachel had never felt so cold, not even in Russia. They were met as they disembarked by a representative of the American Joint Distribution Committee seeing to the refugees and were taken to a small ryokan on a side street close to the center of town. An elderly Japanese woman, dressed in a dark blue kimono with a pale blue obi greeted them at the door and showed them to their accommodations, a large tatami room with a smaller one separated by a shoji screen. The room was bare except for a low lacquered red table in the larger room and a shelf on which stood a vase with one curving branch casting a shadow on the wall behind it. How different from the overstuffed hotel room in Moscow, with its heavy furniture and thick drapes. But where would they sleep? There was no bed visible, no chairs, no closets. The woman bowed deeply and retreated from the room. Rachel's spirits sank; they were alone in a strange land. She walked over to the window and looked out onto a small courtyard with a rock garden and several dwarfed trees. A gentle snow was falling.

"Well," Aleks said, "I'll go out to the reception room and try to find out where we can get something to eat." But before he could cross the room, two women had appeared their hostess and a much younger woman, probably her daughter. They were followed by a man bearing their suitcases. And suddenly there was a flurry of activity. The man slid open a screen on one wall of the room which was apparently concealing what passed for a closet, and deposited their suitcases inside. The younger woman pulled out a futon and some sheets from a similar closet in the alcove and made up a bed on the floor, pointing to Rilka, indicating this was where she would sleep. "Yukiko," the older woman said pointing to herself. "Keiko-san," she said, pointing to the younger woman. "Hayaki-san," she said pointing to the man.

Yukiko motioned Rachel to follow her to the bath while Hayaki now produced a heavy cotton kimono for Aleks. Through motions and sign language, they indicated that dinner would be brought to them. Rachel entered a small ante-room in the bath area outside their room. Yukiko indicated she should disrobe and when she stood naked in the changing room, she saw just beyond it through the open door a deep square wooden tub with a cover on it. Yukiko took off the cover to reveal a steaming bath filled to the top, with a wooden scoop beside it. Yukiko dipped the scoop into the bath water and poured it over Rachel, who let out a gasp as the hot water scalded her. But with the next scoop she was adjusted to the temperature and when she finally stepped into the deep bath, she at last was able to shake off the piercing cold she felt upon their arrival.

When she came back to their room, dressed in a heavy navy blue and yellow yukata-type kimono, her feet clad in tabi, the sock that divided the big toe from the rest of the foot, and zori sandals, she felt warm and wonderful. Aleks and Rilka meantime had unpacked some of their belongings and Rachel tried to bring some order to this unpacking while Aleks and Rilka took their baths. Keiko placed cushions for them at the low table and they sat on the floor somewhat uncomfortably when she brought up their meal. Keiko giggled as they tried to use chopsticks, but she showed them how and Rilka was delighted. They ate pickled fish and all sorts of unfamiliar food, but after drinking cup after small cup of hot sake both Rachel and Aleks felt wohlbehagen, an overwhelming sense of well-being.

After two nights at the ryokan, the Jewish agency arranged for their trip to Kobe, where they would stay until they left Japan. In Kobe they settled in to a hotel where other refugees from Poland who had arrived before them were housed. Thanks to Dr. Kotsuji Setsuzo, Kobe welcomed the Jews. Dr. Kotsuji had been educated in America and held a doctorate in Semitic studies from Berkeley. He persuaded the Japanese Foreign Minister Matsuoka to let the Jewish refugees stay in Kobe until they emigrated, and Matsuoka agreed if the Kobe police would agree. Kotsuji got the Kobe police to agree, though it cost him a good deal of money. The Jewish Community of Kobe, known as Jew-Com, provided funds for the refugees and help with Japanese officials. As the evils in Europe multiplied, so multiplied the kindnesses of those who rallied to save lives out of their convictions and their humanity. Now Rachel and Aleks could take a deep breath and prepare for their future. These were good times for Rilka, too; Rachel was happy that the Gordineks were also at the hotel so Rilka had Lusia to spend time with. There were, in fact, a number of children Rilka's age, six and seven-year olds, and they ran around the hotel playing hide-and-seek and other games of their own invention.

Rachel and Aleks went to the refugee relief offices on Yamamoto-Dori Street to try to get news of Sofie and Mama and Papa and of Aleks'sisters. But there was no news of their families, only the news that the Russians had sought Aleks' arrest in Vladivistock just days after he had left for Japan. They also inquired about passage to America, and were informed they would have to go to Tokyo.

The refugees took part in various activities organized in the community center in the same building as the refugee offices. The community center had been established by Anatole Ponevejsky, a long-time resident of Japan, and now it served the refugees. One of the activities was a sight-seeing trip to Kyoto. A group of eleven of the adults, along with Rilka and Lusia and a boy called Nadek, went by bus to the Kinkakuji Temple. The Golden Pavilion, rising three stories, was perfectly reflected in the pond on which it was situated and the shingled roofs and golden walls of the upper stories took their breath away. Rocks, artfully placed, rose from the pond, and the trees along the shore looked like they were growing upside-down in their pond reflection. What a magical sight! The tour guide took a picture of the whole group standing on a small bridge across the pond with the Temple in the background.

Rachel liked to go to one particular park near their hotel. She and Lusia's mother and the two girls strolled down the winding paths and returned the curious smiles and bows of the Japanese mothers tending their children. The sun shone on the melting ice. The dwarfed trees cast small shadows on rock gardens and streams gently flowed down little hills and gathered into sparkling pools. The beauty around her calmed her.

Aleks had bought a small English-Japanese book and started studying Katakana. It was a simpler script than Hiragana or Kanji and he thought he could master some of it. Rosenblum the engineer laughed at him indulgently. "Why are you bothering? You will leave here soon."

Aleks wanted to eat in a Japanese restaurant outside of the hotel. He and Rachel went out late in the afternoon, leaving Rilka with Lusia. The hotel concierge had recommended a restaurant well-known for its variety of noodle dishes and wrote the name in Japanese on a slip of paper on which he drew a rough map. They followed the street outside their hotel, made several turns onto smaller streets and pretty soon were lost in a maze of narrow alleys and small side streets. As they stood on one corner trying to figure out which way to go next, a Japanese man in Western dress approached them and bowed deeply. Aleks bowed. Rachel bowed. The man bowed again, till Rachel giggled at all the bowing but had no idea what the man wanted. He took the slip of paper Aleks had been looking at, then nodded. "Ah so deska," he said and motioned for them to follow him. They walked behind him, turning right on the next street, then left, then straight for some blocks and on and on till they were hopelessly confused and getting a little worried. At last, they arrived at the restaurant, the man indicated they should go inside, bowed deeply and walked away in the direction from which they had come.

"How amazing," Rachel said. "He went so far out of his way just to show us!"

"And that," said Aleks, "is why I am learning Katakana."

The men from the Mir Yeshiva, with their full beards, in their black suits and black hats, walking three or four abreast on the streets, drew little groups of Japanese whose curiosity conquered their shyness. They took photographs and asked for autographs. And the Mir men freely signed their names. They were completely unselfconscious, these Mir Yeshiva students and their Rabbis, and they performed their religious duties steadfastly, studying and praying, swaying back and forth as they prayed. Their certainty of purpose impressed the Japanese, who considered them "Holy Men." Rachel, observing, envied that certainty of purpose, though she had scorned this religiosity that reminded her of Zarki, just as she had envied Jakob his certainty of purpose about going to Palestine, just as she had admired Aleks' certainty of purpose when he wrote those political articles in Czestochowa and when he worked in the Ministry in Warsaw. She herself still had no other purpose than to survive and to see Sofie and her family again. That vision of something important, monumental, outside of her being eluded her, but she understood it and desired it. It's men that have the purpose, she thought. The men she knew had that vision, but not any of the women, except maybe Karola.

Their twenty-one day transit visa expired. They went to the government office accompanied by a JewCom member and had it renewed for a week. Every week Aleks went and had the visa renewed for one more week, but they knew they had to make arrangements to leave. One day they traveled to the steamship company offices in Tokyo to book passage to America. They were to stay for two nights at a small hotel. That evening, together with the Gordineks and another couple who had traveled with them, they were invited to a Kabuki performance. They were to meet to their host, a member of the Jewish community in Tokyo, at the clock tower of the Ginza Wako building. They left the hotel in plenty of time and walked around the Ginza, stopping in the shops along the way. There was a stall selling chestnuts and both Rilka and Lusia wanted some. The vendor pulled out the hot chestnuts and wrapped each one individually in beautiful paper with a leaf pattern on it and handed them one by one to the two girls. They walked through the Matsuzakaya department store and as they wandered between the aisles, a young man in a store uniform approached them and bowed. "Please to follow me," he said in slow English which Rachel understood. He took them to the top floor and into a large room filled with games and toys and in the center was a small enclosure filled with multicolored rubber balls among which children jumped and rolled around and slid into each other. Though Rilka and Lusia did not go inside, they were fascinated. A playground in a department store!

At the Kabukiza Theater some people sat on chairs, others on cushions. The actors wore elaborate costumes, lavish makeup, faces painted white, eyebrows turned upward, exaggerated in black paint, the beautiful women played by men in their exorbitantly colored kimonos, speaking in stylized, strange voices accompanied by music on instruments the refugees had never heard before. It was such a spectacle that they were all entranced, but it went on for hours and hours and Rilka and Lusia were getting restless. Vendors of oranges and sweet drinks walked up and down the aisles and people came and went in and out of the main theater area, apparently not worried about missing any of the action. Rilka and Lusia also got up to walk around the area, but eventually, after three hours, they all left while Kabuki continued.

The next morning the Gordineks obtained passage on a passenger ship to Los Angeles. Aleks obtained cheaper tickets on a freighter to Seattle that carried passengers. They returned to Kobe and made ready for their departure at the end of March.

It was all so accidental, Rachel thought, so accidental that they were still alive. The ship they had been on from Vladivostock to Japan sank on the voyage immediately following theirs. It was sheer chance that they were here in Japan, getting ready to go to America, and yet ... and yet. After all, Rachel's fierce determination made her leave Moscow against all medical advice. Had they caught a later train across Siberia, they might have been on that sinking ship. Was she totally powerless or totally powerful? A dangerous train of thought, because if she was totally powerful, then it would have been within her power to save Sofie, and she hadn't. She was pulled backward by the recurring nightmares of Sofie left behind, of her parents' unknown fate, and she was pushed forward, to America, by her daughter's future, by her husband's and by her own strong will to survive, and more than survive, to live.

And so, when at last they stood at the railing of the Hiya Maru which would take them across the Pacific Ocean, when the loud blasts from the foghorn signaled their departure and the freighter slid out of the dock, they were cut loose, like the ship, from the moorings of Europe.

PART III

America

-18-

New York—1941

The train pulled in to Grand Central station at seven in the morning. Neither Rachel nor Aleks had much sleep on the trip to New York from Seattle where the Hiya Maru had docked on a wet, gray day, in a soft impenetrable mist. They had looked with wonder at the scenery as the train sped through the majestic Rockies, the open, vast plains, the rolling hills. But mostly they marveled at the openness of the people, their unembarrassed friendliness, their boisterous children. They had been up for two hours already, had washed, combed, straightened out their clothes, and watched the sun rise over well-kept fields, small towns nestled in valleys, early forsythias coming into yellow bloom along the roads running parallel to the train tracks. Rachel thought of the three of them as encased in a glass bubble, perpetually rolling along in the world, observing the life outside but not a part of it, never stopping long enough to establish a footing, to come to rest. Where would they rest? How would they establish themselves, starting out with no roots here?

When they arrived in New York, Rachel made no move to get off the train. Rilka was getting her own little bundles together and Aleks was taking packages down from the overhead rack, but still Rachel remained in her seat.

"Let's go," Aleks said. "Everyone else is off the train already."

"Why rush?" Rachel said despondently. "No one is waiting for us." But she got up and slowly followed him down the platform.

All at once, she spied a small group of people at the end of the platform, waving to them. "Oh my God," she said in astonishment. "It's Dr. Lazar, and the Biebers! How did they know? They must be here for another reason." But she began to run towards them.

A group of Aleks's friends, refugees who had arrived months before and who had found out from HIAS when Mischler was arriving, came to greet them. Rachel was once again, after so long a time, sparkling, alive, joyful. They were whisked off to the Lazars' home and served breakfast, and there was the telling of stories and much laughter, and a constant stream of visitors to see Aleks and Rachel, eager for news of the war, news of others left behind. At last one of the men said he had a car and would take Rachel to look for an apartment. Aleks and Rilka stayed behind while other friends dropped in and Rachel went off in the car, stopping in one brownstone after another and inquiring if there was an apartment for rent.

Within a couple of hours she had found a vacancy. It was a third floor walk-up in a somewhat dilapidated brownstone on West Seventy-fourth Street. The living room was long and narrow with a shabby couch, which opened up into a double bed, against one wall. It was covered with faded green fabric. Round lace doilies were scattered on the back of the couch, on each of the two heavy armchairs and on several little occasional tables placed around the room. Rachel's friend sighed and began to leave. Rachel went over to a bay window that looked out onto the street. A small kitchenette was at one end of the apartment with a curtain separating it from the dining area, which contained a maple table jutting out into the living room, with four mismatched chairs around it. On one side of the living room a double glass door led into an alcove which held only a narrow bed and a small dresser. The bathroom, down the long narrow hall, was to be shared with the tenants of the other apartment on the floor. The rent was $72 a month.

"A front apartment! I'll take it," said Rachel.

She was exultant when she came back to the Lazars'. "Isn't it wonderful?"

They gathered all their belongings, the few suitcases they had, and were saying goodbye, when the phone rang and Artur Lazar went to answer it. It was a Polish journalist, an old friend of Aleks's; he and another journalist from Czestochowa wanted to see him.

"Invite them to our home tonight." Rachel said.

"But we haven't even moved in," Aleks protested.

"By this evening we'll be ready," she insisted.

On the way to their new apartment she stopped at Woolworth and while the car waited, Rachel bought some glass plates and cups and utensils. At the bakery next door she got cake and at a little grocery on the corner, some milk and tea and fruit. That evening, Rachel entertained the two journalists.

"Our first night in America, and I'm entertaining guests in my own home, on my own plates!" Rachel said, delighted with herself and with the world.

"You are given lemons, and again you make lemonade!" Aleks kissed her.

❦   ❦   ❦

The refugees gathered at the Polish Jewish Club on Sunday afternoons, for tea and cakes and to exchange news from Europe. On Friday nights, they stopped in after nine, and sat at little tables, engaged in discussions of the war and of business. A hierarchy began to emerge, at first subtle to newcomers, but becoming quite clear as Rachel and Aleks grew familiar with the members: the old hierarchy of success. It was difficult for all of them, Rachel realized, with a new language, new customs. All of them had lost their old status. In Europe they were all addressed by one title or another—Engineer Blaustein, Professor Hirsch, Magistrate Fein, Attorney, Senator—here they were nothing. Their former positions, and their current pretensions about them, would have been looked upon with amusement by Americans. So they had only each other to look to for validation of their identities, acknowledgement of their true worth and achievements. But now, in this new country, those old positions, those old titles meant little; it was money and success that counted. And some of them were getting there, through different routes. The doctors took some refresher training and set up practices. True, most of their patients were other refugees, but they made money, they lived well, and above all, they had high social status. There were those who went into business and prospered, importing all sorts of things, selling vast quantities of merchandise during these times of shortages. They moved into large apartments on Riverside Drive, or even Park Avenue, in elevator buildings, and their wives wore fur stoles. At the Club, they were sought out. They became smug, but also they exhibited a sense of noblesse oblige, but only up to a point: the "oblige" referred to a generosity in giving advice, the "noblesse," to their sense of themselves.

The lawyers fared badly—their skills were not transferable. They, like Rachel and Aleks, were on relief from HIAS, till they found something. And also, there was a counter-hierarchy, the hierarchy of intellectuals, who sneered at the businessmen.

"He is prosty," Aleks said of Gordinek—simple, a Philistine. "I was at his apartment, a very elegant place, Persian carpet, chandeliers, on Park Avenue! And there was a whole wall of books, beautifully bound, engraved leather. I thought I had misjudged him. Here was a man who had a whole magnificent library. I pulled a book out of the wall to leaf through it—and it was empty! Imagine, just a box for show. Here he is pretending he has all those books, and they are only decoration!"

Aleks sometimes went to the Writer's Club on weekday nights. Rachel encouraged him to go. There he was greeted warmly. It was a different atmosphere. The arguments were louder, more impassioned, more concerned with socialist politics, Yiddish writers, hollow-cheeked poets. They knew of Aleks, they had read his column in Czestochowa, his writings in Warsaw. They welcomed him at their tables, but they couldn't help him find his place.

"I don't belong there," he told Rachel. "They know what they are doing; they are writing or they are dreaming of writing. I have to make a living. I don't know how they manage it."

"You should write too, Aleks. It's what you do best. Or go to the Jewish Committee. There must be a special job for you. You know so much. They should be overjoyed to have you!" Rachel said.

"If they want me, they know where to find me. No one is offering me anything."

"You have to push yourself, Aleks. You're always waiting for them to find you; you have to find them! They're jealous of you. You know more than any of them."

Rachel got a job selling advertising space for a Jewish newspaper. She wanted to save some money so she could enroll in the Trafagen School and learn to make hats. "Hats?" Aleks said disbelievingly. "Why hats?"

"I like fashion and maybe I'll become another Lilly Dache. I will have the highest clientele. And you can become very rich in that."

Aleks was finally persuaded to write a book on the History of Judaism in Poland, and spent his days between the library doing research and the apartment where he typed on a battered but workable Underwood he had obtained from a friend in the Writer's Club. In the evenings they would meet friends and walk up and down Broadway, from 72nd street to 96th street, talking, debating, stopping in at the cafeteria on Eighty-Third Street for tea and cake, or at the little coffee shop on the west side of Broadway. Always they would run into someone else they knew, from Poland or Russia or Japan. Rilka had found a friend in school, Elzbieta, who was exactly her age and who also could speak no English, and the two girls introduced their parents to each other. Somehow, everyone on the West Side knew everyone else. They had come from different towns and different strata in society, but they had a common bond in their refugee status. But still, there were the rich and the poor. Elzbieta lived in an elevator building in a large apartment with river view, Rilka in a walk-up, in two rooms, always messy.

Rachel hated being poor. She said to Rilka one day, "Go to the grocery and get a loaf of rye bread and a container of milk. Tell the grocer I'll come by tomorrow and pay for it."

"I have to do my homework," Rilka said.

"It's just on the corner. It'll take you five minutes."

"I have a stomach ache," Rilka said.

Rachel sighed. She knew Rilka hated to go without enough money to pay. She went herself.

"I forgot my purse," she said to the grocer. "I'll stop by tomorrow."

"All right, all right," he said, not looking up at Rachel. He was putting up price signs on bins of fruit and vegetables. A teenage boy, the grocer's son, made his way past Rachel with a carton he was delivering. There were no other customers in the store.

"Thank you," Rachel said. "I'll be here by tomorrow evening."

"I know you will. But you can pay me at the end of the week. Don't worry."

They lived on relief money from HIAS and on Rachel's small earnings from the newspaper advertising. She had thought it would be for a month or two at most, but now it was eight months already.

Rachel stood behind a long table, laden with moon-shaped, sugar-sprinkled cookies, long strips of apple strudel, and slices of pound cake, and poured tea from a large, silver-plated samovar, donated to the Club by Genia Jaster, the wife of one of the refugees who had made money in Shanghai. Jews who had not left Japan before Pearl Harbor were sent to Shanghai, where many died of typhus and others became rich. Rachel had volunteered to be a hostess on the last Sunday of every month. There was a pleasant din all around of mostly Polish conversation, with occasional English sentences. It was a large room in a residential hotel on Seventy-Second Street, and in one corner a gramophone was playing softly and two couples were dancing a foxtrot. Rilka was playing chess with Elzbieta in another corner and some adults were giving them advice on moves, much to the girls' annoyance. They had just learned to play chess and it was all they did in every spare minute. Checkers was no longer of any interest to them. Lusia, the Gordinek's fifteen-year-old daughter, her long blond hair glowing, her overly large bosom shaking as she laughed, was surrounded by gangly boys. The Gordineks were playing gin rummy with the Lazars and a bridge game was in progress at the table next to them.

The late afternoon autumn sun threw shafts of light onto the polished wooden floor through the parting of the heavy velvet drapes. Aleks, sitting at a table near one of the windows, was half bathed in a beam of illuminated dust particles while the other half of his face was in shadow, giving him a mysterious look. He sipped his tea from a glass and was engaged in conversation with two gentlemen whom Rachel didn't recognize. She had been standing at her post for nearly two hours and her feet hurt. She decided to take a break and brought her cup of tea and a plate filled with little cakes to Aleks's table. The men rose as she approached and Aleks held out a chair for her.

"Jake Goldfarb," one of them bowed and introduced himself. "A pleasure, a pleasure," he said with a strong Yiddish accent. Jake was portly, slightly balding and well-dressed in a pinstriped suit that made him look a little thinner.

"Aaron Duellen," the taller of the two men added, as he took Rachel's hand and lightly kissed it.

"Jake is in leather goods, mostly from Brazil. He sells to all the big department stores," Aleks explained.

"There is a lot of money to be made now," Jake said. "The big problem is suppliers. I can sell anything, but to get the merchandise … ah, that's not so easy. The importers are in the driver's seat now—they act like God, debating what jobber they'll sell to and who they won't. I told your husband to come and see me, maybe we can do something together."

Rachel raised an eyebrow. "My husband is writing a book."

"A book? What kind of money can he make from a book?" Jake patted his stomach with satisfaction. "Aleks, you come to my office tomorrow, we'll talk business. You come to this country—you have to establish yourself, *then* you can write a book!"

"Why don't you import directly from Brazil? Why buy from the importers? "Aleks asked.

"More risky," Jake leaned back in his chair and lit a cigar. The smoke made Rachel cough. "The importer has to lay out the money. I buy after I have a deal with the retailer. Practically no risk and easy to make money."

Aaron turned to Rachel, "And what are you doing, Madame Mischler? Are you tending your kitchen, like most of these ladies here, while waiting for your husband to write a book?"

She looked at him with annoyance. She didn't like being made fun of, but she noticed he was smiling kindly.

"I am learning to make hats," she said, thrusting her chin up in the air.

"A beautiful woman like you, making hats! You don't need to make hats; you should have someone make them for you. You should be in business, not learning a trade. Take me: I came here a year ago, and now I am very well off. People respect me. What you need in this country is money. Money talks."

"And how did you make all this money?" Rachel asked trying for sarcasm in her voice, but finding herself very interested.

"A jobber—I'm a jobber also. Jake complains about the importers. We jobbers are just as bad. I decide where to sell and how high I can raise my prices. Corsets and brassieres, that's what I sell to the stores, all over the country. But I have my problems with suppliers too. My suppliers are factories and they decide what jobber to sell to. It's all the same, big fish deciding which little fish to eat. Come to my office next week. I know a lot of people. I'll introduce you around. Who knows? Something may develop."

Rachel felt a surge of excitement. Possibilities opened up before her. If she could only relinquish those notions of the need for intellectual superiority, of contempt for business. She was too sensitized by Papa's constant ups and downs before the war, by the borrowing and expanding and contracting, the uncertainty, and the illusions. And yet it was all so familiar to her, and so tempting, that ever present hope of getting rich, of never having to forget her purse when she went to the grocer's. Actually, she could easily relinquish her snobbish notions for herself; it was only Aleks whom she needed to keep untarnished. But even that was a mixed urge. She wanted him successful too.

"I'll come to see you," she said excitedly to Aaron. "Next week. And Aleks, you must see Jake. Tomorrow. Oh, how lucky we met you today. And we weren't even going to come, but it was my turn to serve. You never know what's around the corner. That's what is so wonderful about life."

Dr. Szosznitzki came to the Club on a September Sunday. He sat at a table with Aleks, surrounded by refugees, talking about the Sunday *Times* article reporting his information about the ghettoes. It appeared in the back of the paper, on page 31, but everyone there had read it:

> They are starving, they are dying, 500,000 in that little area in War-saw. There is a wall around it, from Dzika Street to Grzybowska. All Jews must wear the white armband with the blue Star of David. Or they are shot. Bodies are left on the street.

Szosznitzki had been there in the beginning; he had lived under the German occupation for several months. He had been a member of the executive committee of the Jewish Council before escaping. He had reliable sources.

"Sofie is there," Rachel said. "I sent packages every week, or a little money when I could. Of course I never knew if they got there, but they must have. Now we can't anymore. It's not allowed by the U.S. government to send money abroad. Something must be done! Perhaps Mama and Papa are there also. I have not heard anything from them."

"There is a ghetto in Radom," Szosznitzki said. "It is closer to Zarki. Perhaps they are there. There are seven thousand Jews in Radom. They are totally destitute."

"It's not possible, not possible …" Rachel murmured.

She thought of the last time she had been in Zarki, that summer when she had returned from England, before the nightmare began. She had taken Rilka with her. "Ruchele, Ruchele," Mama had cried when Rachel came through the door, unexpected, and had kissed her on her cheek, her neck, her hair. Mama had fussed over Rilka. She set before her a big plate of boiled chicken from the soup pot, with the dill clinging to it. Rilka ate half the chicken and sucked on the chicken feet with delight. "I want more lapki," she had said. In Mama's garden tall sunflowers grew and Rachel had bent their long stems so Rilka could pick out the black seeds. Rachel felt herself dissolving into Mama, felt that flow of adoration that exuded from Mama's soft body into her own, saw Mama looking at her with such untarnished, unconditional love, that she cried in pain and regret that she hadn't told Mama that she knew, she knew about that love, she too felt it, even if she didn't visit Mama enough, even if she hadn't seen Mama for months, she returned that love … and now it was too late, too late to tell Mama. Now Mama was in the ghetto in Radom—or worse.

Rachel was preparing a sweet carrot pudding for Thanksgiving.

"Not carrots," Rilka said impatiently. "Sweet potatoes."

"I don't know what sweet potatoes are. How can potatoes be sweet? This will taste good." Rachel was trying to do it right but this was not her holiday. Rilka had insisted on Thanksgiving. She had been cutting out paper turkeys for two weeks. She practiced poems about Pilgrims in her poor English and she had a walk-on role in her class play. She spent most of her time with Elzbieta and the two of them were not befriended by the other children. But they did not seem to mind; they had each other. And in fact, it seemed to Rachel, they liked their separateness. But Rilka wanted a turkey and all the trimmings. Rachel bought a large chicken, a capon really. There were only three of them and it was cheaper. Rachel kept a little notebook where she entered every penny spent, subtracted it from the week's allotment, and knew she did not have enough remaining for a turkey.

"A small deception leads to big deceptions," Aleks had said when she told him about the turkey. "You should tell her the truth. If we can't afford it, we can't afford it. She is old enough to know that."

"But it's harmless. A little fantasy doesn't hurt either. And if she believes it is a turkey, then it is. What does it matter what it really is? It really is what she thinks it is."

Aleks had kissed her neck, "Perhaps you're right. You have that talent for creating your own reality to suit you. It's a gift."

In the evening they sat down to Thanksgiving dinner. Aleks wore a navy blue suit and a tie and made Rachel put on her black dress with the white lace collar, though she protested there were only the three of them, why dress up.

"I dress for myself—and for you. You know the story of the British gentleman whose ship sank and he was stranded on a desert island. He dressed in a tuxedo for dinner every night. To represent the British Empire and civilization. Of course it's a good thing his butler and his trunk were stranded along with him."

Aleks gave a lecture on American history while Rilka fidgeted.

"I know all that," she said. "I know more than you. We learned it in school."

"Well," he concluded. "The Pilgrims gave thanks for landing safely in America and we also give thanks for landing safely in America."

Rachel took the bird out of the oven and put it on a platter. It was golden brown, with crisp skin and a delicious smell, but it was small.

"That looks like a chicken," Rilka said.

"It's a turkey," Rachel said. "Haven't you ever seen a turkey?"

"I saw pictures of a turkey and it was much bigger and fat across the chest."

"It's a turkey. You wanted a turkey, so I got you a very special turkey. But since there are only three of us, it's a small turkey."

"Well, it tastes good," Rilka acknowledged. "But it's so familiar. I expected, well, something different."

"You can go to school and tell them you had Thanksgiving turkey, just like everyone else."

They had been in America only nine months before Japan attacked Pearl Harbor. "How could this happen," Rachel asked Aleks, "when the Japanese were so good to us? How is it possible? They must already have been planning this when we were there." But four days later America, already at war with Japan, declared war on Germany and everyone in the refugee community welcomed this news, convinced now that the Nazis would soon be defeated.

Every day Aleks went out to look for suppliers of leather goods for Jake, to talk to importers, to try to learn how to start his own business. He was not writing at all now, and he hadn't yet earned a penny. And he was getting more irritable every day. He and Rachel argued over small things, often yelling at each other while on the radio the salubrious voice of Gabriel Heatter droned on in the background, bringing more news of defeat in Europe.

"Open the windows," he said one night after dinner.

"You're not a cripple. Open them yourself. You could help me a little, instead of telling me what to do. The sink is full of dishes and you sit there and read a newspaper!"

"Why does it get to be such a mess in the first place? Why don't you clean up when you work?" He waved his hand towards a pile of clothes tossed onto a large armchair, to the dinette table, covered with the paraphernalia of her hat-making. She had gone to see Aaron the week after they met at the Club but he was busy and nothing had come of it. She had decided to stick with making hats.

"I work hard enough." She was shaking with anger. "I go to school, and every day I try to make some money for us. On top of that, I shop and cook. I take care of everything Rilka needs. All the other wives sit around and play cards with each other! And you, you never finish anything! If you stuck with the book, you could get a job at the Jewish Agency, instead you run around with Jake. He won't help you. He's out for himself, and you're so naïve, you don't even see it!" She turned her back to him and bent over the sink. Her eyes filled with tears.

Rachel was in her nightgown, her robe, half open, drawn loosely around her. Wearily she walked over to the dinette table and began to throw into an empty carton the pieces of felt, ribbon, plastic fruit and flowers, bits of straw facing which she used to concoct those wildly imaginative, monstrously absurd hats, with plumes and clusters of plastic cherries and feathers at jaunty angles. How sad it was, how sordid, how hopeless. Aleks came over and put his arms around her. She leaned her head on his shoulder and all her muscles sagged. He stroked her hair, and with the deepest sorrow in his voice, said softly, "It will be all right. It will be all right. Things will change."

The next morning Rachel went to see Aaron. She lived in the valleys between defeat and hope. After that sad evening her determination had increased. She decided she would convince Aaron to let her be a rep, to sell his merchandise, to build up her own list of customers. After all, he said he had no trouble selling, only getting suppliers. Aleks also, with new determination, went off to see Jake. Rilka was left alone.

"Go play with Elzbieta—I mean Betty," Rachel said. Elzbieta, who wanted desperately to be an American, insisted everyone call her Betty which she thought was a typical American name, but Rachel was always forgetting. "I'll be back by two."

She convinced Aaron to let her sell and she went off immediately to small shops on Fifth Avenue and Madison Avenue and the side streets. Other reps had already wrapped up the department stores and she thought she could make a niche for herself in areas the other reps wouldn't handle because it was so much work for small sales. She walked all day in the blustery wind but made no sale. Perhaps because it's still part of the holiday weekend, she thought. She would try again on Monday. She got home at five o'clock, tired and discouraged. Genia Jastrzek was sitting on the couch, holding Rilka in her arms.

"What happened? Oh my God, what happened?" she cried.

"What happened?" Genia said harshly. "You left this poor child alone! She thought you were dead!"

"Oh." Rachel breathed a sigh of relief. "I told her I'd be home in the afternoon. Rilka, how silly of you to worry. I said I'd be home."

"You said two o'clock." Rilka accused her.

"It's five now. How can you do that to her? Why didn't you call? Rilka called me an hour ago and she was hysterical. What is the matter with you?"

Rachel flushed. Her brief feeling of guilt gave way to anger. How dare this parasitic woman scold her?

"Genia, I have to work. Someone has to earn money for this family. We don't want to accept money from charities. If you were any sort of person, you would work too. You would at least help your husband. I know he has money but he works very hard for it, while you go out for lunches."

"In my family, women don't work!" Genia said scornfully. "Everyone knows what you are like. No one likes you or Aleks. He just criticizes everyone and thinks he knows more than anyone else. He's a snob and he doesn't have a penny. And *you*—you push yourself into everything and Aleks just hides behind his books. If he had so much brains he would earn a decent living. What kind of husband is he? He should support you and you should take care of Rilka."

Rachel was shaking. She kept her voice low and controlled and her face was white.

"Genia, please don't tell me how to live my life. Is this what you call being a friend? What have I done to you to make you act like this? Please, leave us alone. I must lie down. Please leave now."

Rachel fell on her bed as soon as the door slammed behind Genia, sobbing uncontrollably. Rilka was horrified.

"I'm sorry, Mommy, I'm sorry. I should never have called her. I was so afraid something happened to you. I didn't know what to do. Oh, I hate her, I hate her. I'm going to call her and tell her I hope she dies!"

"No, it's all right. Just get me a poultice, a wet cloth. My heart is pounding. It's all right. I should have called you. Oh, we are so alone. So alone. Only Aleks and you and me. We must help ourselves."

She lay on the bed, breathing deeply. The phone in the hall rang. Rilka got up to answer it.

"It's Daddy. He wants to speak to you right away. I told him you were lying down." She looked frightened again.

Rachel went to the phone. "Oh Aleks," she said, "come home."

"Rachel," Aleks's voice was strong with excitement. "I just earned five hundred dollars! My first five hundred dollars! I got a supplier for Jake, a big importer, and Jake gave me five hundred dollars! This is the beginning! I'm bringing wine, get out the glasses!"

Rachel ran back into the apartment and twirled Rilka around.

"Daddy earned five hundred dollars! Everything will change now!"

-19-

Aaron turned out to be a friend. He set her up as a jobber, taught her about the corset and lingerie business, and in the beginning even provided space at minimal rent, a windowless office, at the farther end of Aaron's full floor suite on Thirty-Second Street and Madison Avenue. She made contacts with a number of bra and corset salesmen to whom she paid a percentage for any sales they made to the stores. Though she had once dreamed of a beautifully decorated room with carpet and flowers and a spotless mahogany desk from behind which she would dispense assignments to her own large staff of reps, she was happy to have this space that was her own, and grateful that Aaron was so kind to her. Late in the morning one day, when she was particularly harassed, the phone rang. Rachel picked it up on the fourth ring. Her desk was cluttered with order forms, ledger books and an old calculator, and she was irritated because she could not find the list of her salesmen that contained their individual commission rates.

"Hello," she said sharply into the receiver.

"Rachel," the voice was low, sure.

Everything stopped. The sound of traffic, blaring and insistent a moment before, was muffled. Only her heartbeat pounded, only the rush of blood in her ears.

"Rachel," the voice repeated, "Rachel, are you there?"

"It's you. How … where are you? How did you find me? Roman, is it you?"

"I'm in New York. It wasn't hard to find you. The HIAS. I know where you live. But I didn't want to talk to your husband! I wanted to talk to you at your place of work. Your boss is a friend of mine. I'll be there in twenty minutes. We'll have lunch at Longchamps."

"Where is Sofie? Do you know where she is? Is she alive? Someone told me she is dead. It's not true. Did you come straight from England? What are you doing here? Do you—"

"Rachel, wait, wait," he laughed, that familiar, deep laugh, that dear laugh, "I'll tell you everything over lunch. No, I don't know where Sofie is. I don't know if she's alive."

Rachel sat at her desk and stared at the wall numbly. All those years, all that had happened in between, and still that same flood of feeling! How was it possible? Oh no, she thought, not the same feeling, only the memory of it. No, she was not going to resume anything. This was just an involuntary response, to be suppressed and controlled. In the evening she would tell Aleks she had run into an old friend from London. She ran into the bathroom, applied lipstick and a dab of powder and rearranged her hat, shaping the broad brim to a more flattering angle. As she entered the restaurant, she saw him talking to the maitre d', came up behind him and touched his arm. He turned to her abruptly. What will happen now, she thought, as his lips brushed against her ear and his breath was hot.

"I have no news for you about Sofie," Roman said when they were seated at Longchamps. They were sipping vermouth in the crowded restaurant. It was a hot late August day. The room was filled with soldiers and sailors and young women in summer dresses. Rachel had taken off her straw hat and it lay on an empty chair next to hers. Her hair was slightly disheveled and little beads of sweat lined her upper lip. She wiped it with a napkin.

"You are especially appealing in the summer time," Roman said. "I never saw you like this."

"Yes, it was spring in London, waiting for summer to unfold," she said in a melancholy tone, her eyes distant.

"And you ran away."

"And it was a good thing! I would have been trapped in London. Aleks would never have taken Rilka out of Warsaw, alone with him. God knows what would have happened to her!" She shuddered. "We've heard terrible rumors. And Mama, Papa, what happened to them? Someone in Japan told me they were killed. But how could it be? Why would the Germans have bombed Zarki—it's not near anything, it's such a small village, it's just farms. Someone said they were in the ghetto in Radom. Perhaps they went into hiding. But how did you get out? When did you come to America?"

Roman smiled, "I left London shortly after you did. Went back to Poland, then to America. Just in the nick of time: I planned to go to the World's Fair in New York and managed to get passage from Gdynia on the S.S. Batory in July, just six week before the German invasion. My good luck. The German submarines sank the SS Batory just a few months later."

A gloom settled over them and they sat in silence while the waitress, in her black uniform and perky white apron, served them poached salmon and little new potatoes with parsley.

"I hear from Aaron you are doing well," Roman said at last.

"I am making a lot of money. Aaron let me have my own territory and I have several reps working for me. Goods are so scarce,—as long as Aaron supplies them I make money. And you, how long are you staying here?"

"For the duration of the war. Maybe for good. Depends on you."

"Oh no, no, not me. This isn't London. There can't be anything between us."

"We'll see," Roman murmured under his breath, but she heard him and shuddered.

❀   ❀   ❀

The limiting factor for Rachel's expansion was supply. She had plenty of demand, but supply was severely limited in wartime. And so she welcomed Roman's offer to help. Roman had interests in the factories that supplied Aaron. It was never entirely clear to Rachel what he actually did, but it was clear that Aaron needed him. Roman began to arrange for suppliers of the rubber and materials that went into the corsets and garments, to sell to the factories that sold to the wholesalers who sold to her—under the condition that they would keep her supply steady.

They had lunches at Longchamps or often they sent out for sandwiches and the three of them, Rachel and Aaron and Roman, ate in Aaron's office, the containers of coffee and sandwich bags spread out on his cluttered desk, while they talked about deliveries and sales territories and profit margins. I am having fun! Rachel thought, just plain fun. She knew the fun was tinged with a sexual undertone, the atmosphere charged, made all the more electric by her determined conviction she would not enter into an affair with Roman again. But what a relief it was from the constant worry about Aleks's struggles to earn money. What a relief to recapture some of the excitement of her youth.

Roman asked her to dinner one day and for the first time she was not truthful with Aleks. She told him she had to work late and then wondered why she didn't just say she was having a business dinner with Roman, as she had often done with Aaron, and then knew why she hadn't. They went to the Hotel Des Artistes, and sat in the velvet plush seats, with the gilt-framed, opulent paintings around them. Roman ordered for her, as he had in London, and she liked his presumptive, assured manner. Their conversation about business was surface only. She was flushed with wine and understood it was only a matter of time before she would overstep the boundary.

Rachel was making money and she told Aleks one day, "Let's move from here. We can get an apartment with another bedroom. Then it won't be such a mess and you won't complain." Often when she ran out in the morning, she just didn't have enough time to close up the living room couch where they slept, and he hated to come home to an unmade bed, with clothes strewn over it.

"Rilka should help you more," Aleks told her repeatedly. "She can make the bed when she comes home from school." But Rilka went to Elzbieta's house after school everyday and always tried to come home after either Aleks or Rachel were already there. Rachel was grateful. One friend is enough if it's a good friend, she thought, and she saw that Rilka was happy when the two girls were together, though they were so different from each other. Elzbieta's new American name suited her; Betty, with her wild blond hair, had such an excess of energy that she would run through the streets, her long legs flying, just for the sheer joy of it, while Rilka seemed embarrassed by her ebullience. Rachel was happy they spent every afternoon after school together, playing chess, going to the local library, climbing the apple trees in Central Park. Betty's mother baked a special chocolate cake and gave the girls a slice with a tall glass of milk. Rilka loved the ice cold white milk combined with the rich, swirly frosting on the cake.

"Well, I'm glad you have such a good friend, and that Mrs. Lauber has the time to take care of you. If I didn't have to work, I'd bake too," Rachel told Rilka, knowing she wouldn't. "I'm glad you don't have to be alone after school. I guess Mrs. Lauber is lucky not to have to worry about earning a living. But I wouldn't trade my life for hers!" she concluded, with a defiant thrust of her chin. Her life is so peaceful—and so dull, like white bread. She is a maid to her husband; she has no life of her own at all. My life may be difficult, but think of all the adventures I have had, and who knows what else life will bring. It's always exciting; there's always a challenge. Don't settle just for comfort, Rilka. Be somebody!"

"I love Mrs. Lauber," Rilka said, "and she is not dull!"

Rachel never insisted that Rilka help around the house.

❧   ❧   ❧

At the Polish Club one Sunday afternoon, they held a meeting, unusual because it was really a social club, but the news from Poland was so disturbing that they had to do something. Aleks suggested organizing a committee to send a special message to Roosevelt.

"They have sealed off the ghetto," one of the journalists reported. "The Polish Underground got word out to England, and some other messages got out to Istanbul and to Berne. They are resettling the people from the Ghetto."

"Resettling? Where?" Rachel wanted to know. "They're always talking about resettling the Jews. The Polish Government in Exile talks about it in England: resettle the Jews, to Madagascar, to China, just to get them out of Poland. But Britain won't let Jews into Palestine. Where are the Germans resettling them?"

"They say to the East. The Ghetto Judenrat in Warsaw received an order on July twenty-second that all Jewish inhabitants will be resettled in the East. The Judenrat has to see to it that it will happen. The Jews have to report to the Umschlagplatz and from there the trains take them away, maybe six or seven thousand a day."

"But why are they helping the Germans in this?"

"The Judenrat was created by the Germans to help them govern the Jews. It came from the old Kehilla, the Jewish Community Council, so it was a natural for the Germans. And I suppose the Judenrat people think they can do more good that way, save more people than if they refused altogether. But some of the Judenrat leaders don't think that. Anyway, some people volunteer ... the Germans offer bread and marmalade."

"Bread and marmalade! For bread and marmalade? To Siberia?"

"The hunger in the ghetto is bad, so the marmalade is an inducement. But there are exemptions to resettlement for someone who works for the Judenrat, or who has some essential work in the Ghetto that the Germans want. You know there are quite a few enterprising Germans who have set up little factories in the Ghetto. They use the Jewish labor and make a lot of money shipping things back to Germany."

Maybe Sofie has an exemption, Rachel thought. Or maybe she is at a factory in the Ghetto, or maybe even in Germany.

The journalists were passing around the newspaper. "Nazi authorities in Poland are planning to 'exterminate' the entire Warsaw ghetto whose population is estimated at 600,000 Jews," the Times article reported. Notices had been posted ordering the deportation of six thousand Jews from the Warsaw ghetto to the East. The Polish spokesman had said, "Up to now two trainloads of Jews have departed to their doom without anything further being heard from them."

"I should never have left Sofie," Rachel despaired. "How could I leave without her?

"You couldn't have known," Aleks said. "No one could have known."

But Rachel knew she had failed Sofie, she had failed Mama and Papa. How she regretted all those times she had promised and not gone to Zarki, not spent Shabbos there, let long stretches of time elapse between short visits. Come home more often, Papa had said, Mama wants to see you. But she had always been so busy, so thoroughly claimed by all the elements of her Warsaw life, that she couldn't find the time to go to Zarki. And Mama declined her invitations to Warsaw, and so much life passed by, so quickly and now it was too late. Too late. Oh, if we could only go back to those we love, knowing now what is important. But Mama herself would understand we couldn't redo our lives. You can't put an old head on young shoulders, she would have said.

After Aleks had gotten the large importer of leather goods as a supplier for Jake, and earned his first money in America, he systematically tried to make contact with other importers of leather goods. But it was mostly unrewarding; they all had their own arrangements already and Aleks was a nobody to them, a refugee who did not really even know the business. He made money only sporadically while Rachel's fortunes were rising. One day, however, he obtained a commitment for a large supply from the original importer who had given him his first chance, and he rejoiced. He decided that the only real way to make money was to be an importer himself, but he understood that while he could learn all the laws and intricacies of importing, he was not likely to get backing from the money lenders and so how could he finance such an operation? Besides, what he really wanted to do was write, but how could he make money at that? Who was interested in the history of Polish Jews or in his political opinions? A while before he had gotten a commission to write a chapter for the World Jewish Encyclopedia and he decided he would finish it. Perhaps that would launch him in the direction of his dream. And so he had his foot in both worlds, the intellectual and the business. "Stick to one path," Rachel advised. Mama would have said, "You can't dance at two weddings." Then one of the editors of the Encyclopedia offered Aleks the use of his home in North Carolina where he could have peace and quiet enough to write. He decided to go for a month. Rachel, ambivalently, both encouraged him and urged him not to go.

❧   ❧   ❧

It was early September. Herb Wicksler was the owner of one of the mills Roman dealt with. Rachel had met him through Roman and she liked him. He reminded her of her uncle in England. Herb was a large man, with a big belly, a hearty laugh, and a warm, expansive manner. He invited Rachel to a house party he was having in his Scarsdale home. Aleks was in North Carolina for the week and Rachel said she would come with Rilka. Roman too was invited, and Rachel was relieved Aleks would not be there.

The Wickslers belonged to the Westchester Country Club and they all spent Saturday there. They walked through the wooded paths and sat on the veranda sipping cool drinks in the late afternoon. Rachel watched a tennis match, a sport so foreign to her it was exotic, and Rilka, at first uncomfortable in these opulent surroundings, was laughing with the Wicksler girls as they ran around playing. Rachel realized with a pang of sorrow that she was unaccustomed to seeing Rilka laugh.

They had cocktails in the grand lobby of the club, with its soft armchairs and rich carpets. Two friends of Elena Wicksler stopped by and they greeted each other with a familiarity of long standing, and talked about tennis games and golf and hairdos. Elena was slender and perfectly groomed, even after a tennis game, and wearing exactly the right clothes, understated and expensive. She always wore one perfect piece of jewelry, sometimes a gold bracelet with an inset gem, sometimes just gold earrings to accentuate the bareness of her white shoulders, sometimes a little diamond pendant which sparkled in the hollow of her neck. Her hair was an auburn brown, cut straight and shoulder length. To Rachel, Elena was of another world.

Roman was playing golf with Herb and two of the other Wicksler guests and Rachel did not see him till they were back in the Wicksler house for dinner. He sat on her right and their thighs touched under the table.

Here Rachel felt outside of her own world of work and obligation and that perennial guilt mixed with desire, and so she gave up the struggle and let herself relax and permitted herself to enjoy it all.

"Tell him," Roman said. "It's time to tell him. I don't want an affair with you. I want something more permanent."

"I can't. Not now. I can't now."

"Then when?"

"I don't know. Not now. Oh, Roman, I love you. I love you."

She was burning, her skin was hot and moist, she pressed against him, she wanted to merge with his flesh. Roman's surprisingly small hands stroked her gently. His body glistened in the pale light of the moon shining in through the window of the second floor guest bedroom. Above, on the third floor, Rilka was asleep, sharing a bedroom with the Wicksler girls. Below their window, other guests were laughing and splashing in the pool. It was a cool spring night, but the pool was warmed and some brave souls went for a midnight swim.

Rachel liked the sound of the laughter drifting up. She took Roman's hand away from her body and placed it on his stomach and subdued her own rising excitement. She wanted to relish this moment, to extend it; she wanted a leisurely love-making. But Roman turned her around toward him, and the warm, hard touch of his body roused her and she caught her breath. She pulled out of his embrace, and stretched out on her back, arms spread across the bed, all moist, open, waiting. Suddenly he was upon her, urgently, and she was filled with him, filled to satisfaction, complete, holding him close, the sweat of their bodies mingling, till finally with one great gasp, his full weight was on her, his whole body relaxed, while she was still rising and falling. He buried his face in her hair, and she shuddered with the after-tremors, till at last she pushed him away.

Rachel sighed deeply. "I wish we could just stay here. Block out the world. Just live in this room and make love every night."

"We could," Roman said. "Or close to it. It's up to you."

"What will I do?" She turned away from him, towards the window. He put his arm over her, and they lay together in silence, but then she felt his body stir again, slightly, against her and she said quickly, "Go back to your room, now, before they come up."

She stretched out languorously among the soft pillows after he left. She was content, satisfied, calmed, for the moment. She knew it was only for the moment. Already she was returning to her own reality. She listened to the sounds of the swimming party downstairs breaking up, as the guests dispersed to their separate guest rooms.

What luxury this was! Rachel thought. This large house with its six bedrooms, the canopied beds, the vases with fresh-cut flowers from the garden below, a maid in black dress and white apron serving after-dinner brandy in large snifters on a silver tray.

In the morning Rilka came in to her room and climbed into her bed.

"Are you having a good time?" Rachel asked.

"Yes … I wish I could swim."

"Maybe we can find a camp through HIAS or some other organization. We'll ask Daddy when he gets back."

"No," Rilka said. "I don't want to go to camp."

She realized how little she knew of real life in America. This was real life. These were real Americans, Jews, but not refugees. But how was it that Roman who actually was a refugee did not seem like one; how was it he was so self-confident, so comfortable? Rachel concluded it was his money that made the difference. Being wealthy trumped the refugee reality. I could have this, thought Rachel.

❦   ❦   ❦

She stayed in the office late one evening, waiting for her salesmen to report in, when Roman entered without knocking.

"That's it, that's it," he shouted. "I am finished with him! Aaron can go to hell!" She had not seen him angry before. His face was red, contorted.

"What happened? Calm down, Roman, you'll have a heart attack!"

"He took goods from my factories, and sold them to a distributor in California, without telling me, without telling you. It's against every agreement we made—he is supposed to buy the goods and I get part of the profit from the sales to the distributors. He is a jobber; now he's acting like a factory owner and making a side profit. No more! His supply is finished! Let him get other suppliers. Those southern factories won't sell to him!" He stomped around the small office.

"Wait, wait," Rachel pleaded. "So if he made a mistake, tell him and he won't do it anymore. Don't just destroy everything."

"I will destroy him even if it destroys me, but it won't destroy me! Don't worry, I will come out on top! He'll be penniless. No one can do that to me." Roman had walked out of her office, slamming the door violently behind him, and she understood, with all the implications and ramifications of this flashing through her mind in a split second, that if Roman didn't supply Aaron, Aaron wouldn't supply her, and there would be no possibility of moving to a better apartment. Instead, there would be the trips to the grocer again claiming she forgot her purse. Oh no, she thought, that will never happen again, no matter what I have to do.

But Aaron found other suppliers, and though he was less able to help Rachel with merchandise, he let her remain in her little office in his place, rent-free.

"You are a good friend, Aaron," she told him. "I am blessed in my friends."

"And you are a good woman, Rachel, for all your tumult and fire."

She was grateful for that from Aaron. She did not think of herself as a good woman, not since Roman had turned up again. She was deeply fond of Aaron. He felt like a part of her family, and she and Aleks saw him often. He was not married and he wanted to be part of their lives. He played cards with Aleks at the Club and sometimes took them out to dinner, and sometimes came over for lunch to their small apartment on a Saturday or Sunday. Aleks liked him, even though he never read a book, and even though one day he had said to Rachel, "Marry me, Rachel."

"Are you crazy?" she had laughed. "I'm married. I love Aleks."

"It will be better. I'll give him ten thousand dollars. He can set himself up in business. I'll provide for you and Rilka. She'll have the best education. And it won't be so different. He'll be our friend. Now he is the husband, I am the friend. The other way I'll be the husband, and he'll be the friend."

"You are crazy. I love Aleks and I don't love you," she said. He looked so crestfallen, disappointed like a little boy, that she patted his arm and added, warmly, "But I do love you as a friend."

A few days later when she had come home from work, Rilka was out and Aleks was packing some things into a little suitcase.

"What are you doing?" she had asked.

"Marry Aaron," he had said not looking up. "He can give you a decent life. And I don't want any money from him. What does he think I am? I can't imagine life without you. It is not worth anything. But you have to do what is best for you."

She sat down on the bed. "You are both crazy," she said with amazement, "Crazy!"

Then she got angry. "He called you with this insane scheme? What am I, a cow? That you can sell and barter with? Did you ask me? Did you ask me if I love him? I don't love him! I love you! You can't just hand me over! Oh, I am sick of both of you!" She started for the door.

Aleks stopped her. "Do you love me?" His voice had an edge of desperation, and hope.

"Of course I do. I love you. This is so ridiculous!" He had her in his arms now and suddenly, they were both laughing.

"It's been such a long time," he whispered. "I thought I had lost you."

Aaron had remained the friend and he had let Rachel stay in her little office. But she had no salesmen now,. She herself went around to the stores, but she was just waiting … Roman had promised he would come up with something.

One crisp October afternoon, after Aaron had left for the day, Rachel sat alone at her desk, poring over her list of accounts, when the phone rang.

"Rachel, meet me downstairs in half an hour. I have a business proposition to make to you. We'll have dinner," Roman said in a tone that allowed no disagreement. He refused to come into Aaron's office suite after their fight.

"I have to be home for dinner. I'll have coffee with you. In half an hour."

The moment she hung up, the outer door opened. She felt a momentary fear and thought again she should lock herself in when no one else was around. She was both relieved and distressed when she saw it was Aleks.

"Aleks!" Rachel exclaimed, as he entered her office, "What are you doing here?"

"I thought we could go home together. I'm finished with Jake," he said quietly. "He doesn't need me any more."

"Oh … what does it mean? You don't have a job? What do you mean he doesn't need you?"

"He has one supplier now, a leather goods factory. They have an exclusive deal. There's nothing I can do for him. Don't look so unhappy. I'll find something else." He smiled sadly.

"Aleks, I can't believe it—you got him that supplier in the first place, and now he just dumps you? You can't let him get away with that! He should cut you in on it. You're just not aggressive enough. Why do you take it? Oh, it's awful."

He flushed. "If he doesn't need me, I am not going to push myself. He doesn't owe me anything—I got him a supplier and I made money from it. Now they have a permanent deal. There's nothing that says Jake has to be in my debt forever. You just don't understand those things! Now do you want to go home or not?"

She sighed. "I am meeting someone downstairs. We are going for coffee to talk about a new business. Come with us; maybe you'll learn something. His name is Roman. He's the man I told you about, the one who had the fight with Aaron."

Rachel preceded Aleks out of the elevator, saw Roman in the lobby starting to walk toward her, and stopped.

The elevator man said, "Have a good evening, Miss Rachel." She barely heard him. Later, she thought how rude she must have appeared. She was always so friendly to the elevator man. Aleks was at her side now, and she quickly took his arm. Roman looked surprised for a moment, then his face became impassive.

"This is my husband, Aleks," Rachel said quickly. Roman held out his hand and Aleks took it.

"I hope you don't mind if I join you. Rachel tells me this is a business meeting, but we have no secrets from each other," Aleks said, smiling.

"My pleasure," Roman answered, somewhat brusquely. Rachel said nothing.

"You have been very helpful to my wife," Aleks said as they were walking the two blocks to Longchamps. "We both owe you thanks." Rachel saw Roman's jaw muscle tighten at the word "wife."

"Rachel is a good businesswoman," Roman said. "Our relationship is mutually advantageous."

When they entered the restaurant, Roman headed immediately toward their customary table. The maitre d' nodded a welcome to them. Roman, absentmindedly, familiarly, started to pull out Rachel's chair for her. Just at the moment that Aleks began to do the same on the other side of the table. But Rachel was already halfway to Roman's side. There was a moment of awkwardness, as they all paused, mid-motion. Then Aleks, bowing slightly toward Roman, motioned with his arm to Rachel to take her seat where she was.

"Please, go ahead," he said, but his tone was just slightly colder, his voice had a question in it.

They ordered coffee and pastries. Aleks turned to Roman and asked if he had read a certain book. No, Roman had not read it. Aleks mentioned another book. No, Roman had not read that either.

"It is difficult, when one is engrossed in the daily cares of business, to keep up with what's au courant," Aleks said. "I am always encouraging Rachel to take a little time for that, so she doesn't become so narrow. But it is a struggle. She is busier and busier these days. Well, we are both happy you are helping her." Aleks hadn't touched his pastry, but he signaled to the waiter for another cup of coffee. Rachel drummed her fingers on the table impatiently.

"Roman," she said, "what did you want to discuss?"

"I have another source of merchandise for you., there is more. I am forming a new corporation and I want you to be an officer of it—perhaps Vice-President, or maybe President. No money involved. This is just a title. If you agree, I'll get the lawyer to draw up the papers."

"Why?" Rachel asked. "Why do you need me?"

"I need someone I can trust. A corporation has to have officers. You won't have to do anything." Roman was speaking directly to her, as if were unaware of Aleks's presence.

"Why not?" Aleks interjected. "If Roman needs a favor …" Rachel looked at him in surprise.

"Well, why not?" she said, suddenly gay. "Vice-President! Let's toast Vice-President Rachel!" She raised her coffee glass and clinked it first with Aleks, then Roman. "It's a deal. I get merchandise, and I get to be a Vice-President! Maybe even President!"

Aleks stood up and came to her side of the table and kissed her on the cheek, in a gesture that was clearly possessive.

"I must go," Roman said, rising, and placing a twenty-dollar bill on the table. "No, this is my treat," he quickly pre-empted Aleks's objections, and in an instant disappeared among the crowd of people waiting for tables and nearly blocking the way out.

-20-

On Thanksgiving Day that year, Aaron leaned back in his chair, opened his belt and let out a sigh. "Too much food, Rachel, too good. You worked too hard. I wanted to take you all out for dinner."

"No, no, it is our pleasure to have you as our guest," Rachel kissed him on the cheek.

"And we really had a turkey this year," Rilka said. "Definitely better than chicken." She began to clear the table they had set up in the small living room.

"Rachel," Aaron leaned over to her as he sipped tea from a glass in a silver holder. "You should watch out for Roman. I like having tea from a glass," he remarked, and in the same even tone, "Roman is using you."

"How can you say that, Aaron? He is going to make me President of Lady Ola Lingerie."

"What is Lady Ola Lingerie? President of what?"

"It's a small firm he's setting up. He'll supply me with merchandise and I'll sell it. Roman sells the manufacturers textiles from his mills and in return they'll sell me the finished goods, then I'll sell under Lady Ola Lingerie. But I'll get a new office. It wouldn't be right to use your space. But anyway, Roman will use Lady Ola as collateral to borrow money to expand."

"I see," Aaron said, stirring the sugar in his tea calmly. "You'll be the front for him."

Rachel flushed, "I don't know what you are talking about. You're just angry because Roman cut off those factories to you. But that has nothing to do with me."

"Wait a minute, Aaron," Aleks said. "Aren't you being unfair? Why not give him a chance? You can't judge a person before they do something wrong. So far he's been very helpful to Rachel."

"That's right," Rachel said, her voice rising with excitement.

"Just watch out," Aaron repeated. "There are more terrible things going on. Did you see today's *Times*?"

"Yes," said Aleks. "It is beyond belief that the world reads this and nothing is being done!"

"Where is it? I didn't see it. Is it about Poland? Let me look." Rachel scrambled through the crumpled paper. "I don't see anything."

"Buried on page sixteen," Aaron said.

Rachel spread the paper on the table. It was early evening. The street was quiet. Rilka had gone into her room to listen to the radio. Aleks leaned his elbows on the table, holding his head between his hands, his shoulders hunched forward. Rachel tried to focus on the headline "Slain Polish Jews Put at a Million." She forced her eyes down the column.

~

Plans outlined by Dr. Alfred Rosenberg, Germany's race theorist who says that the Jewish problem of Europe will be solved when no Jews are left. are systematically carried out … The Nazis make it plain that all Jews not wanted for military reasons must die. Poland is now a mass grave. Jews from all Europe are brought to the Warsaw ghetto and separated into two groups: the able-bodied young, and the children, old and sick, who are dispatched eastward to meet sure death … A government report tells how a mass electrocuting was carried out at Belzac. Deportees from Warsaw were packed into a barracks and ordered to strip naked, ostensibly to have a bath—then they were pushed into a room with a metal floor. The door was locked and current was passed. Death came instantaneously. A large digging machine was installed nearby to dig mass graves.

❦   ❦   ❦

At times it seemed impossible to Rachel that her life went on while in Europe her family was perishing. Though often she came home late, most evenings she and Aleks were at home in their small apartment. While Rilka listened to *The Lone Ranger* and *The Green Hornet* on the radio, they talked over their prospects for business. Then Aleks would demand absolute silence when Gabriel Heatter came on, bringing the news of the Soviet troop counter-offensive at Stalingrad in November of 1942. He sat in the worn armchair in the living room, smoking a Pall Mall cigarette; a radio announcer had told him, when they first arrived, that Pall Malls were the best cigarettes and, unfamiliar with the concept of advertising, he took it for the absolute truth and never changed brands. He used a long, ivory cigarette holder, like the President did. At special times there was the elegant voice of Franklin Delano Roosevelt delivering his Fireside Chats. Aleks was totally devoted to Roosevelt and continuously lectured Rilka, who impatiently had to listen, about what made him great, what made America great. When the President started with that familiar phrase, "My fellow Americans," they all three gathered around the radio, silently proud to be addressed as Roosevelt's fellow Americans. He, who had told his fellow Americans they had nothing to fear but fear itself, now discussed his plans to defeat the enemy. He asked his listeners to have a large world map before them while listening to him and there on the radio he gave a lesson in geography and strategy to explain why America had to fight at distances all around the globe. "From Berlin, Rome and Tokyo, we have been described as a nation of weaklings," he said. "Let them repeat that now! Let them tell it to General MacArthur and his men. Let them tell that to the boys in the Flying Fortresses. Let them tell that to the Marines!"

He exhorted Americans to sacrifice and he transformed a sleepy nation into a vast production machine, turning out airplanes, tanks, guns and ships. Rosie the Riveter was on posters everywhere; Uncle Sam warned that "Loose lips sink ships." In school Rilka saved her allowance and bought War Bonds. Along with her classmates, she sang "Oh beautiful, for spacious skies, for amber waves of grain, for purple mountain majesties, above the fruited plain, America, America …"

At the Club, Aleks organized meetings. They put together a petition to President Roosevelt. They went to see Rabbi Stephen Wise, hoping he would have influence, as chairman of the Conference of Jewish organizations. Aleks wrote a piece on the history of Jews in Poland. It was published in the Polish Jewish paper. Only the Polish Jews read it. He had started his own business being a jobber for small leather goods, but he paid little attention to it, preferring to write.

Rachel, on the other hand, plunged into work. She stayed late every night, poring over lists of customers and potential buyers. When Roman came, between his trips to the mills, and took her out to dinner, she called Aleks and said, "Make something for Rilka, I'll be late."

One night she came home after eleven to find Rilka asleep and Aleks not there. She called Genia and then Aaron. They hadn't heard from him. Panic overtook her. She walked across the hall to where those awful Hungarian women lived. She knocked on the door and burst in before there was a response from inside.

In the flamboyantly furnished apartment, with its zebra-striped spread on the couch, its red velvet throw pillows, its ornate reproductions of Renaissance landscapes, were the mother and her daughter. Aleks was sitting at the dinette table, a cup of tea in front of him. Magda, the mother, sat opposite him, her elbows propped up on the table, her head between her hands. She had jet black hair, piled in an enormous pompadour atop her round, powdered-white face, and startling red lipstick. Her eyes looked slightly slanted as she squinted in concentration at something Aleks had said. In her blue-green kimono, she almost had the appearance of a white-faced geisha in a stylized Japanese print. The daughter, Eva, who looked exactly like her mother, but twenty years younger, taller, slimmer, stood behind Aleks' chair and rubbed his neck. They all turned to look at Rachel.

"I was worried about you," Aleks said. "Where have you been so late?"

"You don't look very worried," Rachel said coldly. "I've been working. Someone has to earn a living." She turned sharply and walked out. Aleks came in behind her.

"Those whores, those whores!" she shouted as soon as he closed the door to their apartment.

"Quiet, Rachel, you'll wake Rilka. They happen to be very nice women who are struggling here like we are! You were unspeakably rude! They are always very kind to Rilka. Stop being so suspicious."

"I don't want them near Rilka! Or you!"

"Then be home more often."

"Then be a husband. Act like you have a family."

Aleks said nothing. Rachel lay awake the rest of the night, not daring to move, pretending to sleep. She was full of remorse, she wanted to take back those words, she hated herself, she felt mean and ugly and arrogant. Why did she attack him like that? Was she any better than those women?

Slowly, she rose to her own defense. After all, no other wife worked as hard as she. Even in Poland, when their life was stable, Rachel worked for her clothes, her luxuries. After all, Aleks paid more attention to his political concerns than to her and Rilka. After all, if he had made her feel that she was the prime focus of all his energies and passion, she would never have started that affair with Roman in the first place. But Aleks had always said no one person can own another. No one belongs to anyone else. Well, if he wanted her independent, she was being independent, and he would have to be prepared to take whatever came along with that. Roman didn't want her to be independent. Roman wanted to own her. And she wanted to belong to someone else, she wanted to be supported, taken care of, owned. Why was she even hesitating? Roman and she were perfectly matched, so what was holding her back? She was glad about Magda and Eva; now she could permit herself Roman. But in the midst of these thoughts, she recognized she was rationalizing. Oh, what did it all matter anyway, what did anything matter? She fell asleep towards dawn and when the alarm rang, couldn't get up. Aleks left the apartment before she was fully awake.

-21-

It was a dark and grim winter. The lights were dimmed in the blackout to hide the city in case of enemy attack. Aleks was an air-raid warden and went to training sessions every week. He was proud of performing his civic duty in his new country. He received a certificate of appreciation from Mayor LaGuardia, and he framed it and hung it up on the wall in their bedroom. Rachel looked at it sadly, thinking of the path that led from the highest-ranking Jew in the Polish Government to air-raid warden of his block. Rachel moved in a daze. She felt light-headed, as if floating in some milky suspension; her mind refused to focus. Only her work commanded her attention.

Business was brisk before Christmas and the store windows on Fifth Avenue were decorated with gaudy ornaments, while displaying signs exhorting personal sacrifice for the war effort. She recalled that Christmas so long ago in Czestochowa, tried to imagine the snow crunching under her fur-lined boots, her reflection in the shop window showing her glowing face under Papa's fur hat. Before Aleks, before her life began, at the brink, when everything was possible. But she didn't recognize that person as herself. There seemed to her no connection between who she was now and that young girl. Only the present exists, she thought once again. Did I ever have a life before this life?

But there was a connection! She had thought then how excluded she was by the pictures of the Virgin Mary and Jesus, by the Christian world around her celebrating something incomprehensible. She hadn't belonged then, in Czestochowa. She was really an outsider. Now, here in America, she did not belong either. She had no American friends. She moved only among the refugees. She was a refugee. She would always be a refugee.

❦   ❦   ❦

One sunny day in early April Rachel took the cross-town bus to the East Side at Eighty-Sixth street. The window was slightly open and the smell of spring rushed in with the breeze. She looked up, as if for the first time, and saw the early yellow buds of forsythias flowing over the stone walls that lined the road. The branches, like golden hair, spilling over, were budding! Tiny leaves were emerging from the tree limbs. Rachel took a deep breath and felt a rush of joy, a physical sensation in her stomach, which fluttered slightly, in her heart which beat a little faster, in her head, which cleared, for the first time in months. Unexplained joy, no reason, no cause, arising from inside her body. She smiled, in amazement, with gratitude. The winter was done.

❦   ❦   ❦

On May twenty-fifth in 1943, the London *Times*, which Aleks bought at the newsstand on Forty-Second street, reported two messages from the ghetto in Warsaw. The first, dated April twenty-eighth, stated "Today is the ninth day that the ghetto fights back. S.S and Wehrmacht formations lay siege. Artillery and lame throwers are employed and aeroplanes shower high explosives and incendiary bombs on the 40,000 Jews who still remain here. The ghetto is burning and smoke covers the whole city of Warsaw." The second message, dated May elevnth, said the resistance was nearing its end. In June, the headline read:

MURDER IN THE GHETTOES—WARSAW GHETTO WIPED OUT

From Poland itself the reports, confirmed by independent intelligence, prove that in many towns the worst fears of a few months ago have been realized. German explosives and guns are silent now in the Warsaw Ghetto, after a month of unparalleled murder in Russia. The Red Armies report that when they advanced last winter into liberated villages, they found that the Jewish inhabitants had almost everywhere been murdered by the German soldiers. Russians were hanged and shot as well in large numbers, but for a Jew to escape was exceptional. Allied peoples often are dumbfounded when Hitler continually raves against "the Jewish clique who began the war." Few people can follow the trends in his twisted mind. What is certain today is that the rage has found outlet for itself in a terrible form, not yet to be measured in scope. The ravings have to be taken as statements of a policy systematically applied.

"Sofie …" Rachel wept. "Sofie must have been in the Warsaw Ghetto. How could they resist the Germans? Why didn't they surrender?"

"They fought with homemade bombs, with smuggled guns, against the German tanks. The Germans set fire to smoke them out of the buildings and shoot them as they came out. They held out for a month."

"But why didn't you tell me this?" She felt faint. She had been standing at the window. Now she came over to the kitchen table where Aleks had the newspaper spread out, and sat down heavily in the chair.

"There was nothing anyone could do," Aleks said softly. "Telling you rumors wouldn't help anything."

"Sofie wrote she was going to volunteer for work in Germany. Maybe she wasn't in the ghetto. Maybe she was out. Maybe…." Rachel looked to Aleks for any thread of hope.

"Rachel, you have to put Sofie out of your mind. You are here. Rilka is here. I am here. We have to go on. When the war is over we'll go back to Poland and find who is left."

"No one is left. No one! We're left. We're here. Why are we here? How did it happen that we are alive and Mama and Papa and Sofie and … Oh God, they are all dead, and we are alive."

They held each other, and she was comforted by the warmth of his solid body, his strong arms enfolded her. They were both the same height and her cheek, damp and salty, was pressed against his. The two of them, together, an island in the midst of a turbulent stream rushing past them. They survived, while their world sped toward the rapids.

After Operation Barbarossa and the German attack on the Soviet Union, and now after the German surrender at Stalingrad in February, the first big defeat of Hitler's armies, people had begun to hope that the tide of war had turned. There was talk of an Allied invasion of Europe. The urgency of such an invasion was heightened by reports that Hitler planned to scorch Europe if he was defeated. At the end of September, the Zurich daily, *Volsrecht*, published the newest Nazi battle song, obligatory in all schools in Germany, translated by the American Jewish Congress and published in a Letter to the Editor in the *New York Times* at the end of December:

> We mount the thunderheads of war,
> Valhalla is our destined place,
> The earth be shattered to the core,
> When falls the master race.
> When Etzel forced the Nibelung band,
> His house crashed down in fire;
> So shall Europe, flaming stand
> When German men expire.

Total unconditional surrender by the Germans was demanded by Churchill and Roosevelt.

"My fellow Americans," said President Roosevelt in his fireside chat. "Over a year and a half ago I said this to the Congress: 'The militarists in Berlin, and Rome and Tokyo started this war, but the massed angered forces of common humanity will finish it.' Today that prophecy is in the process of being fulfilled. The massed, angered forces of common humanity are on the march. They are going forward—on the Russian front, in the vast Pacific area, and into Europe—converging upon their ultimate objectives: Berlin and Tokyo. I think the first crack in the Axis has come. The criminal, corrupt Fascist regime in Italy is going to pieces."

Rachel stopped going to the Polish Club. Aleks, on the other hand, went with more regularity. He was invited to give talks on Polish history, on Jewish literature, on the refugee problem. He was a member of a myriad committees, set up, disbanded, re-constituted under yet another name, all trying to decide what they could do to influence public opinion, the government, the bigwigs in the large Jewish organization, on how to help the Jews in Europe.

To Rachel it seemed it was all just words, pointless attempts to delude themselves into thinking that they had any power whatsoever to influence events, a game played by grown men to flatter their own egos. Rachel wanted no part of it. Nor did she want to be relegated to serving tea and organizing soirées, like the other women in the Polish Club. She could understand why no one paid any heed to their opinions. Most of them were ninnies, parasites in Rachel's eyes. They didn't work; they played cards and had lunch with each other.

"The women in my family don't work," Genia had said with contempt for Aleks for not being able to provide for his wife. Rachel knew the other wives in the Polish Club thought the same way. And so did the men. Even among her fellow refugees she was an outsider, different from the other wives, as Aleks was different from the other husbands. Only in Warsaw, only after she had married Aleks, when through him she was near the center of power, did she bridge two worlds, and felt on top.

Now that the course of the war had turned in favor of the Allies, now after D-Day, Aleks and his committees turned to planning for post-war Poland. Aleks wrote an impassioned piece titled "The Polish Government in Exile and the Jewish Question."

The opinion of the Jewish public, after more than twenty years of political struggle in Independent Poland on the minorities question, is alarmed that a new democratic order in Poland might be dragged down and destroyed by riotous nationalistic elements, who at the moment when the fate of nations and civilization is in the balance, have no more important worries than to consider the "Jewish Problem."

The Jews have always manifested their loyalty toward their Fatherland Poland, through sorrow and joy, triumph and despair. There has been no historic event in Polish history in which the Jew has not taken part wholeheartedly, defending his homeland where his forefathers have lived for over nine hundred years. The new Polish "democracy" must be founded on equal rights for the Jews and for all minorities. Sad to state, in spite of the lofty declarations and promises of the Government in Exile, though under the leadership of Prime Minister Sikorski, whose sincerity we do not question, this proof of democracy is not yet forthcoming.

"You would not think of going back to Poland, Aleks?" Rachel asked with some alarm.

"Who knows what will be after the war? This is my country now, but if I am needed … who knows?"

"There is no one left there. I could never go back. What are we, Aleks?" she said angrily. "Poles, Jews, Americans? We're a little of everything and we're nothing. We're refugees. Well, I'm going to stop being a refugee. To belong here, you have to have money. Thank God I'm making money."

"Don't be carried away by money, Rachel. You want to become like that ignoramus Roman? Who doesn't even read a book?"

It was the first time she heard Aleks say anything disapproving about Roman. He surely suspected something. She never lied and she never told and, mercifully, he never asked. But they had begun to lead separate lives, with only Rilka as the locus of their marriage. Rachel loved making money, loved not having to count pennies. Cleaning out a drawer, she found buried under crumpled stockings, a little notebook she used to keep when they first came to New York. She had a stab of pity for the person she had been, who had entered these items "Twenty-five cents—Rilka, three cents cents—New York Times, ten cents—grapefruits." And a wave of pride that she didn't have to do that anymore. And, unbidden and unexpected, a flood of compassion for Aleks.

She thought wryly that she would welcome Karola now, Karola that sharp, brilliant journalist of whom she had been so jealous in Warsaw. Now that Rachel was effective, now that she knew her own strength, she would have welcomed Karola as an equal, as a friend. Karola could advise her what to do about Roman. Karola, with her strong will and hard intelligence, would not tolerate the soft ambivalence that possessed Rachel.

Rachel was floating along, not really wanting to make any decisions. She had an abundance of customers, merchandise from Roman, a growing reputation as Lady Ola. Roman had made her officer of several companies of his, and periodically she received a check for some fee that Roman said was due her. She had insisted to Aleks that they move and found a suitable apartment on the East Side, with a large living room, full of light, looking out on Ninety-Sixth Street and Madison Avenue. It wasn't Park Avenue, but it was close. She and Aleks had a decent-sized bedroom at the end of the long, narrow hallway and Rilka had the maid's room off the kitchen. For the first time since the war began, they all had privacy.

❧   ❧   ❧

Sitting in her office one late afternoon, she picked up the phone on the first ring. It was a mill owner from South Carolina who called and asked to speak to the president of Burbank Manufacturers. Rachel was at a loss for a moment, until she realized that was the latest company of which she was supposed to be treasurer, though she had never seen any books of Burbank. She vaguely understood she was being blackmailed—either she went along with Roman or there would be no merchandise. She suspected there was something shady about it, but she never asked. She needed this self-delusion, because she thought she loved him. It wasn't dishonesty, she decided. There was an air of mystery about him, something secretive that intimated international connections with men of substance. The mysteriousness was part of his attraction, but so was his penchant for being the winner, his effectiveness, and perhaps, most important, his commitment to her and her alone.

The mill owner from South Carolina wanted to know where his money was. Roman owed him for $50,000 worth of "gray goods," unprinted textiles. Rachel knew Roman had recently sold a batch of gray goods to another mill for printing, but it was for $30,000.

"I'll get back to you," she said.

"Don't worry about it," Roman told her when she confronted him over dinner that evening.

"Roman, I don't want to be part of this," she said firmly.

"Don't question me and don't worry about it. It has nothing to do with you."

Aaron explained it to her. "He gets credit on the strength of these shadow corporations he sets up. And then, if he can't sell at a profit, he sells anyway but he simply doesn't pay his bills. The creditor wants his assets. But his asset doesn't exist—it's a shadow corporation. They could sue him, but it would cost them a lot of money, so they just don't give him credit anymore, but he finds other mills who don't know about him. I did try to warn you."

"But is it dishonest? After all, declaring bankruptcy is legitimate. If he can't pay because he can't sell, what can he do?"

"A really honest man would pay off his old debts before running up new ones. You're an officer in these new corporations he keeps setting up."

Rachel remembered that Aleks had given up her dowry so her father could pay off his debts.

❦ ❦ ❦

Roman was away for several months in the winter of 1945, traveling throughout the south, making personal contacts with the mill owners, to some of whom he was still in debt. It was in their interest to keep him solvent or they would never see their money, and so they continued to back him and give him credit. Rachel was no longer involved in his shadow corporations. He had bought a business for her, lingerie and custom-made corsets, but she was paying off his investment, slowly but steadily, and she expected to own it fully within three years.

Sometimes she marveled at the strangeness of fate—how she had envied that Leila, that mousy little guest at her first party in Warsaw, for owning a boutique. And now Rachel had her own salon on Fifty-Fifth Street, just west of Fifth Avenue, and a whole staff. Jean, her manager, supervised the fitter and eight women who sewed the garments. Her clientele was upper-class and included Mrs. Roosevelt and Mrs. Sulzberger, Judy Holiday and other famous people. It was a salon just as she had dreamed of in Warsaw, posh and elegant, and she was interviewed by Women's Wear Daily and photographed at showrooms. She kept the name "Lady Ola." She thought it suited her. "Lady Ola is here," the receptionist would say when she came to the showrooms to buy. But she found the retail and service business hard, and she worked long hours and weekends.

Though she saw Roman less frequently in the course of business, he was always on her mind; when she did see him, she felt the same physical pull that he always exerted on her. But they had not made love for many months. She wanted to feel cleansed, to feel she was a good person, and he did not want just another affair, as he had told her before. Roman was pressing her to marry him and she was in a constant state of agitation. Could she get divorced? What a scandal that would be. But Rilka was almost in high school now; she could withstand a divorce and her life would be better. But could Aleks withstand a divorce? He struggled so with his business and his writing and he loved her and needed her.

She said to Jean, her manager at Lady Ola, one day as Aleks left her store to go back to his office, and she watched him, looking older, looking tired, "Poor Aleks, he works so hard. I wish he didn't have to work so hard."

"Mrs. Mischler," Jean said in amazement. "Why would you be sorry he works hard? We are born to work!"

It was a new perspective for Rachel and it made her feel better.

❈   ❈   ❈

On April twelfth, 1945 the Little Flower, Mayor Fiorello LaGuardia came on the air on WNYC at 6:15 p.m. Rachel and Aleks had hurried home from their offices a couple of hours before as soon as they heard the news; they didn't know what else to do. Rilka had been dismissed from school early. The bells in the churches tolled. Now the three of them listened in silence. "Franklin Delano Roosevelt is not dead. His ideals live. Centuries and centuries from now, as long as history is recorded, people will know Franklin Delano Roosevelt loved humanity. I call upon all New Yorkers to carry on." An hour later Harry S. Truman was sworn in as the thirty-second President of the United States.

❈   ❈   ❈

Soon after, it was V-E Day. Europe was in ruins and no one knew if any of their family members survived. On May eight, 1945, the same day that the headlines proclaimed that the war in Europe was over, an article by C.L. Sulzberger inside the paper had another headline: Oswiecim Killings Placed at 4,000,000.

> More than 4,000,000 persons were systematically slaughtered in a single German concentration camp—that at Oswiecim in Poland, near Krakow—from 1939 to 1944. The Germans thus accomplished with scientific efficiency the greatest incidence of mass murder in recorded history.

-22-

Aleks brought flowers on Friday nights and they always had dinner together. Rilka set the table with a white tablecloth in the large dining room of their new apartment, usually just for the three of them, though sometimes Aaron joined them and occasionally a friend of Aleks's from the Club. It was a custom Rilka really instituted.

"The Laubers always have Friday night dinner. They have wine and candles and challah. We should have it too," Rilka insisted. Both Rachel and Aleks actually liked the idea and it became the one sure evening when they would be together, like a regular family, and Rachel felt like a real wife when she covered her face with her hands and blessed the Shabbos candles.

One Friday night, when there had just been the three of them, after dinner when Rilka went off to see Elzbieta, Rachel was leaning over the table, gathering up the cake crumbs from the tablecloth. Aleks had cleared the table and was carrying a small tray with wineglasses and dessert plates and she looked up and saw his face, caught unaware, as he headed to the kitchen. It had a look of such sadness that her breath caught. Not resignation, but sorrow borne in solitude. She suddenly became him, as if she were standing in his shoes, contemplating a life without her. And she felt a flood of love for him at that moment.

She walked over to him just as he was putting the tray on the kitchen counter, and kissed his neck softly. He turned and kissed her hair, and they stood wordlessly, close for a moment, then she went back to the dining room and rearranged the silver candlesticks, with the candles still burning. She saw that love for another could be nothing more than self-love, because it was she who was inside his very being at that moment of empathy. So perhaps that flood of love had been for herself. Perhaps that is what real love is, being so merged with the other person that self-love and other-love is indistinguishable. She had never felt that way with Roman.

❦   ❦   ❦

Rachel walked up the steps of the Plaza Hotel and headed toward the Palm Court. The war in Europe was over. It was a perfect day in June. The yellow forsythias, always a symbol of renewed life to Rachel, blossomed in Central Park, and the "doroshkies," the horse-drawn carriages for tourists lined Fifty-Ninth Street near the hotel, waiting for customers. The harnesses of the horses were gaily decorated with flowers and the drivers gossiped together and gave Rachel appreciative looks as she passed them.

Inside the hotel there were officers everywhere, army, navy, greeting each other, meeting women dressed in bright spring dresses, wearing short white gloves. There was a festive air in the grand, plush lobby. Enormous flower arrangements in huge vases were displayed in the Palm Court and the sounds of the tea orchestra playing Strauss waltzes greeted her, as she walked through the balustrade and glanced around looking for Roman.

"Madame?" the maitre d' bowed slightly, "May I help you?"

She spied Roman sitting at a side table and he half rose as he saw her.

"Over there," she said to the maitre d', and strode buoyantly across the large room toward Roman's table.

She wore a wide-brimmed beige straw hat, a pale peach French-cut suit, with a flared skirt, and a silk blouse accented by a double string of pearls, with the wide gold bracelet Roman had given her. A tall, exceptionally good-looking naval officer, sitting alone, looked at her intently as she passed his table, and she smiled down at him. I'm past forty, she thought! She felt beautiful and sophisticated and worldly and important, and not like a refugee.

She approached Roman's table at the far end of the Palm Court and felt that welcome tinge of sexual excitement, heightened by her recent good fortunes in business. Roman had already ordered a glass of sherry for her.

He started speaking as soon as she sat down, while she removed her gloves.

"Rachel, I'm going back to England after the summer, on the first sailing after the holidays. I want you to come with me. I am not waiting any longer. No, listen to me," he held her wrist across the table as she started to speak. "I don't mean for a vacation. I mean as my wife."

"A divorce ... Roman, in a month?"

"Don't be foolish. I know you can't get a divorce in a month. Your coming with me will establish adultery and abandonment. The divorce won't be hard to get."

"Adultery! My God, Roman. How could I do that to Aleks?" She took a big swallow of the sherry. Her hand trembled and she spilled some. She put her napkin over the stain on the tablecloth. Why did the prospect of divorce appall her so? Certainly she had contemplated it.

"Rachel," Roman's voice brought her back to this moment. "Rachel, why do you act so naïve?" He was exasperated. "What do you think you are doing? This is 1945. You don't have to wear a big red A on your bosom. You say you love me. I want to marry you. What is stopping you? In any case, Rachel, I am getting married," he said with a tone of finality.

In spite of herself, she smiled at his determination, his self-assurance that she would do what he wanted.

"No, you don't understand," he said, interpreting her smile correctly. "I mean I am getting married. My cousin has someone in mind for me. She's in Switzerland," he continued. Rachel was stunned. "She was in Poland in hiding through the war. Now she's in Zurich."

"You would marry someone you don't know?" Rachel said incredulously.

"I want you, Rachel. But I want a family. This woman is thirty-two years old. She comes from a fine background. I can't wait for you any longer. I don't think you'll have the courage to leave him."

"I don't know what to say. How much can you love me if you would just take any woman you don't even know in my place? One is the same as the other! No, not the same—the other is better, she's younger."

"Don't be bitter, Rachel. I want you. You can make up your mind and come with me. Then I will write my cousin and tell him to forget it. And I will never speak to him again about it. But I have to tell you, if I marry this woman, it is over between us. We will not see each other again."

Though they were living on the East Side now, on they still went to Rosh Hashanah services in the specially set-up ballroom of the old Ansonia Hotel just west of Broadway, as they always had when they lived on the West Side. Aleks loved this service, with some English, with some drama and a more literary symbolism, and of course with Jan Bart the cantor. But getting to the services presented a problem, since riding on a bus was proscribed on the High Holy Days, but the walk both ways, on both days of the Jewish New Year, from east 96th street to west 73rd street seemed too long. Aleks determined that on the morning of Rosh Hashanah they would ride to the services but walk back through the park in the afternoon. Rilka, imbued with the spirit of the Lauber family who were strictly orthodox, protested vigorously.

"It's so hypocritical! If you're observing Rosh Hashanah you can't ride. You're just making up your own rules. It's disgusting!"

"It's more difficult to be a Reform Jew," Aleks told her. "If you're orthodox, you know exactly what to do in every instance. You have no choices to make. If you're Reform, you choose the essence, the meaning. You decide what makes you a Jew. Besides, if you're so certain that it's hypocritical, why did you put up such a fight when you had to go to orthodox Hebrew school?"

"If you're so Reform why did you make me go to Hebrew school?" Rilka had rebelled and fought and complained when Aleks had made her go to the West Side Institutional Synagogue after school three afternoons a week to learn Hebrew.

"Because you have to be educated before you can choose to reject orthodoxy. If you don't know anything, you can't choose anything."

"Life is so much more difficult if you have to choose," Rachel sighed.

Rachel told Rilka, "What you learn is always with you, all your life. You can have money and lose it, you can have youth and beauty and that goes, but what you learn stays with you. It's your very own for all of your life and no one can take it away from you." Rachel believed that completely, but it struck her that she was speaking words that belonged to Aleks. In some important sense, her view of the world was through his eyes. She believed she didn't really exist before she met Aleks. It was he who taught her about everything. She discounted the young girl she had been, reciting poetry with Pavel in the forest, or the nascent persona who was a pioneer in Palestine with Jakob. Had she gone with Jakob, would she be seeing the world through his eyes? But she had had no idea who Pavel really was or even Jakob. She had incorporated Aleks into her and now she spoke his thoughts. Who was she herself then? Who was she when with Roman? Who was that woman who lived in action, and brimmed with passion at his presence? If she went with Roman to England, would she view the world through his eyes, those hard and practical eyes, focused on winning and succeeding, those eyes that saw the world as it really was? Would she become Roman? But what was the reality? Was Aleks's guiding myth, the value on learning, a rationalization because he was unable to succeed in America? No, he always held it, when he was at the peak of his success in Warsaw. But now he should have adapted. This was not Warsaw. Here money counted. So she debated with herself the entire week between Rosh Hashanah and Yom Kippur, trying to figure out who she was, knowing that after the Day of Atonement, she would have to face the answer.

❦   ❦   ❦

On the eve of Yom Kippur, they walked into the great lobby of the Ansonia Hotel, with its rococo turrets and towers, and took the elevator to the third floor where the services were just beginning. The vast ballroom, brightly lit with three enormous crystal chandeliers, was filled with over a thousand people. There was a hum of conversation as people greeted each other and exchanged news of families. Aleks and Rachel, with Rilka walking behind them, made their way toward their reserved seats. The din began to subside while they were still walking up the aisle, and people rose in an undulating wave, starting from the front as they saw the cantor and rabbi take their places at either side of the raised platform which served as the bima. The cantor, weighing over three hundred pounds, white robed and wearing a large, tall satin hat, converged with the rabbi, walking from the opposite side, in front of the Ark. They opened it, revealing the three Torahs Scrolls clothed in elaborately embroidered satin covers, capped with their great silver crowns. Assisted by officers of the congregation, they removed the Scrolls from the Ark, unclothed them and laid the largest center one on the reading stand in front of the rabbi. The cantor returned to his place.

Into the silence of a thousand people, the lone, pure tenor voice of Jan Bart broke through with the first mournful chant of the Kol Nidrei prayer.

"Kol Nidre-e-ey," the cantor sang in minor key, drawing out the notes which hung on the air like spun silk threads, vanishing … Absolve us of unfulfilled vows. Absolve me, prayed Rachel silently. Jan Bart, huge and solemn, swayed back and forth in his white robes and huge high white hat, and repeated the Kol Nidrei chant two more times, his operatic tenor voice gathering strength each time, ending with force. May we be absolved of them.

Everyone sat down and the evening service began. This was a special Day of Atonement, the first after the end of the war. Aleks refused to ride on Yom Kippur, though not on Rosh Hashanah, and so on the final Day of Awe, they would not ride. Since the whole of the next day till sundown would be spent fasting and at the services, they would stay overnight with friends on the West Side. Rachel and Aleks went to Aaron's apartment on Eighty-Sixth Streetto spend the night and Rilka went to the Laubers, grumbling about more hypocrisy, but pleased to be going to Betty's house.

The next day was crisp, brilliantly sunny, and as they walked towards the Ansonia down Broadway, they passed their friends going to various synagogues in the area. Everyone was dressed in their finest clothes. The women wore large hats with broad brims and new suits. The young girls strolled along Broadway in their new outfits, blushing and pretending to ignore the young men who walked purposefully with their fathers to the services. But outside the synagogues, the young people dawdled before going in and talked to each other and laughed and during the whole long day of services, there was much coming and going among the young people.

Inside, the cantor intoned, "Prepare to meet Thy God, O Israel ... This is the day of awe ... This is the day of decision ... This is the Day of Atonement." He swayed and beseeched, and pleaded and prayed, sometimes sobbing, sometimes praising creation in his purest, most lyrical tones. On this day, after the war, when the horrors of the concentration camps had been revealed, inside that room there was weeping and profuse sorrow, on this day when sins are confessed and forgiveness sought, the divine decision made: who shall be inscribed in the Book of Life for the year to come and who shall not. God is praised, sins are confessed, forgiveness sought, life examined and acknowledged to be fleeting. Rachel, enveloped in her thoughts, in this communal crowd still alone, with her own life and her sorrows and sins, wept for Sofie, wept for Mama and Papa and Aleks and Rilka and wept for herself. But not for Roman; she did not weep for Roman. At this moment she hated Roman for making her become the deceitful person she was. "For transgression against God, the Day of Atonement atones; but for transgressions of one human being against another, the Day of Atonement does not atone until they have made peace with one another." Could she atone to Aleks, to Rilka?

> "O soul, with storm beset, Thy griefs and cares forget!
> Why dread earth's transient woe,
> When soon thy body in the grave unseen
> Shall be laid low,
> And all will be forgotten then, as though
> It had not been?"
> Wherefore, my soul, be still!"

She read the meditations during the Memorial Service, tears running down her cheeks.

"Therefore, rebellious soul,
Thy base desires control;
With scantly given bread
Content thyself, nor let thy memory stray
To splendors fled."

If she could only stop wanting so much, stop caring so much. Oh no, her own rebellious soul intruded, no, God help me never to stop wanting. That is death—to stop wanting, to stop caring.

As the sun was setting Rilka, who had been outside most of the day, came down the aisle and made her way to her seat next to Aleks. He insisted she be there for the concluding Nieleh service, so they could end the day together. "Shema Yisrael," Jan Bart sang. "Hear O Israel: The Lord our God, the Lord is One."

An old man standing beside the rabbi put the curved ram's horn to his lips and blew a long clear note on the shofar. Aleks turned to Rachel and kissed her, while she had her arm around Rilka and the three of them stood hugging each other while the rabbi pronounced the benediction. Rachel looked at Aleks. His hair was gray at the temples and thinning on top, but his shoulders were straight. Rachel had a vision of Aleks in the Great Synagogue in Warsaw, when he was young and hopeful and she was a new bride. "Rejoice, O bridegroom, in the wife of your youth, your comrade," the men had sung.

They filed out and the crowds streamed down Broadway. It was dusk and some of the food stores began to re-open. They stopped in Sammy's and picked up schmaltz herring and black bread, and took the bus across town on Ninety-Sixth Street. Aaron was coming to break the fast with them, and they waited for him before taking that first bite of food and drinking a glass of slivovitz. There was nothing like that first taste of the salt herring on black bread spread with butter.

It was late at night, after they had eaten, after the final cup of tea and slice of nut cake, after Aaron left, and Rilka went to sleep, that they cleared the table together, not speaking, both aware that on the next day, they would face the unspoken future.

-23-

Rachel returned home from work earlier than usual the day after Yom Kippur. Aleks was already home and greeted her at the door.

"There's a message for you. An undelivered telegram. From Poland."

"From Poland? Who could it possibly be?"

"Solarek—maybe he's answering our cable—at last!"

Senator Solarek had returned to Warsaw after being freed by the Russians, they had been told. He was an old friend from Aleks's days in the Ministry. They had sent him a cable to find out if he knew anything about the family.

"Oh, he must know something then, he must have found out what happened to them all." Rachel stood in the middle of the room, paralyzed.

"Don't expect too much," Aleks said, retracting his earlier excitement, as Rachel's face drained of blood. "It must be a return of the one we sent to Solarek. They probably couldn't find him. After all, we just sent it care of the Joint Distribution Committee. The chances are a million to one that they actually located him. All those displaced persons. Impossible! We were foolish to even try. Anyway, they'll redeliver the telegram tomorrow."

"It can't be. They would have said it was returned. No, I can't wait. I have to find out." She picked up the phone and called information, then Western Union. She tapped her pencil on the table edge nervously.

"They're closing," she said, "I'm going down there."

"Wait till tomorrow," Aleks said. "If they're closed it will be a wasted trip."

"No. I'm going to the main office." She grabbed her coat and ran out the door.

All the way down to Wall Street, as the subway roared and lurched, she forced her mind to stay blank. She concentrated on the ads along the subway wall. She looked at Miss Subway. This month it was a pretty girl with short dark hair and an upturned nose. They always have upturned noses, thought

Rachel. Miss Subway's favorite hobby was sewing doll's clothes. She had a vast collection and had won prizes. This was her other life, when she wasn't being secretary to an important lawyer.

Rachel emerged from the subway, amid a crush of people, like ants she thought, and ran off to the telegraph office. It was closed. She rang the bell urgently and a man came to the door. He was tall, with a blond mustache and unruly hair, about forty or so, and he stooped a little, as if he could barely fit in the room.

"We're closed."

"I must come in. There was a telegram for me, from Poland."

"Well, you'll have to wait till tomorrow. All the telegrams that were undelivered are sorted in their sacks for tomorrow's delivery."

"Let me in. Please."

She pushed her way in and he let her pass into the vestibule.

"Lady, I can't do anything about it."

"You don't understand. It's from Poland."

"So, it'll wait till tomorrow."

She was crying. Now she knew it had to be from Moniek. She was convinced it was from Moniek. "They were all killed. I heard they were all killed. It's from someone who knows. I have to see it."

"I can't do anything," he said, but his voice was wavering.

"Then I'll wait here till tomorrow," Rachel said with determination." I'll sleep in the lobby. You can't force me out." She moved further inside.

"Lady, please, what can I do? I'll be fired if I tamper with the mail. I'm just on night duty. Go home, please go home."

"Tell me who it's from. Just tell me what it says. You don't have to give it to me. Just find it and read it. Then you can put it back. My parents were killed. Please."

He must have seen the newspaper photos of the concentration camp victims. He couldn't possibly ignore her desperation. He stood uncertain of what to do. Rachel kept pressing him. "Please, please. You must do this for me."

"Well," he said. "I could lose my job." But he went inside the large room, behind the counter and she waited. He came back in few minutes, the longest few minutes, and held out a piece of paper on which he had transcribed the contents of the telegram.

"Zyjemy. Rodzice nie." Rachel's eyes read each word separately, in order, as she forced herself not to look to the end of the line at the signature before she absorbed the contents. "Alive. Parents not. Sofie."

"Oh," she said, "Oh."

"Are you all right?" he held out his arm and helped her sit down. "Is it bad news?"

"Yes, oh my God, yes. My parents are dead. No! No! Sofie's alive!" Sofie's face came into focus in her head, Sofie in the doorway of their apartment in Warsaw, looking startled. She had put the image out of her mind for years now; she had refused to let it intrude into her vision, so that she thought she had forgotten what Sofie looked like. Then unbidden, in a flash, a flickering image appeared on the screen of her mind, of Sofie shorn of her hair, taut skin covering visible bone, mute, the unspoken accusation only in her silent haunting look, and Rachel shut her eyes tightly against the image and the overwhelming black deep pit of sorrow and fear inside her as she held the copied telegram.

"Are you all right?" he repeated.

"Yes, yes," Rachel looked at him in wonder. "She's alive. Sofie is alive. I knew it! I always knew it!" She threw her arms around the man, hugging his chest, her head barely reaching his shoulders bent forward to receive her. Her face was wet with tears and she laughed with an edge of hysteria. "She's alive."

"Lady, I'm happy for you. That's great. That's great. Let me get you a drink of water." He turned to the water fountain, but Rachel saw his eyes were brimming over. "Thank you," she said, "thank you. I must use your phone."

"Sure, sure," he was ready to give her anything. She called Aleks.

"Sofie's alive. I'm coming home."

❦   ❦   ❦

Rachel took a taxi home, caution to the winds, what does it matter what it costs, what does it matter, Mama and Papa are gone, but Sofie is alive. On the long ride home however, she puzzled over the meaning of the telegram. "Alive" it said. In Polish, "zyjemi" was plural. Who was alive, Moniek? David? Not Mama and Papa, the cable was clear about that, but which of her brothers? Or only Sofie?

When Rachel arrived home after the nearly one hour's ride from downtown in the traffic, Aleks had glasses of brandy set out and Rilka was making little canapés. Aaron was there and some journalist friends of Aleks and the neighbors from the floor below. The phone was ringing. Aleks picked it up and she heard him telling the news to whoever was at the other end. She walked in, and they each rushed toward her and hugged her, and everyone was crying and laughing and drinking. People kept coming in—Aleks must have called the whole world.

"We'll see if we can get her to Switzerland, then maybe South America," Aleks was making plans. It was not possible to get into the U.S. under the immigration laws.

"Cuba," someone said. "It's closer. You can get into Cuba."

Cuba, Rachel thought. I will see Sofie, I will see her.

"We'll contact the Displaced Persons Bureau tomorrow. We'll start everything tomorrow."

"Yes," Rachel said, looking Aleks, "We'll start everything tomorrow."

-24-

The first uncensored letter from Sofie was seven pages. Rachel read it out loud, for Rilka to hear also.

After the Germans sealed off the ghetto, I moved from one apartment to another. They kept making the ghetto smaller. First one street was shut off, then another. The wall around the ghetto had only two gates and to get out to work you had to have a special permit to pass through the guards, but soon no one could get out. Every day they took thousands of people at the Umschlagplatz. Then we didn't know where; now we know.

The uprising lasted nearly four weeks. I don't know how the Jews got ammunition; they smuggled it in over the year. Those who could get out to work brought back bits and pieces of things from which they made bombs, guns. The fighting was awful—dead bodies lying in the streets, weeping everywhere, but the German tanks came and we had no chance. When they came in to the ghetto, I was living in a room with so many people. We heard the Germans coming up the stairs and we put a heavy dresser against the door, hoping they would not bother to come in, since they were just running up and down the stairs, shouting "Heraus, heraus." We didn't breathe, we kept completely still, but they knocked the door down and took us all.

They took us to Maidanek, the concentration camp in Lublin. The women were separated from the men. We lived in wooden barracks, slept on straw in cubicles built against the wall. I had a top cubicle and the lower onewas occupied by some women from Lodz—it was like a platform in the wall with straw in it. Three women slept in each. It stank. The toilets were holes in a wooden block down the center of the back end of the barracks, no covers, all open. Everyone fought not to have to sleep at that end where the toilets were. Eventually, we worked it out that we would take turns so that no one would have to sleep there more than one time every twelve days.

They had "selections" and they would come to take away the sick. Every day we heard shooting. The ones they took away did not come back and we knew they were shot. One day the commandant announced that two hundred volunteers were needed for work in the ammunition factory. Whoever wanted to volunteer should register with the barracks guard. The women in my row said, "It's a trick, they want two hundred corpses!" Others said, "Don't volunteer for anything. Keep quiet, don't let them notice you." But I didn't listen. Nothing could be worse. I didn't care if I died. At least being shot would be quick. It didn't matter to me. I signed up. Early the next morning, before it was even completely light, I went to the wire fence in front of the third barracks.

There were already people waiting there, and within a few minutes, there were maybe five thousand people surging forward, waiting, crushing together. In spite of all the rumors about the Germans' tricks, they all "volunteered." The Germans came in several cars, and the commandant looked at the huge crowd and said, "Only two hundred," and they cut off the first two hundred. I was among them, pressing forward. I thought I would be trampled—everyone wanted to be in the first two hundred. But I got through and they put us into several trucks. Before we pulled away, I saw them herding the others together. I heard shots, and more trucks were pulling up and people were being loaded onto them. Later we learned they took the other people to the forest and made them dig trenches and shot them into the graves they had dug.

Meanwhile, we were driven to a factory and there I worked along with the rest. It really was an ammunition factory. We were given some lunch there so we were well off. There was no food in the camp, only a thin watery soup and a slice of bread, stale and hard. In the factory we got potatoes and once in a while some chicken even. Every evening we were put on trucks and returned to Maidanek. Then the

Russians were coming nearer and we were evacuated to Buchenwald. Since I had experience in munitions work, I was one of the lucky ones who were allowed to work in Leipzig. Everyday we were taken by trucks from Buchenwald to the factory in Leipzig and back again at night. Buchenwald was worse than Maidanek even. The stories and rumors were terrible. I tried not to make friends with any one because they could disappear the next day and never return. But there was one woman, Rivka, who I shared the straw mat bed with. She talked to me constantly and told me about her family. Her husband was mayor of their little town and he had the duty to provide people when the Nazis demanded five hundred workers one week, a thousand the next. Her husband had to choose. He tried to protect his family, but in the end they took him off to a camp or maybe shot him, who knows, and they sent her older son to some other camp and her mother-in-law and her two-year-old boy went to Auschwitz—she heard this from a prisoner who had been transferred from Auschwitz to Buchenwald, and her they took to Buchenwald to work in the munitions factory. The other prisoner told her how the mother-in-law saved the boy. When there came for a selection for the children—a selection meant the gas chamber and the ovens—she gathered straw from the other bunks in the barracks and piled it into hers and hid the boy under the straw. She didn't know if he would suffocate, or cry out, or be found, but they didn't find him. Later the mother-in-law was taken, and the boy was taken care of by another woman. So Rivka didn't know if he was alive still, but she hoped. She still had hope. She sang softly at night, in our bunk—she had a lovely, soprano voice—"Yingele, yingele," an old Yiddish lullaby, "Sleep my little child, do not fear." I'll always remember her voice. It kept me going. Rivka had hopes that the Russians would come soon and free us, and she would find her child. Whenever we had an extra ration, she shared it with me, gave me a little extra piece, she thought I was so thin, she was afraid I could not go to work and then it would be over. I gave her some warm socks I had hidden and an extra sweater I had worn underneath my clothes. So we helped each other.

Then I became sick with typhus. That was the dreaded thing. The guards came everyday to look for the sick people and they took them out and shot them immediately. I was very sick, full of fever. I couldn't get up. Before the guard check Rivka dressed me and combed my hair, and got me up. I couldn't stand, but she held me up and sat me at the long table with her where we had what they called breakfast. And she kept me up straight with the back of her hand, so when the guards came they didn't see that I was sick, and so she saved my life.

All this time, Rachel, did I think of you? No. Well, in the beginning, yes. I wondered where you were. Were you caught? Were you in another camp? Were you in Siberia? Were you dead or alive? After the ghetto uprising it was all hopeless. I stopped thinking. I did not think of anything. I made my mind blank. But I did not want to give up. I wanted to live. Why? What did I have to live for? I don't know, but I wanted to live. So I made my mind a complete blank, and I thought only how to survive to the evening, how to survive through the night.

Then, when I had the typhus, I was too sick to care, but Rivka saved me.

Then there were rumors that the Americans were coming and that we would be liberated. The commandant announced we were to be evacuated. So all the women's barracks were moved out. They didn't want to leave any evidence, I guess. We marched on the road through the forests outside of Leipzig, but at the end of the afternoon, we were told to turn around and march back; it had been only a rumor about the Americans. The same thing happened two days later. We were not working in the factory anymore, because all the Germans were trying to leave before the Americans arrived or maybe the Russians. While we waited in Buchenwald, there were plenty of guesses and rumors. Someone said the next time they march us out it will be to shoot us all—we will die in the forests. Someone else said no, they want to give us alive to the Russians. Someone else still said absolutely no, they don't want any of our stories to get out. At this time I thought, how silly to die now. We are almost free. To die just at the end, what a waste, what a laugh.

We marched in rows of five. I was the second from the right side of the road, and the three other women were on my left. Rivka was the one next to me. We were not supposed to talk while we marched, but we did whenever the guard was enough ahead of us, we whispered and we decided that when we came to the part of the road that was narrow, we would slip out to the right, the whole row of us, and we would run into the forest and hide. The whole row had to do it together and then the guards wouldn't notice a whole missing row. If only one or two women slipped off the guards would see very quickly that a row was not complete and that someone had escaped, and then of course there would be shooting and dogs and that would be the end. But if we all went, we had a chance. We knew that part of the road was about an hour's march away. It was a dark and cloudy day. I was terribly nervous. I thought it would be silly to try to escape and get shot, now so near the end, but then I thought, otherwise we will be killed anyway, so what do I have to lose? Then all of a sudden, Rivka on my left gave me a slight shove with her hip, and the woman on my right was already slipping down a slight embankment into the forest and I was right after her, then the other three women after me, and we lay flat on the ground as the ranks behind our row closed in and the space we left vanished almost immediately. As soon as the long column of women had passed us, we crept further into the forest till we could no longer see the road, and stayed there until dark. Then, when it was dark and still, we emerged from the forest and ran down the empty road till we came to a farmhouse on the left side of the road. We knocked on the door. We were quite desperate and knew we ran the risk of being turned over to the Nazis.

It was a German farm woman who opened the door. She took one look at us, how thin we were and looking like skeletons, with our prison clothes torn where the branches had caught them. "Komm herein," she said, her eyes wide. Her husband stood behind her. "Komm herein," he repeated. We came in and the woman made us sit down and gave us big bowls of soup wile her husband cut chunks of black bread for each of us. I can't tell you how heavenly it tasted. The warm soup, rich with chunks of meat in it, flowed into my stomach and I felt like it was life flowing inside me. They were so kind to us. Their eyes were fixed on us, with such pity in them. But at last, after we ate and after we got cleaned up a bit, the wife spoke to me in German and said we had to leave. They were afraid for their lives if the guards came looking for us and found us there. She told us there were some Polish workers who had taken a castle on a hill beyond the next town and that we should go there. She gave us some clothes of her own and we pieced them together so we wouldn't look too strange and then we set off for this old palace that had been the home of some German baron or bount. It was abandoned except for about twenty Polish men who had been working for the Germans in some factories and who left when the Germans ran away because the Russians were coming. We reached there just as the dawn was breaking. There was an eerie light setting off the castle's silhouette. I thought we were in another century. We stayed in the cellar of that castle for two nights and then the Russians came and liberated us. How we loved the Russians! Young men, tired, smiling at us, showering us with whatever they had, candy, vodka. They were angels from heaven!

Their officer came and asked where we were each from and helped us to find trucks or cars or carts or whatever could get us back to our towns. I made my way back to Zarki. I had to see what happened to our family. Our old house was partially destroyed. There was a wall and a gate in the wall. I heard a dog barking. I could look over the low wall. It was a little dog, running back and forth on the path inside the yard. There were some flowers growing on the left side of the path and on the right side was the door to the living room. My breath stopped. I couldn't knock on the door. I imagined Mama and Papa inside. I saw you, Rachel, on your wedding day. I was dizzy. I thought I had to walk away, but then I forced myself to push open the gate and knock on the door. A tall man, dressed in farm pants and a blue shirt, with a big mustache opened the door. Behind him stood another man who looked just like him only younger, and a woman, blond, full-bosomed, in a wide skirt. They said nothing, just looked at me. I am Sofie Jonish, I said. I used to live here. Do you know where my family is? The older brother opened the door and motioned me to step inside. It was our old living room, but not our room. None of the furniture was ours—only the sideboard, that big heavy piece Mama used to put the fresh bread on Fridays. The younger man pointed to the older one. My brother hid them, he said. At first I thought they were hidden right there in the house. Then they made me sit down and gave me tea and a sweet cracker and told me how the older man had hidden David and Moniek in the barn in the fields just outside the town. For two-and-a-half years they lived in the barn under a trap door under a cow. The trap door was covered with straw and the cow stood over it and the Germans never found them. I cried as if my heart would break, not even so much for David and Moniek, but for these people, Polish farmers, simple, who risked their lives and brought food to them everyday and took out buckets of their waste every day for nearly two years!

The older brother told me they had left some time ago and he didn't know where they were now. Mulek and Schlomo went into the forests and the younger brother thought they had joined up with the partisans. But Mama and Papa—I cannot bear to write this, I cannot bear to think it—Mama and Papa were taken to the ghetto in Radom and Papa died on the transport to Treblinka. Lucky for him that he didn't see what happened to Mama.

Now I am in Warsaw, writing you this. I found where you were. There is an organization to trace relatives. I found you. Now I think all the time I believed I would find you. But maybe that is just a story I tell myself now that I am alive, against all expectation. Anyway, I have a chance to go to Switzerland and I will go. There are no Jews in Poland.

I will cut these years out of my memory. I will not speak of them. I will erase them and I will start a new life.

"We will start a new life," Rachel said to Aleks and put down the letter.

❀　　　　❀　　　　❀

"Why did you stay?"

Rachel was silent for a long moment. Finally she said quietly, almost as if talking to herself, "How could I go? I couldn't leave you."

"Out of pity, then? Or guilt."

"No. Well maybe, that too a little. But that was not it. That was not it at all. After what we've been through together—we survived together. For better, for worse."

"He could have given you everything you wanted. I have nothing to give you. In Poland it was different, but here, well …"

"Aleks," Rachel sighed. She was at peace, the turmoil of the last week evaporated. "What is a life after all? Money is good to have, but what does it mean? There has to be some meaning. How could I leave when things are bad for you?

Never! I would hate myself all my life. No one knows me better than you. You are my anchor, and I am yours. I couldn't cut such ties. Remember when we first met? In that club in Czestochowa. You were giving a lecture—all the women were around you. You hardly paid attention to me …"

"I paid attention. You were the most beautiful, such burning eyes, such a proud chin, and such nerve—you pushed your way right through the crowd. And then you flattered me. I doubt you even heard my lecture!"

They lay quietly for a while, in their separate beds. The moon's light filtering through the gauze curtains illuminated the room, casting shadows.

Rachel said softly, "It was out of love I stayed."

Aleks turned toward her in the semi-dark. His hand touched hers across the small space between their beds. "You have always been my best friend."

When we are young we invent our lovers. Rachel invented Pavel, ascribing to him a romantic nature that perhaps did not fully exist. She invented Jakob, seeing in him the rough masculinity she yearned for at that time in her life. Even with Aleks, it was his wisdom, sophistication, and standing that she fell in love with. And perhaps he invented her too, in all her tempestuousness and beauty, la femme eternelle. In all of these fantasies there was the element of truth, like a grain of sand around which the oyster fashions a pearl; but they hampered embracing the underlying humanity in the existential yearnings of "the other." Perhaps such inventions are an essential ingredient of that initial "chemistry" but ultimately, Rachel at last discovered that love begins when invention ends.

978-0-595-41727-8
0-595-41727-2

Printed in the United States
217220BV00001B/65/A